My stomach clenched.

There were four glass fronted freezer cases, two on my left, two on my right, and a long, narrow table in the center of the room. The freezers were the kind you see in grocery stores except that these didn't contain pizzas and frozen peas and ice cream. One was filled with arms, one with legs, one had four torsos lying flat on racks, and the last contained about a dozen heads. The heads all looked exactly alike and they were all Edgar Parmenter.

From "Piecemaker"

Managansett Press

Don D'Ammassa is the author of:

Horror
Blood Beast
Servant of Chaos*
Caverns of Chaos*
Wings over Manhattan
The Gargoyle
That Way Madness Lies*
Little Evils*
Passing Death*
Date with the Dark*
The Devil Is in the Details

Science Fiction
Scarab
Haven
Narcissus
Translation Station
The Sinking Island*

Mysteries
Murder in Silverplate
Dead of Winter*
Death at the Art Gallery*

Fantasy
The Kaleidoscope*
Elaborate Lies*

Nonfiction
The Encyclopedia of Science Fiction
The Encyclopedia of Fantasy and Horror
The Encyclopedia of Adventure Fiction
Masters of Detection Vol I*
Masters of Detection Vol II*

*published by Managansett Press

THE DEVIL IS IN THE DETAILS

DON D'AMMASSA

"Amy's Pupill" first appeared in Noir, 1993
"The Devil Is in the Details" first appeared in *Whispered from the Grave*, 2000
"Literally Speaking" first appeared in Eldritch Tales, 1990
"Moloch's Furnace" first appeared in After Hours, 1993
"Next Door Neighbor" first appeared in 100 Wicked Witch Stories, 1995
"Payment in Arrears" first appeared in Aberations, 1993
"Piecemaker" first appeared in *Blood Lite 2*, 2010
"The Piggy Bank" first appeared in Horrors: 365 Scary Stories, 1998
"Puppets" first appeared in Bizarre Bazaar, 1993
"Wings Over Manhattan" was first published as a chapbook by Dark Moon Books, 2010
All other stories appear for the first time in this volume.

Managansett Press First Edition 2015

THE DEVIL IS IN THE DETAILS

CONTENTS

THE DEVIL IS IN THE DETAILS

Rachel Cox had been fascinated by ghost stories ever since she'd precociously read *The Turn of the Screw* by Henry James at the age of eleven. Much to the dismay of her mother, a librarian, and her father, a high school English teacher, she had indiscriminately devoured the works of M.R. James, Mary Wilkins Freeman, H.R. Wakefield, August Derleth, and Oliver Onions along with the more acceptable Edith Wharton. Her favorite movie was *The Haunting* and her favorite television program was *Buffy the Vampire Slayer* which, in her opinion, needed more ghosts.

With adolescence had come boys and for a while it appeared that Rachel's obsession had passed. True, she changed partners much more frequently than did her friends, and always on her own initiative, having failed to find any depth within the boys she dated. Her father considered this inconstancy an asset; he was not thrilled with the prospect of becoming the second most important male in his daughter's life. On the other hand, her mother blamed Rachel's stubbornly boyish figure and urged her to take more pains with her appearance. "It wouldn't hurt you to put on a few pounds either."

Through high school and then college, Rachel nodded and smiled and went her own way, rarely dating the same young man more than twice. If she was troubled by the lack of a permanent relationship in her life, she concealed it even from herself. Somewhere in the recesses of her mind she may have wondered why she never seemed to find anyone with the qualities she sought, but it had never occurred to her to define what it was that they all lacked. Had she done so, she might have realized that she was fixated on a literary device rather than reality.

During her senior year at Brown University, she sold the program code for a computer game she called *Ghost Lover* to a software company. Much to her chagrin, it eventually reached stores as *Blood Wraith*, but a major studio bought the film rights three months later, and Rachel was halfway to being a millionaire the day she received her diploma. The software company wanted a sequel and Rachel was happy to oblige, but found that there were too many distractions living at home in Providence, where her parents seemed more than ever determined to provide guidance, welcome or not.

She had been tentatively looking for an apartment when the Upson Downs house was put up for sale.

"I just want to look around inside," she told her mother. "I know it's much too big for me."

"What's the attraction anyway?" Her mother tapped the picture in the real estate handout with her forefinger. "It's an ugly building and according to this it needs considerable repair."

"The Downs house is haunted, Mother." She spoke as though that fact explained everything, and perhaps it did. "Samantha Downs was brutally murdered in 1946 by her ex-boyfriend. Her current lover arrived too late to save her, and he and the murderer had a terrible fight. Payne, the killer, died immediately, and Matheson lasted only a few hours, just long enough to tell the police what happened. Since then, no one has lived in the Downs for more than three months."

"Sounds distinctly unwholesome, and I thought you'd outgrown all that." Maureen Cox frowned and turned away. There was no answer that would have satisfied her, so Rachel didn't even try.

She fell in love with the Downs house immediately, and bought it after minimal discussion, at a price ten thousand dollars higher than the agent's most optimistic prediction. Her parents disapproved, but Rachel didn't argue, just went on with her own business wearing a faint smile and an air of distraction. She moved in the day after signing the final papers.

If ever there was an individual predisposed toward contact with the ghosts of the departed, it was Rachel Cox. She bought every book she could find that dealt with the Downs murder case even peripherally, and she knew the principle characters better than many of the living people in her life. Samantha Downs, the last of an aristocratic family fallen on hard times, had scandalized her friends by having an affair with Lawrence Payne, a petty criminal prone to violence and suspected of more serious crimes. His demeanor was described as "quietly smoldering" in at least three of the popularized accounts, capable of exploding into "disproportionate fits of rage".

During one of these, he broke Samantha's arm, which act finally convinced her to break things off.

During the stormy relationship with Payne, only one of Samantha's former friends remained close. Perhaps because of this loyalty, Damon Matheson was the one to whom Samantha turned following the breakup. Their friendship grew to love and they had announced their engagement only a few days before Samantha's death. It was in fact generally believed that this was the event which precipitated Payne's final crime. Matheson arrived at the Downs house just as Payne was about to make his escape. The two men fought, Matheson was fatally stabbed, but collapsed only after throwing his opponent down a staircase. Payne suffered a broken neck. Matheson then crawled into the bedroom and called the police, who arrived moments before he too expired. Samantha had been beaten to death over a period of several hours, and had suffered other indignities about which Rachel's books were rather vague. Although she was not ordinarily interested in the lurid details surrounding crimes, she was distressed at the lack of detail because it prevented her from attaining full empathy with the victim, which she considered essential to making contact.

Disappointingly, Rachel's first month at Downs house passed without incident. She was systematically refurnishing the house exactly as it had been on the night of the murder; using photographs and a detailed floor plan included in one of her books. She hadn't found the right dining room furniture yet, and she'd decided to cheat and use modern appliances for the kitchen, but the bedroom was very close to perfect and she was methodically working on the living room and front hall.

One hot August night, things changed. It was quiet both inside and out. The television was off and there was almost no traffic on Main Street even though it was early evening. Managansett seemed to have been arrested in time and, surrounded as she was by period furniture, Rachel easily imagined herself back in the 1940s. The only building visible from her bedroom was the Sheffield Library, which had been closed for the past two years and didn't even have security lights any longer. The humidity was overwhelming and she was regretting having decided to forego air conditioning as part of her bid for authenticity, but despite the heaviness of the night she finally drifted off into a light sleep.

She woke suddenly, absolutely convinced that someone had touched her as she slept. Her head rose cautiously from the pillow. A rose tinted lamp glowed from the bedside table, a modern reproduction but very similar to the one Samantha Downs had used when reading the detective thrillers to which she had been addicted. Nothing moved except for one of the floor length drapes which trembled slightly as an anemic night breeze slipped in through the window. The room was sparsely furnished and there was no place for anyone to hide except for the mahogany wardrobe near the opposite wall, or possibly under the bed. Rachel considered both possibilities unlikely, but at the same time she found it difficult to dismiss her experience as a dream. She had felt fingers pressing firmly into the flesh of her left arm, a sensation so distinct that it lingered even now.

After several tense minutes, she settled back, closed her eyes. "Samantha! Was that you?" She whispered into the room, then waited. Almost an hour passed and she was still waiting when she fell asleep again, and this time she didn't wake till morning.

Rachel made an effort to work on the program code, but the computer seemed so out of place in the small sitting room which served as her office that she made little progress. Samantha had called this her sewing room, but there was no record of it ever having used it for that or any other purpose, and Rachel concluded that her anachronistic hardware would be least intrusive here.

Frustrated, she went for a walk, but less than two blocks away she turned hastily back to the house. If Samantha's spirit remained nearby, it might attempt contact at any time, day or night. It would be terribly tragic if she missed this opportunity out of boredom or restlessness. So instead of enjoying the sunlight, she spent the rest of the day wandering from room to room, imagining how each had looked five decades earlier, and wondering if she had dreamed that faint touch.

She went to bed early, but found herself too excited to sleep until she poured herself a large glass of brandy and drank it down. Rachel was a light social drinker at best and the brandy made her head swim so alarmingly that she collapsed onto the bed, hoping that she wasn't going to be sick. It had the desired effect, however, and a few minutes later she was sleeping soundly.

The room was entirely dark when she woke this time, not to a touch but to a sound no longer present. She might have drifted off immediately if it hadn't been for the darkness. The rose hued lamp had been lit when she closed her eyes; she was absolutely certain of that. Could the bulb have gone bad? She rolled over on her side and turned the ornate switch. It clicked and the lamp brightened immediately, then slowly faded back to darkness.

Rachel was still mildly befuddled by the brandy and lying motionless, propped on her side, when she heard the sobbing. Somewhere in the house, although she couldn't quite tell the direction, someone was crying - a woman, not a child. It was one of the oldest clichés in ghost story fiction, and she'd have rolled her eyes in amusement if this was part of a movie. But in real life, it sent an equally predictable shiver down her spine, not of fear exactly, more like excitement tinged with anxiety.

"Samantha? Is that you?"

The sobbing continued for a few seconds, then came to an abrupt stop.

"Samantha? I'm a friend. I want to…to help you, if I can." She waited through a full minute of absolute silence. "Can you hear me, Samantha?"

Something fluttered at the open window, a night bird or perhaps even a bat, startling Rachel momentarily before it passed on. She shook her head as the tension ebbed, wondering if she'd imagined the sobbing, was already easing back down onto her pillow when fingers closed around her left wrist. For a split second, Rachel wanted to pull her hand away, roll off the bed, and run from the house. Even without the lamp, the moonlight illuminated the room enough to prove to her that she was alone on the bed. But the sensation of fingers pressing into her flesh, though weak, was persistent and unmistakable.

"Can you speak to me, Samantha?" Her mouth was so dry that it took two tries before she could get the words out. There was no answer. "Can you at least hear me? Tap your finger if you can hear what I'm saying."

But there was no tap, and the sensation slowly faded away until Rachel was once more quite certain that she was alone in the room. This time it was almost dawn before she got back to sleep.

The next day seemed to pass with funereal slowness. Rachel ordered a pizza for lunch because she didn't want to leave the house, and ate the leftovers cold for supper because she didn't have a microwave and wasn't sure how to reheat it in the oven. The evening seemed to stretch on endlessly before the shadows finally congealed into full darkness, and then she felt so tautly awake that she doubted she could ever drift off to sleep. She was considering another brandy when her eyes closed and her breath evened.

Her eyes slowly opened in the darkness hours later and this time there was no doubt in her mind at all that she was not alone in the bedroom. The moon was full and she'd left the curtains open; a column of dust motes danced suspended in the cool blue light. Rachel felt not the slightest alarm, but excitement made her pulse race and her hands trembled as she pulled aside the single sheet with which she'd been covered. Sitting on the edge of the bed, she slowly let her eyes trail around the room, seeking some indication of the presence of her visitor.

There! At the corner of her vision, something moved, but when she turned, it was gone. She stared into the beam of light from the window, trying to recapture what memory said was an abnormality. Her concentration became almost a hypnotic force of its own, and it was never afterwards able to pinpoint just when it became evident that something anomalous was happening in front of her. A shape was forming within the dust, not distinct enough for her to identify but clearly human. Rachel discovered that by letting her eyes unfocus slightly, she could better see the outline, which was clearly that of a slender human being.

"Samantha?" she whispered, and as she did so, the "head" shifted position slightly. "Can you hear me?" For a few seconds that seemed endless, there was no change. Then the "head" quite distinctly nodded once, then again, then burst apart as a flutter of breeze from outside tugged at the curtains. Samantha waited for almost an hour, waited until her neck was stiff and her forehead pounded sympathetically. Then she lay back crosswise across the bed and closed her eyes. But she was still awake when the sun came up.

Rachel spent most of the next day studying photographs of Samantha Downs' bedroom, even though she already knew the details intimately. She was convinced that the closer the parallel between the past and the present, the easier it would be to make contact. There were a few minor inconsistencies, quickly corrected, but ultimately she acknowledged that there wasn't much improvement possible.

While nibbling at a late, light, cold, and not particularly nourishing supper, Rachel had an idea. Leaving her unfinished meal on the table, she half ran to her small office. There, within a few minutes, she had cut all of the better snapshots of Samantha Downs from the books and magazines she'd collected. Clutching them in one hand, she ran to the bedroom where she methodically laid them in neat rows atop the bedspread.

For the next hour, she studied Samantha's delicate features with a hungry intensity and attention to detail that would have made the finest artist jealous. She memorized the shape of the woman's eyebrows, the slight asymmetry of her mouth, the position of two birthmarks, one on the jaw line, the other just below an earlobe. Rachel kept at it until she could see each photograph in her mind just as clearly as she could with her eyes. Satisfied for the moment, she swept all but the three best photographs into a pile and set them on her night table. Then she climbed into bed and propped the last three up against the base of her reading lamp. She fellt asleep while staring at them.

This time there was no sense of transition. One moment she was asleep, the next she was awake, convinced that someone had called her name. Clouds obscured the moon tonight, but the lamp remained lit, although its light was oddly subdued. A playful breeze stirred the curtains, and shadows moved along the walls. All but one. A single columnar shadow remained motionless at the foot of her bed, a murky darkness through which Rachel could not see the far wall. It was roughly human in size and shape, but with no distinctive features. Biting her lip, she turned to the pictures at her side and concentrated, once more drawing the essence of Samantha Downs' physical appearance to the forefront of her mind. When she felt she had captured it, she turned back to the indistinct figure at the foot of her bed, and gasped.

Samantha Downs stared down at her. The image shimmered slightly and had a tendency to fade if she stared too hard, but it was unmistakably the image of the woman from the photographs. She was dressed in blouse and slacks, her hair cut unfashionably short, hands clasped loosely at her waist.

"Samantha?" Rachel sat forward, but as she did so, the figure seemed to recede. "It's all right. Don't be afraid of me. I want..." But Rachel was dismayed to discover that she didn't know exactly what it was that she did want. "I want to help if I can."

The apparition lifted its head slightly and Rachel read an expression of unhappiness that was so deep that she instinctively extended one hand sympathetically. Again, Samantha seemed to draw back, although only her head actually appeared to move.

"I won't come any closer." Rachel withdrew her hand and sat back. As she did so, Samantha's head turned toward the door and something in her posture changed.

"He's coming." It was a whisper so thin that it wasn't quite sound. Rachel felt rather than heard the words.

"Who's coming, Samantha? Is it Damon?"

Rachel had hoped to reach the ghost of Samantha Downs because the woman had lived in this house for her entire life. The possibility that her lover's spirit might have remained behind had always seemed slight to her, given the fact that he had only been a visitor within these walls. In fact, there was some question as to whether he and Samantha had ever been intimate. Some of those who wrote about the affair speculated that her unpleasant experience with Lawrence Payne had led to an aversion to sex which Matheson had been patiently dealing with, and there was a good deal of evidence supporting this position despite the announcement of their intentions to marry.

"He's here." As before, the words were barely perceptible, completely empty of emotion. Samantha's eyes expressed deep sadness, and Rachel felt her own eyes stinging. How tragic, to have finally found the right man after such a terrible mistake, only to have happiness stolen at the last moment, and in such a horrible fashion. But even as she felt sympathy for the nebulous figure in front of her, Rachel found herself wondering about Damon Matheson. Could his spirit really be trapped in the house as well? If so, was it possible that she might see his manifestation? The thought filled her with an entirely new kind of enthusiasm, and for a few seconds she forgot all about Samantha Downs.

When she recollected herself, she was completely alone in the room. "Samantha! Come back!" But the shadows remained perfectly ordinary for the rest of that night.

Nothing happened for the next several days, although Rachel sometimes woke in the morning with fragments of images in her head. Samantha was calling to her without words, or standing over her sleeping form, sometimes accompanied by a larger, less distinct figure. Sometimes the latter was there alone. Rachel didn't know whether these were dreams or wishful thinking or some sort of subliminal communication. Each night she concentrated on the pictures and sometimes she had the sense that Samantha was nearby, just beyond the borders of perception, but that she was somehow prevented from penetrating the barrier between them.

During the days, Rachel worked on her program code and actually made some progress. She had thrown out the original story line and was now working on a new one which had strong parallels to the Downs murders. Her mother called to ask her to lunch, and Rachel begged off; she hadn't left the house in two weeks now. Three bags of groceries remained in their bags on the kitchen table where the delivery man had left them. Rachel had made only a half hearted effort to put the items away, abandoned even before she'd dealt with everything requiring refrigeration. A faint odor of decay permeated the kitchen and was insinuating itself into the rest of the house.

On the eighth day following the manifestation, she changed her tactics. All of the pictures of Samantha Downs went into the drawer of her night table. In their place were several photographs of Damon Matheson, including the only one which he shared with Lawrence Payne. The two men stood shoulder to shoulder, but Rachel thought that she could see signs of revulsion in Matheson's face and the position of his body, as though he'd been forced to touch something repulsive. Matheson was a tall man, dark and handsome, of moderate build. At first he seemed to dwarf Payne, who was several inches shorter. But then one noticed the breadth of Payne's shoulders, the solidity of his trunk, the blazing intensity of his eyes. Rachel, like Samantha, thought that Matheson would certainly be the more responsive, thoughtful lover, but she also understood the earlier affair with Payne. This was a man around whom things happened, lively, exciting things that reminded you that you were alive. It was a pity that he had allowed his obsession to destroy himself, and the others.

Rachel sat up in bed, sipping brandy and studying the pictures of Damon Matheson until her vision began to blur and her head tilted to one side and then she was asleep. The photograph of Damon Matheson fell from her limp fingers, balanced for a few seconds on the edge of the bed, then dropped to the floor. A cloud obscured the moon.

Absolute silence disturbed her sleep. Rachel opened her eyes to a room filled with shadows, shadows so deep and thick that she could almost feel them pressing against her body. Then she knew that she wasn't really awake, but wasn't quite dreaming either. And once again, she was not alone.

The presence that hovered around her was larger than that of Samantha Downs, but lacked the detail of the earlier apparition. Rachel knew that this was a man even before the first touch, a light pressure on her right thigh that might have been a cupped hand. It remained motionless at first, then moved steadily up to the curve of her hip, across the plain of her stomach, ever higher until Rachel felt the unmistakable shape of a hand closed around her right breast. She could see the indistinct form of a man standing over her, which was peculiar since her eyes remained closed.

The pressure remained constant but no longer moved, and Rachel sensed that she was expected to do something now. Although she wanted to open her eyes, she was afraid that if she did so she would see nothing and that the experience would end in disappointing reality. "What is it that you want me to do?" she whispered softly, shifting her body, trying to intensify the pressure on her breast. The touch was cool but waves of warmth spread from the point of contact, and the sensation felt wonderful beyond anything in her previous experience.

Rachel felt her own hands moving over her body and then the kiss of the night breeze told her that she was naked and she wondered how that had happened because she couldn't remember taking off her nightgown, but perhaps she had, and besides it didn't seem particularly important now because the pressure was moving again, and there was another just like it on her opposite thigh, and this one moved between her legs and the night became electric for some undefined period of time and when Rachel finally fell back into full sleep her body was slick with sweat.

She went to bed early the following night with the photographs arrayed around her, but her eyes kept straying back to the one in which the two men stood side by side. This captured the essence of Damon Matheson more completely than the others, or at least that's what she told herself as her eyes kept sliding across the page to the dark browed visage of Lawrence Payne. He was actually rather ugly, she decided, almost apelike, but undeniably a source of great personal power. It was such a shame that he was unable to control the violence within himself. Matheson on the other hand radiated calmness and self confidence and a more controlled power, a strength that she believed she had felt the previous evening.

Sleep was a long time coming, but it came at last. Rachel dreamed of Matheson and knew she was dreaming; the images lacked the substance of the previous night's encounter. With that realization came a fading, and just before everything dissolved, she caught a glimpse of Lawrence Payne's face hovering disembodied in the distance and felt a shiver of anxiety. Then the dreamscape was gone and she fell back into unawareness…

…and woke in a cold sweat.

She was naked and shivering despite the mugginess of the night. Rachel lifted her head from the pillow, still not sure if she was asleep or awake, and then felt the hands on her body even before sensing the dark shape hovering above her. There was still no detail to the form, but the two points of contact with her body were undeniably hands now, large and powerful hands that moved gently at first, but with increasingly urgency as the seconds passed.

"Damon," she said, trying to will his face to solidify out of the darkness, but no sooner had she spoken than the hands grew more insistent, less gentle. She hissed with surprise as one breast was clutched almost painfully and a second unseen hand moved across her ribs with bruising force. And then some greater weight was pressing down on her thighs and for the first time Rachel felt a hint of alarm, a dawning fear that perhaps she had gotten involved with something beyond her, something not amenable to control.

"Damon, stop it! You're hurting me!" Still she whispered, reaching down to grasp wrists that weren't there. Her hands pressed right through the shadowy arms without having any effect on the apparition's ability to touch her. She tried to twist out from under, but there was no physical body to contend with here, nothing to provide leverage. Rachel was fully awake now, but the transition had no effect on her situation. If anything, the shadowy hands were more insistent now, and more solid than ever. Fingernails scraped across her chest and throat and she was pushed back down onto the pillow, and the weight on her thighs grew even heavier. Rachel began to panic, windmilling her arms through her phantom attacker, apparently with no effect.

Then there was a sense of movement at her side and a faint voice whispered "No!" A second blurred form emerged from the shadows, this one with an identifiable face. The ghost of Samantha Downs merged with the amorphous shape above her and there was a brief swirling in the air as the two merged and became one, then slowly faded away, taking with them all of the pressure on Rachel's body. And just before the night returned to normal, Samantha Downs gave Rachel her final warning. "You brought the wrong one."

Suddenly free, Rachel leaped from the bed and ran to the bathroom where she vomited a mixture of brandy and undercooked food into the toilet. It wasn't until she was standing in the shower, letting the cool water revive her, examining the darkening bruises on her body that she allowed herself to think about what had just happened.

"My God! I brought back Lawrence Payne." The thought staggered her sufficiently that she almost lost her footing. She spent the rest of the night sitting in a chair watching bad television programs with every available light turned on.

It didn't seem quite as bad in the daylight, but if Rachel had entertained any doubts about the danger in which she'd placed herself, she had only to look at the bruises on her breasts and thighs, or the scratches on her left side to remind her. But even though she did not intend to give Lawrence Payne another chance to touch her, she still remained determined to contact the spirit of Damon Matheson. That first night's encounter had been gentle and delightfully erotic, and she was willing to risk a great deal to pursue it. But Rachel wasn't foolhardy.

She removed the picture of Payne from her bedroom and those of Samantha Downs as well. All of her concentration tonight would be reserved for Damon; she would shut out the others entirely to avoid distraction. Tonight she would see his face; she was sure of it. As the day progressed, she grew increasingly confident of her ability to make the connection, but oddly nervous, like a bride on her wedding night or a teenager waiting to meet her blind date. The daylight seemed to drag on endlessly, and her efforts to distract herself by working on her program code were dismal failures. At last the sun began to drop and Rachel settled into bed. She concentrated her will and mentally erased the images of Samantha Downs and Lawrence Payne, concentrating instead on Damon Matheson, determined to fall asleep with his face foremost in her memory.

And for the first time in her life, Rachel experienced insomnia. She tossed and turned and tried to relax and looked at the clock's slow progress and then tossed and turned some more. Eventually her inability to drop off made her more anxious and less relaxed and she felt trapped in an emotional spiral that had no discernible end. Midnight came and she was still alert, though nearly in tears from frustration. As the minutes continued to pass, she began to resign herself to failure, at least for the night.

But even as she considered defeat, something stirred in the corner of the room. For the first time, the manifestation began while she was awake, and that very fact reassured Rachel, convinced her that now, finally, complete success was imminent. The disturbance grew larger, reared up man-sized and moved toward her, and she tried to make out his face. As before, there were no details, but the shape seemed more solid than before as it approached, looming above her.

"Welcome, Damon," she said warmly and then the face began to resolve itself. For one terrifying moment she thought it was Lawrence Payne standing there but then the features grew distinct and the handsome features of Damon Matheson looked down at her. Rachel sat up, let the strap of her nightgown slide down one shoulder so that one breast was bare, then raised her arms to welcome him.

Matheson's ghost rushed forward to embrace her and this time he was so solid that she was overwhelmed and fell back, striking her head against the headboard sharply enough that everything in the room grew much darker and she realized that she was going to black out. "No! Not now! It isn't fair." But she only thought the words because she was already slipping away.

Her first sensation when she recovered a murky consciousness was that her head hurt. The second was that the rest of her hurt quite a bit as well. Rachel opened her eyes in darkness, lying on her back in the center of her bed with her head lying in the cradle of her forearms. There was no movement in the room, and she resigned herself to having lost Damon once again.

It hurt to breathe and she tried to bring one hand down to touch her aching side, but her wrists were firmly held in place by some restraint she could not see. When she tried to turn over she discovered that her ankles were similarly encumbered. Rachel's mouth was dry and when she licked her lips, she tasted blood, and that was sufficient to shock her into full awareness. For several seconds she tried to free herself, to no avail. Her struggles had wakened other discomforts; her ribs were bruised, her lip was swollen, and there were sharp pains in her right knee as though something were out of place.

Rachel lay still, trying to compose her thoughts, and as she did so, a form stepped into her line of sight. For one terrifying moment she thought that it was Lawrence Payne standing there, but she concentrated on her memory of Matheson's face and tried to impose it by force of will, apparently with success. The swirling shadows seemed to war within themselves at first, but eventually Damon's handsome, rugged features emerged and stabilized.

"Thank God!" The sense of relief was dizzying. "Damon, you have to help me. Help me the way you tried to help her."

And Matheson smiled and leaned over Rachel and then his arm rose and his fist descended in a brutal blow that broke her nose, and in the few seconds that elapsed before the next struck her she realized two things. One was that the police had been misled back in 1946. Lawrence Payne had not murdered Samantha Downs; he had tried unsuccessfully to save her. The other was that Rachel was finally going to find out the long suppressed grisly facts about Samantha's death in excruciating detail.

PIECEMAKER

It was supposed to be routine surveillance. The insurance company rep is a friend of mine and she hands me off a job from time to time even though the company refers most of its cases to the bigger investigators. It involved a questionable worker's comp account. You know, some bozo claims to be unable to work so he can collect, and meanwhile he's in his back yard building a patio. That sort of thing. It usually meant sitting in a tree or some other concealed spot with a camera for hours or more often days.

This time it was a little different. When I read the case summary, I glanced up at the rep. "Is this some kind of joke, Brenda?"

She looked uncomfortable. "We think there's some kind of hanky panky going on." Brenda was the kind of girl who said "hanky panky." She also described her job as "rinky dink."

"According to this," I waved the single sheet of paper at her, "the subject lost an arm in an industrial accident and you tell me the company wants to cut off his benefits if he doesn't come back to work?"

Brenda's eyes skittered away from mine. "There have been some contradictory indications. He might not have lost the arm after all."

I was beginning to think this was a joke. "Color me stupid, Brenda, but couldn't you just send your adjustor by to visit and find out for sure?"

She sighed but still wouldn't look me in the face. "We did that. Mr. Parmenter was very cooperative, even took off his shirt to prove that the arm wasn't just strapped to his chest."

"Then why do you need me? Obviously the poor sod deserves whatever he's getting from you people."

"Ordinarily, I'd agree with you. But there have been reports…"

She summarized them. I thought she was crazy and said so, but the company was willing to pay me so I didn't argue. But I planned to pad my expenses to punish them for wasting my time.

Edgar Parmenter was – or had been – a mechanic at Eblis Manufacturing up north in Managansett. He'd been servicing a rotary polishing machine when the safety brake on a cart of brass fittings had failed. The cart sideswiped him and his right arm had been pulled into the gear box and severed just below the shoulder. The arm itself had been crushed to pulp. He had declined to be fitted for a prosthetic arm and naturally he couldn't return to his former profession.

Sounded pretty cut and dried. The spanner in the works was that two delivery men and three neighbors all insisted that Parmenter had two perfectly functional arms. Two of those neighbors had seen him doing laps in his swimming pool and one of the deliverymen insisted that Parmenter had shaken hands normally. Brenda's boss wasn't sure what was going on, but it sounded fishy to him and he'd suggested that it hadn't been Parmenter who'd been injured at all, but someone taking his place that day.

I drove by Parmenter's house as soon as I left Brenda's office. It was in an attractive, older neighborhood with big yards, lots of trees and shrubs. I spotted a few places where I could probably lurk in the shadows for a while, unless someone went for a walk or looked too closely, and decided I would have to use the van.

The van is specially equipped, of course. Zippy Electrical Contractors don't really exist, but it looks real enough. The rear and side windows are one-way glass and there are mountings for still and digital cameras and a comfortable seat. I hate using it. It gets stifling in the heat and even when the weather is cooperative, the hours of inaction are boring and demeaning. Try pissing into a plastic jug all day and you'll see what I mean.

Parmenter's house wasn't far from a convenience store and I figured I could park there for the better part of a day without attracting too much attention. There'd be a nice clear shot through the rear window. I still wasn't quite sure what I should be looking for. I mean, if Parmenter had a one-armed double, how was I going to be able to tell which was which? I was more than a little irritated with Brenda and her boss as well. After all, someone had lost an arm, so why did they care who cashed the check?

Morning found me in my Zippy uniform, parking as planned. I got a bite almost immediately. Parmenter – I recognized him from the file Brenda had provided – came outside and picked up the morning paper. His body was angled so I couldn't see clearly, but it did not appear that he was symmetrically equipped. I snapped a couple of photos just to be doing something, and to justify the larger than conscionable bill I planned to submit for this job.

He came out again about an hour later, arranged a sprinkler on his lawn, and turned it on. For just a second or two he gave me a great view and I took still pictures and a short digital recording. There was no doubt that his right sleeve was full, but it could have been a prosthesis of some sort, even though he hadn't officially been provided with one.

The morning dragged on into afternoon and evening with no further sight of my quarry. By the end of the following day, however, I had plenty of proof that the man living at 332 Starfish Lane had two working upper appendages. I had clear pictures of him reeling in a hose, carrying a trash can, even raking leaves. Unfortunately, I also had clear pictures that proved he was an amputee, including one in which he'd answered the door bare chested with a bandaged stump. I was quite sure now that there were two separate but very similar men living there. Parmenter was an orphan with no known relatives, but I supposed he might have run into his long lost and unknown identical twin. But which of them had lost the arm?

I didn't dare use the van again. A couple of the neighbors had given it odd passing looks already. That was fine with me. I wasn't going to solve this problem from a distance. It seemed to me that the insurance company was going to have to pay someone regardless of whose arm had been torn off, but my own curiosity had been piqued and I planned to satisfy it on Brenda's dollar.

Friday morning I had a Mr. Messenger plaque on my car. I stopped in front of Parmenter's house and walked up to the front door carrying a package addressed to Prudence Tessworthy at 332 Starfish Lane. I rang the bell.

Parmenter showed no sign of recognition when he answered the door. I smiled professionally. "Is Prudence Tessworthy at home today?"

Parmenter, whose right shirt sleeve was rolled up and tied off just beneath his stump, frowned at me. "Never heard of her."

It was my turn to frown. "Are you sure? This is the address on the package."

"Positive." He smiled politely and started to close the door.

"Excuse me," I said hastily. "Do you know if anyone by that name lives in the neighborhood?"

"Sorry, no." He didn't sound sorry.

"Maybe someone else in your household would know. I'd really appreciate it if you'd ask."

"I live alone. Try Mrs. Richardson in the red house at the corner. She knows everyone's business." And the door closed.

Now that Parmenter had seen my face, my options were more circumscribed. What I really wanted was a picture of the two Parmenters together. Then it would be up to the insurance company to sort out which was which, and whether either of them deserved further compensation.

I drove away slowly, as though looking for another address, but I was actually examining Parmenter's property in more detail. The back yard was surrounded by eight foot tall stockade fencing and invisible, but I had already noted one vantage point. I drove to the office, changed the signs and plates on the van, and drove back masquerading as Northeastern Telephone Services.

I've climbed telephone poles in the past, and I'll probably do it again in the future, but I've never liked it. With a pouch of tools – including a camera with telescopic lens – slung around my waist, I ascended to just below the wires where I could hopefully pass for a legitimate serviceman.

As expected, I had a great view of the rear of 332 Starfish Lane. Parmenter had a nice pool – now covered for the season, a small patio, a fancy grill and smoker, and a gazebo. Although it had been warm and calm all week, it suddenly turned frosty and windy and within an hour I was freezing my butt off. There was no sign of life at Parmenter's all morning and I descended stiffly to pee in my jug, eat some junkfood, and decide whether I wanted to continue my vigil.

The afternoon was more positive in a negative sort of way. Parmenter decided to grill himself a steak.

He only had one arm when he started up the grill. I surreptitiously snapped pictures with which to impress upon Brenda my devotion to my job. He went back into the house and returned a few minutes later with a nice looking steak on a platter, condiments, and a can of beer. This time he had two arms. Okay, I told myself.

They're both there. He's only cooking one steak, but it's big enough for two. If I could catch the pair of them splitting it and toasting each other with Budweisers, I could call it a day.

Parmenter sat and read a magazine while the steak sizzled on the grill. I could almost taste it from my perch. After a while, he turned it over, then went back into the house, returning almost immediately with another beer. He still had two arms. He was still alone. And he stayed that way. Damned if he didn't eat the entire steak, then shut down the grill, police up his dirty dishes, and take everything inside.

I wondered if maybe his partner was a vegetarian.

He made one more brief appearance a few minutes later, apparently checking to make sure everything had been tidied away. This time he was sporting an empty sleeve and I snapped a picture or two reflexively.

I descended before the sun did, and I was not happy. I would turn in my photographs and the insurance company could refuse to pay the claim, but Parmenter almost certainly would appeal and when his one armed version showed up for the hearing, the outcome would be inevitable.

Back at the office, I printed out copies of all the pictures and arranged them neatly to present to Brenda. It was only then that I frowned, noticing an anomaly. In the last two shots, taken from the telephone pole, it was quite obvious that Parmenter's arm was missing. Except that this time it was the left arm.

Sometimes I use bad judgment. This was probably one of those times. I was watching Parmenter's house again from my own car parked just down the street when I saw his Ford back out of the driveway and head off toward the interstate. Without consciously planning what I was going to do, I found myself walking briskly along the sidewalk. Pretending that I was doing nothing out of the ordinary, I rang the doorbell and waited. There was no answer. It only took a few seconds to circumvent the lock; if I surprised Parmenter's partner I'd have some explaining to do, but curiosity had overwhelmed my good sense.

The house felt empty. "Is anyone home? Your front door was wide open." I waited a few seconds and there was no answer to my lie, so I closed the door behind me. The unwisdom of this was apparent by then, but I was committed.

A quick search of the house – both floors – turned up no sign of Parmenter number two, or anyone else. Only one bedroom was in use, one set of clothes, one toothbrush in the bathroom, one dirty coffee cup in the sink. Every bit of physical evidence suggested this was the home of a rather boring bachelor.

Then I found the arm. It was lying at one end of the couch. I assumed that it was a prosthesis and reached down to pick it up, but recoiled slightly when I touched the wrist. It was much more lifelike than I had expected, even felt humanly warm to the touch. I started to draw my hand back – and the damned thing grabbed me!

I must have looked pretty stupid, dancing back and waving my arm wildly. Its fingers were interlocked with mine and even as my head told me that it was just some sophisticated piece of metal and plastic, the rest of my body insisted that this was a living creature. I fell over an end table and banged my hip, then brought the disembodied arm down against the floor hard enough to break two of the fingers with audible snaps. It bounced once and lay on the rug. I had just convinced myself that it had been an automated electronic reflex when the arm flipped over and began walking toward me on the tips of its fingers.

If I had run for the front door, I would almost certainly have made it, but I was so shocked and revolted that I retreated into the tiny kitchen at the back of the house, a strategic error since there was no other exit except the door to the basement. I grabbed a carving knife from a rack beside the sink but the ambulant arm stopped in the doorway. I'd have sworn it was crouching but how can an arm crouch? I resisted the temptation to warn it off. No ears, after all.

Then I heard a car drive up. Parmenter was back.

I replaced the carving knife hastily and opened the basement door. The steps were clean and straight and barely creaked as I descended. I heard the door from the garage open just as I reached the bottom. Footsteps sounded above my head.

It was gloomy down there, lit only by narrow slits of daylight through windows set in the foundation. There was a work table right in front of me and a washer dryer combination and furnace. The bulk of the basement was concealed by cheap paneling. I found a door, not locked, and slipped inside. Fluorescent lights hung from the ceiling, two of them illuminated, enough to give me a good look at my surroundings.

My stomach clenched.

There were four glass fronted freezer cases, two on my left, two on my right, and a long, narrow table in the center of the room. The freezers were the kind you see in grocery stores except that these didn't contain pizzas and frozen peas and ice cream. One was filled with arms, one with legs, one had four torsos lying flat on racks, and the last contained about a dozen heads. The heads all looked exactly alike and they were all Edgar Parmenter.

I'm not sure how long I stood there, almost as frozen as the contents of the freezers, before the door opened behind me.

"Oh dear. You shouldn't have come down here, my dear sir."

I turned slowly. Edgar Parmenter stood in the doorway and he was holding a handgun in his left hand. His right arm hung at his side, two of the fingers obviously broken.

"What the hell is all this?" My voice was a quavering croak.

Parmenter seemed perfectly relaxed. "None of your business, actually. You should have picked another house to burglarize." He frowned. "That was you posing as the messenger the other day, wasn't it? I thought there was something odd about you."

I didn't correct him, hoping he'd underestimate me. "You're right. Look, whatever you're doing is no skin off my nose. I'll just get out of your way." I took a step forward and the handgun came up smartly.

"I think not. Please walk to the other end of the room, turn and place both hands on the wall while I think about this."

I did as I was told and for a few minutes we were both lost in thought. Parmenter found himself first. "You've chosen a very awkward time to intrude in my affairs. I have an appointment which I really can't skip. Turn around please."

I thought he might shoot me right there and then, but he had other plans. "Be so kind as to take one of those torsos out and place it on the table for me."

Although I was still convinced that these were artificial body parts, I flinched when I touched the torso. It wasn't as cold as I expected, more like a refrigerator than a freezer, and not particularly heavy. But it did feel like human flesh and I couldn't completely suppress my revulsion.

"Now a pair each of arms and legs. And make sure you get a left and a right for both sets."

Parmenter then directed me to insert each severed limb into the appropriate place on the torso. I gaped at him in astonishment but when I tried I found that the truncated bones sort of locked into place and when they did so, flaps of skin folded over to conceal the seams.

"And finally a head. Any one will do."

This was the worst part of all. The head was so lifelike that I almost dropped it. It also fit into a socket and snapped into place. The result was a perfect imitation of a dead human body. But it wasn't human. And it wasn't dead. The eyes popped open almost as soon as the head was attached.

"Damn, it's cold!" It was Parmenter who spoke, but not the Parmenter who held the gun. The figure I'd assembled on the table sat up abruptly and looked around. "What's going on?"

The first Parmenter gestured toward me with his weapon. "I have a problem."

The second gave me a quick look. "So I do. What am I going to do about it?"

The first sighed. "That's up to me. I have to meet with my case manager this afternoon and I don't have time to deal with this, so I'm going to have to do it for me."

The new Parmenter slid down off the table. "Why do I always have to solve the problems? Why can't I think of something for a change?" There was a cabinet under the table from which the naked Parmenter took out a set of clothes and began dressing.

"I do my part. I all do. Just take him someplace and kill him in an hour or so. I'll have a perfect alibi."

"If I say so."

Once the second Parmenter was dressed, the gun went from one to the other, but remained pointed at me. "If I take the car, how do I take him anywhere?"

"I'll call a cab. But be careful that no one sees the car. They'll trace it back here."

The first Parmenter vanished upstairs and the second eyed me dourly. He was still shaking with the cold, but not as much as before. "Look," I said. "Why not let me go? I won't say anything. No one would believe me and I'd have to admit that I was trying to rob the place."

"I'm afraid I can't take that chance. Upstairs now, and slowly. I'd rather not make a mess down here."

The first Parmenter threw me a set of car keys when we reached the top of the stairs. "I'll see me when I get back. Be careful."

I had to cooperate, play for time, watch for a chance to take him by surprise, so I climbed behind the wheel of Parmenter's station wagon while he took the passenger seat. "Where to?"

"Take Route 13 north."

Neither of us said much for the next twenty minutes. Parmenter turned on the radio and it was Patsy Cline singing "I Fall to Pieces," which I thought appropriate. We headed north out of Providence and then took the exit for Managansett. Parmenter directed me onto a back road that bypassed the town center and looped out toward the reservoir at the far end of town. The road didn't lead to much of anyplace else and we saw no traffic at all toward the end of the trip. Following instructions, I pulled over into a lightly wooded area and stopped.

"Get out."

I let my shoulders slump and dropped my chin, trying to project resignation as I opened the door. Parmenter was already turning to do the same when I slammed my right elbow back hard, taking him right under the chin.

I had hoped to knock him out. The result was not quite that. His head literally popped out of its socket, struck the roof of the car, and bounced into the back seat. I was too relieved to be shocked, or perhaps I was just inured to shock, but I expected that to end the struggle. Unfortunately, now that Parmenter's body – this body – was warm, it apparently no longer needed the head to function. But it did need the eyes to see with. Two bullets smashed through the windshield and a third through the roof.

I opened the door and half fell, half slid out onto the ground. Two more shots sounded and I made my way on all fours into the shelter of a small copse of trees. When I looked back I saw a rather foreshortened version of Parmenter. He had managed to get out of the car and was now groping around in the back seat, presumably searching for his head. I suppressed an hysterical laugh and tried to assess my options.

I could run, of course, but if I tried the road, Parmenter could chase me down in the car. I hadn't had the foresight to take the keys out of the ignition. Assuming he got himself reassembled, that is. The alternative was to hide until he gave up and went away. But Parmenter seemed to be having a great deal of difficulty reclaiming his head, and I decided to go on the offensive.

I stood up and sprinted toward the car.

Parmenter was bigger than me, even without his head, but an organized minority can always overcome a disorganized majority. I knocked him to the ground with my initial charge and then kept kicking and punching until his body stopped trying to get up. Then I knelt on his back and took one arm in both hands. Since the head had disengaged so easily, I figured, maybe the limbs would as well. I exerted pressure and torque and there was a slight pop. Parmenter was one armed again.

The other three limbs were even easier now that I had the hang of it.

I bundled the body parts into the trunk and drove back to Providence, intending to go to the police until I realized how my story would sound. An examination would certainly prove that Parmenter was not human, but if I drove up to a police station with what appeared to be a disassembled human body, I'd be behind bars really fast. I finally decided to park the car at Parmenter's house and place an anonymous call to the police. They'd conduct a thorough search, find the basement, and what happened after that was anyone's guess.

But it didn't quite work out that way. When I arrived, I decided to take one last look, still not quite convinced that this wasn't all some elaborate hallucination. As soon as I turned the key, the trunk popped open, forced from within. Two arms tumbled out onto the ground and one snagged my pants cuff and held on until I kicked it with the other foot. I backed away, decided discretion was the better part, and went to retrieve my own car. I never called the cops.

There's not much more to tell. I delivered the photographs to Brenda, along with an invoice, but did not tell her what else I'd discovered. She called me back a few days later to say that Parmenter had vanished, his house had burned to the ground, and the company had no place to send its checks.

That was almost a year ago and no one has seen Parmenter since, but over the course of the last few weeks, I've been feeling increasingly uneasy. Private detectives often develop a kind of sixth sense and I was sure I was being watched. I spent a lot of time looking into my rearview mirror, installed a security camera at my house, and paid attention to my surroundings when I walked on the street, but I never spotted anything out of the ordinary.

Until this morning. In among today's various bills and junkmail was a small package with no return address. Curious, I found a knife and cut through the tape. Inside was a small, rather fancy cardboard box. I opened it and discovered that it contained a single, ordinary looking replica of a human eye. That was startling enough in itself, but then the most unexpected thing happened.

It winked at me.

CHOICE CUTS

Tabitha Claremont didn't discover her unique gift until she killed herself, which might have been tragically ironic except that it didn't end her story.

Her childhood could not be described as a happy one. Arthur Claremont was a violent man who treated his wife and daughter with no more respect than he did any of his other "property", and Lucille, his wife, was a passive woman who accepted her lot without complaint. If his particular style of physical discipline was not quite legally abusive, it veered very close to the impermissible and might have crossed the line dramatically if Tabby had not been such a frail, sickly child. As it was, there were layers of scar tissue on the skin of her psyche, if not her body. Like her mother, she adapted to her environment, and by her early teens she understood her father well enough to avoid giving him more than occasional excuses to resort to his particular concept of discipline.

Adolescence brought improved health, and she had inherited her mother's strikingly attractive features, but the earlier illness and an unsettled home life had taken their toll. She stood slightly above average height, but remained thin and awkward. Her father forbade cosmetics or jewelry, her clothing was dowdy, and her lifeless hair was almost invariably tied in a pony tail. Since she had never been allowed to play with other children outside of school, Tabby had no real friends, and her reluctance to participate in class – even though she was otherwise an excellent student – exasperated most of her teachers. There had never been a boyfriend, not even casually. Her father would not have approved even if her gaunt appearance and determined isolation had not proven to be adequate safeguards against involvement.

The first stirring of discontent occurred while she was seventeen. It started when she developed a not very well concealed crush on Jeff Schofield, who sat opposite Tabby in study hall and who occasionally engaged in whispered conversations on trivial matters that somehow seemed to her wonderfully important at the time. The fact that he was going steady with Valerie Cottrell bothered her not in the slightest; she decided he was staying with the cheerleader only to avoid hurting her feelings.

That particular fantasy died when Valerie suddenly dropped out of school to deal with her unexpected pregnancy.

Although Tabby felt crushed by the revelation, the genie was out of the bottle and would not go back. She transferred her affections to Terry Brady, class president, a boy with smooth manners and a possibly genuine good nature. Terry also had a girlfriend, whose existence Tabby managed to rationalize away with little difficulty, but her efforts to insinuate herself into his life were unproductive. She had managed to speak to him a half dozen times, but on each occasion he had been unable to remember her name.

That's when Jessica Calvert touched a match to tinder. Jessica was not the most popular girl in school, but she ruled her own small clique and had a considerable male following, more through the power of her personality than because of her indifferent looks. She would never be an outstanding student, but when it came to sizing up people around her, Jessica was in her element. Tabby was sitting in the cafeteria, poking at her lunch and sulking because her latest encounter with Terry hadn't gone any better than the previous ones, when Jessica slid into the seat beside her.

"Looks almost edible today, doesn't it?" She nodded toward the anemic blob of beef stew on her own tray.

Tabby blinked. "Yeah, I guess."

"So you're interested in Terry Brady. Maybe I can help with that."

Tabby went from being aghast that someone knew her secret, to wary about Jessica's intentions, to excited that someone actually thought she might have a chance to win his affections.

"Why don't you come over to my place after school today?" suggested Jessica when the period ending warning bell sounded.

"Oh, I can't!" There was a note of panic in her voice. "My father wants me to come right home." For a second her face fell, then she brightened. "Listen, he's going out of town in the morning and he'll be away for a whole week. How about after school tomorrow?"

The date was set and Tabby spent the rest of the day enjoying a mild euphoria that didn't escape her father's notice. "You're looking pleased with yourself today. What's going on?"

Years of practice carried her through. "I did really well on my history test first period. I was a little worried about it."

He made a disgusted noise. "History won't help you find a job or get a husband." No longer interested, he turned back to the television.

The following night, Jessica introduced Tabby to the wonders of makeup, showed her how to rearrange her hair to better advantage, and told her about a house party that weekend. "Tommy Reed's parents are out of town. Everyone's going to be there."

Tabby felt simultaneously excited and depressed. "I don't know, Jessie. I hardly know Tommy and he didn't invite me."

"Well, he invited me and said I could bring a guest. And since that jerkoff Parker and I split up, I was planning to solo." When Tabby still seemed reluctant, Jessica leveled the heavy artillery. "Terry's going to be there, and he's coming by himself."

"I thought he was going out with Sherry Nelson?"

Jessica raised one hand and wiggled it ambiguously. "Rumor has it they're not getting along. And she's in Vermont with her family this weekend."

And so it came to pass.

Even with her father out of the picture, Tabby had to be cautious. Her mother was incapable of keeping a secret, so Tabby pretended to have a headache and announced she was going to bed early. Then out the window and four blocks over to Jessica's house for a quick makeup application and a borrowed dress. She was so excited that she could feel her heart racing.

The party was loud and crowded, but the Reeds lived all by themselves at the end of a private road and there were no neighbors to complain. Tabby allowed Jessica to lead her from room to room, and stood by while her companion exchanged hugs and occasional kisses with several of the guests, some of whom were strangers to Tabby. The makeover job was effective. Patty Grimes didn't recognize her even though they had known each other since first grade, and at least a few of the boys made tentative overtures, all of which she ignored or rebuffed. She was only interested in Terry Brady.

Who didn't appear to be present.

"He's coming later, I promise." Jessica led her to the dining room. There was a large punch bowl and Tabby was thirsty, but her first sip burned on the way down.

"There's something wrong with this."

"No, dear. That's just the vodka."

The second sip tasted slightly better and she really felt thirsty, but she was also depressed. She had risked her father's wrath and Terry wasn't even here. Despite Jessica's promises, she felt sure that he wasn't coming. On top of that, when she finished the glass of punch, she discovered that Jessica had abandoned her. Feeling even sorrier for herself, she returned to the punch bowl, then found a spot in a corner where she could sit on the floor and escape notice. And for the next hour, that's where she stayed, except to get up every ten minutes for a refill.

When she rose for the last time, her legs were unsteady and she almost fell, saving herself by grabbing a floor lamp which rocked and clattered threateningly. She steadied herself and took a few steps, and then noticed that the room was slowly beginning to spin around her, and the spinning seemed to move up the walls to the ceiling and then down through her head into her stomach.

"Oh my God!" She pressed one hand over her mouth, panicking, and bolted toward the front door. There were shrubs out front, she remembered, places where she could be sick in privacy. But she didn't make it that far. She was halfway down the front steps when the pressure became too great and her body convulsed and the poisonous bile in her stomach exploded out of her mouth.

And sprayed all over a very surprised looking Terry Brady.

Tabby found the strength to run off, hoping that he hadn't recognized her in the darkness, but convinced that he had. She was sick and disoriented and wandered aimlessly for more than an hour before she got her bearings and set off for home. It was well after midnight when she reached the house, her stomach still rolling, her head pounding, exhausted and dispirited, convinced that she had just ruined her life beyond any hope of redemption. Her mother would long since have gone to bed, so she let herself in through the front door.

She never noticed her father's car in the garage, and when she saw his suitcase in the front hall, she simply stopped, dumbfounded. She was still standing there when he came to the top of the stairs and turned on the light. "Tabitha? What the hell are you doing down there?" His voice held that slight tremble that always preceded violence. Something snapped inside her when she heard it this time.

She turned on her heel and rushed out through the still open door, running through the darkness, not having consciously chosen a destination. But when she found herself trudging up the dirt road to the old quarry, she knew immediately that this was right, that she had gambled and lost and had to pay the penalty for her foolishness. "If only I hadn't listened to Jessica," she thought. Tabby didn't hesitate more than a second before throwing herself off the lip toward the jagged rocks below.

And found herself sitting in the school cafeteria.

"Looks almost edible today, doesn't it?" Jessica nodded toward the anemic beef stew.

Tabby blinked. "Yeah, I guess." Had it all been a daydream of some sort?

"So you're interested in Terry Brady. Maybe I can help with that."

Tabby thought about it. "Not really. Thanks anyway." And she turned so ostentatiously back to her food that Jessica froze, then shrugged and moved to another table.

There actually was a party at the Reeds that weekend, and for a while Tabby was convinced that she really had died and returned to life in her own past. But as the months passed, she decided that she must have heard about it earlier and stitched it into her daydream. Dream or not, it changed Tabby dramatically. She was no longer quite as frightened of her father, and her newfound self assurance seemed to disconcert him. He displayed no more respect for her than he had before, but his contempt was more circumspect. Her interest in boys didn't exactly atrophy, but she set it aside for the time being, concentrated on her grades, and won a nearly full scholarship to Brown University.

Her father was furious and told her she couldn't go. "You're not going off to live with a bunch of hippies and dykes!"

Tabby, who now called herself Tabitha, didn't argue with him. She simply packed her bags and moved out while he was at work one day. He followed her to Providence only to be arrested, twice, once before and once after the restraining order. The last she heard from him was a terse letter forbidding her to ever speak to either of her parents again.

Halfway through her freshman year, Tabitha began dating James Nicholson, who described himself inaccurately as a pre-law student and carefully avoided mentioning that he was on academic probation. Nicholson was very much like her father, physically domineering, fixed in his opinions, unable to accept alternate viewpoints. She quickly fell into the old pattern of subordinating her own interests and needs, abandoning her old friends and adopting his, even modifying her stance on public issues. The only ground she still held solidly was on sexual matters. She was no prude and Nicholson had enjoyed considerable liberties, but the final bastion remained intact.

"Come on, Tabitha. You're not going to tell me you want to wait until we're married, are you? I can't think of anything more awkward than two virgins trying to make love for the first time on their wedding night."

She held out until they'd been dating a full year before finally agreeing to spend a weekend at a rented cabin in Vermont. They saw very little of the autumn foliage that was theoretically the justification for the trip, and Nicholson proved to be a surprisingly ardent and experienced lover. Until that weekend, she had thought she was in love with him; by Sunday night, she was certain of it.

A few weeks later, two days after discovering that Nicholson had at least one other current paramour, Tabitha sat in her dorm room, staring at the prescription she'd been given by the doctor at the health center. The good news was that she hadn't tested HIV positive; the bad news was that she had a serious venereal disease.

"If only I hadn't gotten involved with him," she thought, over and over again, as she drew the warm bath and set a row of razor blades out in careful order on the side of the bathtub.

As before, Tabitha felt a sudden sense of unreality. A moment ago she had been lying in the bathtub, watching her blood swirl through the hot water, and now she was standing in the quadrangle, facing a handsome young man with a crew cut. "Nice to meet you, Tabitha. I'm James, James Nicholson. I'm studying law. What's your major?"

She regarded him solemnly for a moment. "I'm majoring in asshole recognition," she said at last. "And you're flunking out."

Tabitha graduated from Brown with no boyfriend but a degree in liberal arts. She struggled to find a job for more than a year before accepting a clerical position at Eblis Manufacturing. To her dismay, James Nicholson was working there as well, in middle management, but their paths rarely crossed and they never spoke. She dated two of her co-workers, neither very seriously, but one of them introduced her to Kevin Chilton, a suave, soft-spoken, handsome stock analyst who eventually slipped past her defenses and captured her heart. The resemblance to her father, both physical and otherwise, was not lost on her this time, but he was a gentler, more refined version, and she grew comfortable with him. His opinions were completely petrified, but he didn't bridle in the face of disagreement, he seemed genuinely interested in her as a person and viewed her political and philosophical shortcomings as quirks rather than personality flaws. He was also a gentle and considerate lover who always used a condom. They dated for over a year, took a short break from each other, then reunited.

Two months later, while sitting on the end of a pier on Block Island, he proposed to her and she accepted.

Their marriage, like most, was neither completely happy nor unhappy. They argued at times, occasionally with considerable heat, but he never struck her, often apologized for his tone, although without ever admitting that he might have been wrong. Tabitha fell into her old habits without feeling any discomfort. Their friends were all his business associates, he administered the budget and made all the financial decisions, and she ran the house subject to his approval. She wanted children, but he didn't, so she stayed on the pill even though it caused her to gain weight which he then remarked upon, although he never quite criticized overtly.

For the most part, Tabitha devoted herself to making Kevin happy. She entertained his friends, even the ones she didn't care for, listened attentively to his complaints about his job, national and local political issues, the liberal media, and the shortcomings of what he called "the great unwashed", the public in general. She let him choose which television shows to watch, which movies to attend, which wines to drink, and where they would spend their infrequent vacations.

She considered herself a devoted, dutiful, and happily married woman. Which is why it came as a particular shock when he told her he wanted a divorce, that he'd been seeing someone else for almost two years. He promised to divide the assets fairly, but as it happened he had taken out a second mortgage on the house, used up most of their savings, and what was left would mostly go to their divorce lawyers. Tabitha was so completely taken unawares that her mind closed up like a shell and she was often unaware of her surroundings. It was in such a state that she stepped off a curb in front of a delivery van, resulting in a hip so badly broken that she could expect to experience mild pain for the rest of her life.

Tabitha still believed that her earlier experiences were dreams or illusions or faulty memories, but just before she took the overdose that killed her, she wondered if this was really going to be the end after all. "If only I hadn't agreed to marry him."

Kevin Chilton would remark to the end of his life that he never understood why Tabitha responded to his marriage proposal by pushing him off the pier.

Tabitha Claremont's friends speculated that she might be gay after she broke up with Kevin. She refused all advances from other men and confined her social life to women, although there was a palpable distance even there. Something else had changed as well. Kevin had talked about his work, and Tabitha remembered enough to make some very profitable investments in the stock market. Within two years, she was living on her earnings and had taken Gretchen Foster as her partner in a small investment firm that very quickly became a major success. After four years, their joint assets were well over two million dollars, initially the product of Tabitha's foresight and later of Gretchen's savvy. The partners trusted each other implicitly and there were rumors, unfounded, that they were lovers as well. If Gretchen had had her way, they would have been more than rumors, but Tabitha had grown wary of close human entanglements, and a respectful friendship and business relationship was the most she would allow.

The trouble started during their fourth year together, although Tabitha only realized that in retrospect. She had become progressively less involved with the firm, partly because she no longer had much to contribute, having used up all of her secret memories, partly because Gretchen had become more obvious about her romantic feelings. Tabitha had been forced to rebuff her rather bluntly, and Gretchen had not reacted well. She was clearly deeply depressed, was less careful about her appearance, and became increasingly drawn and subject to emotional outbursts. Tabitha finally decided to take an extended leave of absence, hoping Gretchen would work things out on her own while she was gone. If not, it would be time to consider dissolving their partnership.

She returned from Europe to find Gretchen hospitalized. The doctors were less than forthcoming, but Gretchen's parents reluctantly admitted the truth. Their daughter had turned to drugs as solace for her unrequited love, or perhaps the latter was just an excuse. In any case, she would be unable to return to her normal life for months, perhaps years.

Even worse, as Tabitha discovered during the course of the next several weeks, Gretchen had managed to lose most of their joint assets. She wasn't quite bankrupt, but she was definitely broke.

This time Tabitha knew exactly what she needed to do. She found a stash of Gretchen's drugs in the back of a file drawer and brought them home with her.

"If only I hadn't decided that I needed a business partner," she said aloud, and turned to the array of plastic bottles.

She was standing on a crowded bus and this transition startled her more than had any of the previous ones. Was this when I decided? Did I really make a choice that would affect my life so significantly while riding on a bus? It must have been so, but it would be so no longer. She would manage her own affairs.

Tabitha liquidated all of her assets in order to have a kernel of cash from which to expand her fortune. She made an appointment with a stock broker, most definitely not Kevin Chilton, and overrode his objections to her investment plan. Two weeks later, she realized that while little time had passed in the world around her, subjectively she had lived several years since her now non-existent marriage to Kevin Chilton, and during the interim, some of her memories had lost their crispness. She had misjudged the timing on her investment in Lexico and misremembered the name of the small software company which had evolved into a major behind the scenes player. Instead of the steady growth she expected, she found herself on a rollercoaster of gains and losses, with the latter eventually prevailing. To add insult to injury, Gretchen Foster and her lesbian lover, Amanda Raymond, had become significant players in the investment world.

She was bankrupt by the end of the first year, and the only thing that prevented her from committing suicide once again was a fluke memory. Sometime during the course of the next two years, she could win the lottery. She knew it with absolute certainty because the winning combination had included her social security number, a coincidence that had marked itself indelibly in her memory. Although she couldn't remember the exact date, all that was necessary was that she be patient and play her number every time the jackpot started to rise.

It took eighteen months, during most of which Tabitha lived in a decaying tenement, relying on welfare money to pay her bills. During that time she was twice assaulted for what little money she carried and once raped by a drunken lout who left her with herpes and a broken hip, odd echoes of lives she had now never lived. She supplemented her income by waiting tables part time at a disreputable restaurant and endured rudeness and occasional obscene propositions from the surly clientele. The world appeared united in oppressing her, and small misfortunes were magnified in her mind to major transgressions. A barking dog followed her home one day and that evening she threw him a ball of raw hamburger laced with rat poison. A neighbor accidentally splashed her with water from a puddle and under cover of darkness she slashed all four of his tires. She had no friends, several enemies, and most of the other people who knew her thought she was mildly scary. Only the promise of the lottery kept her from killing herself again, but at last her number came up and her take, after taxes, was slightly over eleven million dollars.

Tabitha was dismayed but not entirely surprised to discover that her good fortune was insufficient compensation for all she had suffered. During the eighteen months of poverty, she had had ample time to reflect on her life, and the indignities and humiliations she had experienced were now swollen, cancerous tumors threatening to burst and overpower her with rage and hatred. She had often ameliorated the pain by fantasizing her vengeance on those who had wronged her, and now she had the means to make those dreams real.

Her father was beyond her reach, having died of cancer two years previously, but the others weren't.

She bought the old Swanson place in Managansett, her home town, partly because it was familiar, mostly because it was remote enough for her purposes, an old farm house on the outskirts of the reservoir. It cost more than she expected to clean the place up and make it presentable, but that didn't matter. She had concocted a new plan, one that would make her present fortune seem penny ante. For the time being at least, the money was secondary.

Except in the case of Gretchen Foster, it was not difficult to entice all of her invitees to a weekend party. Terry Brady had married Jessica Calvert, which made it very easy to invite them both up for an informal high school reunion. She lured James Nicholson with a job offer and Kevin Chilton with the prospect of managing her newly acquired portfolio of stocks. Gretchen politely declined the same ploy, insisting she had enough clients already, so Tabitha went to see her and make the invitation personal. Whatever physical chemistry had attracted Gretchen in the now defunct timeline was still functioning, and Tabitha played to it, eventually receiving a promise that Gretchen would attend.

The five guests might have been puzzled by the makeup of their group, but they didn't have time to think about it. The wine served at their first meal was drugged and when they awakened, they had all been securely bound.

She spent five days exacting her revenge, one day for each of them, and when she was done she left a mess behind that even the seasoned local coroner would find disturbing.

Tabitha drove down Reservoir Road, headed for her mother's house. She knew that once she died and was restored, all of her work would be undone, but she would still have the memories of these five days, and that would sustain her, allow her to live with the resentments that boiled within her. Memory would do something else as well. She had learned her lesson this time. On the seat beside her was a slip of paper on which was written the string of numbers which would win her a lottery prize of nearly two hundred million dollars, a number which no one had played and which had come up the day after she had decided not to go to her father's funeral. There were enough sleeping pills in her purse to kill her several times over, once she was sure the numbers were etched into her memory. There was also a loaded revolver with which she planned to shoot her mother, the woman who had never stood up for herself, and who had allowed her daughter to be turned into a perpetual victim.. But victim no more.

"I just have to remember that damned number," she whispered aloud. The nagging fear that she would forget it had become a looming threat, the very thought of which caused her mind to go blank. Even though she had studied it for more than an hour already, she wasn't quite certain of the first digit, and she turned her head, reached down for the reassuring hard copy, and as she did so a sports car shot out of a side street, slewed across the road, sideswiped her car just solidly enough to send it crashing into one of the oversized maples that lined the street.

In the last few painful seconds before consciousness faded, Tabitha had the presence of mind to whisper one last sentence. "If only I had attended my father's funeral." But she knew instinctively that it wouldn't work unless she died by her own hand.

When she opened her eyes, she found herself in a bed. The room was very unfamiliar, just a blank white wall and some curtains. A voice sounded from somewhere out of her line of sight, but she couldn't turn her head to look.

"Her eyes are open, doctor."

"It's just reflex. It's not likely that she'll ever regain consciousness. I'm sorry, detective, but the paralysis is complete and permanent."

"Well, it's just as well. It'll save the state the cost of the trial."

"You're certain that she killed all those people then?"

"Absolutely. She made no effort to cover her tracks. Her fingerprints are everywhere, in the blood, on the bodies. What's left of them anyway."

"She must really have hated them."

"As far as we can tell, three of them were complete strangers. I guess this just proves that winning the lottery doesn't solve all your personal problems."

The voices were fading, as though the speakers were going away, and Tabitha never did see their faces.

She realized the truth then. She was paralyzed and likely to remain that way until she died. And if she didn't die by her own hand, she wasn't going to be able to come back. She was trapped this way for the rest of what would undoubtedly be her final life.

"If only I hadn't looked away at just that moment," she thought to herself.

But she had.

MOLOCH'S FURNACE

The silent factory stank of ancient dust and drying oils, with just the slightest acrid hint of blood.

When Captain Samuels approached the rookie cop posted at the entrance, the young woman almost challenged him before recognizing his deeply scarred face. "Sir!" She snapped to attention, stiffening her back and staring at an invisible target somewhere over his right shoulder.

"Relax...Wheaton," he had to lean forward to read her name tag. Maybe it was time to accept the inevitable and have his eyes checked. The progressive deterioration of his body was annoying and increasingly undeniable. "This isn't the army, you know. Where's Caulfield?"

"Inside, sir." Her attempt to relax was largely unsuccessful.

Samuels let his eyes wander to left and right, scanning the dirty walls of Eblis Manufacturing, illuminated in places by the dim security lights set along the perimeter of the property. "That covers quite a bit of territory, Wheaton. Can you be a little more specific?"

"Yes, sir. Sorry, sir. Straight ahead once you're inside, then take a left at the second aisle and follow it all the way to the back. It's...he's in there, sir."

Samuels hesitated a second. "You've seen it, haven't you, Wheaton?"

The young woman nodded, and even in the artificial light, he could see that she was losing color. "Only from a distance, sir."

"And I imagine that was quite enough. Carry on." And he stepped through the doorway.

It was dark inside, windowless, the walls and equipment painted drab, unexciting colors. There was dirt everywhere, so thick on the floor that its surface was rough and treacherous. Samuels had toured the factory on a previous occasion. The manufacturing process fascinated him, the featureless skids of brass and lead and other metals were transformed by their passage through a series of loud, dirty, chaotic production departments, emerging as highly polished, silver and gold plated giftware, elegantly packaged and ready for the stores.

Caterpillars and butterflies. Diamonds formed from ancient coal.

There were voices in the distance, indistinct. Flashes of light strobed irregularly, police photographers plying their trade.

Huge mounds of machinery lurked in the corners. The walls were decorated with faded posters advocating safe work habits and quality awareness. Samuels turned at the second aisle and emerged into an enormous work area, metal frame ceiling thirty feet above a concrete slab. At least a dozen technicians and police officers were in sight, but the usual chatter was muted.   Lieutenant Caulfield had been standing quietly to one side, moved forward to greet his superior.

"Good evening, Captain. Didn't expect to see you here." Didn't want to either, no doubt. It could be interpreted as criticism of Caulfield's handling of the case. This was, after all, the third incident, and they were as much in the dark as ever.

"Who was it this time?" There was no point in reassuring the detective; he'd just interpret it as evidence he was under a cloud.

"Security guard, name of Olson. Probably attacked while he was making his rounds, either here or in one of the two departments beyond." He gestured vaguely.

"Can't you narrow it down a little further than that?" Samuels tried to keep his voice neutral.

"Not yet. We're still missing parts of the body."

Samuels grimaced. Point to Caulfield. "Give me the short version, Glen. I don't want to be in your hair any more than you want me there."

Caulfield put hands in pockets and pursed his lips. "Some of this is just guesswork."

"I won't quote you."

"All right. Olson came on duty at eleven last night, right on time according to the log. Sergeant Vernon's on his way over to interview the man he relieved, but everything seems to have been routine. Sometime between midnight and two, Olson started his rounds. He's supposed to do one circuit in each two hour block, with random routes and starting times."

"Was he armed?"

"Yes. Didn't do him much good. Anyway, we don't know specifically where he was attacked, but we're pretty certain it was on the ground floor, even though we found the time clock up on a mezzanine in the next building."

"Might have dropped it running away."

"Not with his heart jammed inside it, he wouldn't."

Samuels made a disgusted noise. "This is the same as the others then?"

"I'd say so. Olson was attacked, obviously, but there's so much damage to the body, I don't think we'll ever know exactly how or when he died. The largest concentration of blood is back there, where his torso was crushed in a punch press, but Dr. Kai believes the limbs and head had already been removed at that point. Probably the sexual organs as well, although we haven't found those yet."

"Wonderful. Who called it in?"

"Shift supervisor came by at 3:15 when Olson didn't answer the phone. Says he'd caught Olson sleeping on the job a couple of times and came by to check."

"Christ, doesn't he read the papers?"

"He's a retired first sergeant, Captain, and probably an alcoholic. I could smell it on his breath."

"Anyone notify Olson's family?"

"Not that I know of. Apparently his wife was killed by a drunk driver earlier this year and they didn't have any kids. We're working on it."

"Is anyone here from the company?"

Caulfield nodded. "Nicholson's up front in the offices. Didn't have the stomach to stay here." He made a sour face. "Couple of the lab boys are pretty shaky too. The smell's bad and some of the things that were done with the body are sick. Olson's arms were propped up so he was holding his own head in his hands."

Samuels left a few minutes later without approaching the remains. Even from a distance, the stink had become unpleasantly intrusive.

This was the third grotesque killing to take place inside the factory since the beginning of the summer. The first victim was a teenage prowler named Carl Ross who apparently ran away from his abusive father and gained access through a second story window.

Someone had used a jigsaw to cut him into so many pieces that it had taken the authorities three days to gather and tag them all from where they'd been scattered throughout the five buildings that made up the factory complex.

Victim number two was an exterminator. He'd been passed through by the guard on a Sunday morning and never came out. The coroner believed that the entire body had been recovered from the compactor, but it was difficult to be certain. Even after his not particularly bereft wife was sober and reasonably attentive, she'd been unable to positively confirm the body, although the dead man's fingerprints had proven conclusive. No clues, no suspects, no apparent motive.

And now the third.

Samuels would have preferred to leave the entire mess to Caulfield but despite an unusual willingness by the news media to downplay the more dramatic aspects of the story, enough of an uproar had been raised to result in strong, ongoing pressure to close the case. If there wasn't movement soon, he'd have to start dealing with questions for which he had inadequate answers.

They didn't find Olson's missing organs until almost noon the following day, when one of the technicians got more than he bargained for from a candy vending machine.

Samuels authorized the posting of two police officers inside the factory. Lab reports began to accumulate, providing no new information. Even the cause of death was described no more specifically than "massive generalized trauma".

Two frustrating weeks passed.

It was just after one o'clock on a Wednesday morning when the phone rang. Samuels rolled over in bed, aware that a call to his unlisted number at this time of night meant bad news.

It was Caulfield, his voice so hoarse it was almost unrecognizable. "We've had another one, just like the others."

"At Eblis?" Of course it was at Eblis. "But there's no one there except.."

"Yeah, we lost one of our own this time."

Rookie Julie Wheaton wasn't supposed to wander out of sight of her partner, but he'd gone to use the restroom and she was missing when he returned. The other officer had made a brief search before realizing something was wrong and sounding the alarm. By then it was too late.

Samuels didn't go to the factory, but he showered and dressed and drove to the station, just to be doing something, waiting impatiently for the phone to ring, for Caulfield to tell him that this time, at last, the killer had made a mistake, left a clue, a bloody fingerprint, the imprint of a sole on the oily floor. He'd even be happy with a wisp of hair or a torn piece of cloth.

The phone never did ring; Caulfield reported in person.

"Anything?"

Caulfield shook his head and slid into a chair. "I'm putting in for early retirement first thing tomorrow." He didn't look as though he was kidding.

"What's wrong, Glen?"

"What's wrong?" The detective's eyes blinked rapidly and his voice shook with stress. "I've got an officer's blood painting the walls of a factory, Captain. I've got parts of her body packed in fucking gift boxes. Her head was in a coffee pot, most of it anyway. The eyes and ears were hidden in pillboxes and the tongue was in a bud vase."

Caulfield's voice had continued to rise and Samuels gestured for him to calm down. It didn't work.

"He skinned her, Captain. After she was dead, I hope. He cut out her heart and put it in one of those big foil covered boxes with embossed flowers all over it, then gift wrapped it with her own skin. Even tied a pretty bow to finish it off." The detective was leaning forward across the desk now, his eyes fixed. "Do you know what he used to tie that bow, Captain? Her fucking intestines, that's what!"

Caulfield requested that he be taken off the case; Samuels refused. They weren't friends, but he had no better investigator. The state police had casually offered technical assistance, but they were dragging their feet, still angry because the local Chief had publicly criticized their efficiency in an earlier case.

Political bullshit, and he'd just lost an officer.

"Do you know why Wheaton was a cop, Captain?"

Samuels shook his head, waited patiently while Caulfield gathered his thoughts.

"She was gang raped at fifteen. Identified three of her assailants, but they never even came to trial. The attorney general's office decided they couldn't make it stick. Officer Wheaton...Julie...said she wanted to be there for someone else next time."

Or even the score, Samuels thought, but didn't say.

Although he'd had less than two hours sleep the night before, Samuels remained at the station until nine o'clock. On his way home, he stopped at the Main Street Cafe, realizing he needed to eat before collapsing into bed.

When he returned to his car a few minutes later, a large wrapped deli sandwich in one hand, he saw Julie Wheaton watching him from the shadows.

Or maybe it was someone else. Certainly the face was the same, the general shape of her body, the color of her hair. But even in the poor light and from a distance, there were differences. Her posture was alert, with confidence rather than nervous uncertainty, the angle of her chin higher, other subtle changes in posture, shoulders, the position of her arms, the way she stood there.

Watching him.

Samuels dropped the sandwich through the open window and started in her direction. She nodded, not acknowledging him but responding to some internal stimulus, and then she was moving away, not retreating, but not hesitating either.

"Hey! Wait!"

Samuels quickened his steps, but she was around the corner of the building before he'd closed the gap significantly. When he reached that point seconds later, an automobile emerged from the side street, and he saw what was unmistakably Julie Wheaton sitting in the passenger seat as it passed him. He also saw the driver's face in profile, male, young, hair long and unkempt. Also familiar, although it took a few seconds before he dredged the name out of his memory.

Carl Ross. The first person killed at Eblis Manufacturing. And Wheaton had been the fourth. Were the other two also wandering around in the darkness?

"Of course we're certain of the identification. I realize you're under a great deal of pressure, Captain Samuels, but I resent the implication that we might have mishandled such a basic question.

You've worked here for how long now, two years? Long enough to recognize the thoroughness of my staff."

Dr. Kai was obviously angry, but not as much as might have been expected. His team's inability to find anything even remotely resembling a clue in the residue of four separate murders had made him defensive and uncharacteristically deferential.

"I'm not being critical, Doctor. I just don't want to leave any possibility unexamined. The state of the bodies...I wondered if that might have been designed to conceal their real identities."

"Impossible. We've recovered virtually all of the digits, Captain, the fingers. And in three of the four cases, dentition as well. Not to mention DNA."

"But what if someone altered the records?"

Kai shrugged. "The prints were checked through the federal integrated identification system, the dental records with family physicians and, in two cases, military records. We found a scar on the appendix of the second victim which matched his medical history and the DNA samples all matched. You are stipulating a rather unlikely scenario, Captain. Do you have reason to do so?"

"No, not really." Samuels sat back in his chair. "Just closing loopholes, no matter how tiny."

After Dr. Kai allowed himself to be soothed and ushered out, Captain Samuels sat back in his chair, stared up at the ceiling, and wondered if this was finally the case he'd been waiting for, the reason he'd pursued a career in criminology, moving restlessly from one jurisdiction to another.

Two days later, he saw Julie Wheaton again. She was sitting in the front room of his apartment when he opened the door, her face quite recognizable in the dim glow cast by his security light.

"Come in," she said quietly, but with a voice that clearly expected obedience. "Close the door."

He did as he was told.

"How did you get in here?" He wasn't armed, hadn't carried a weapon routinely in years. His eyes strayed to the locked cabinet in the short rear hall. "Who are you?"

"You know who I am." Was there an undertone of amusement? He wasn't certain.

"I know who you're *not*."

"You're making a simple situation unnecessarily complex, Captain Samuels. Believe the evidence of your eyes."

"Believe that a woman who was murdered and dismembered has somehow reassembled herself?"

"Believe that appearances are sometimes deceiving, that reality sometimes exceeds experience, that humanity transcends these frail envelopes." She touched her hand to her chest.

"Why are you here? What do you want?"

Something moved in the darkness of the far hall, another intruder, one who stepped forward just far enough that his profile was visible. Samuels recognized him immediately. Edgar Haynes, a professional exterminator until his untimely death at the hands of a still unidentified murderer.

"Are you afraid of dying, Captain Samuels?" Wheaton, or whatever it was that looked like Julie Wheaton, hadn't moved.

A few seconds passed before he answered. "Everyone dies."

"True enough. But death can be a transition rather than an ending."

Samuels licked his lips, trying to analyze his situation. Were they planning to kill him in order to conceal the fact of their existence? But then, why reveal themselves in the first place?

"I suppose you're going to tell me you know from experience, right?"

Haynes, or whatever it was that looked like Haynes, made a short, throaty sound that might have been a laugh. Wheaton uncrossed her legs and stood up, gracefully, calm and self confident, but without offering any overt threat.

"Come with us, and find out for yourself." Haynes moved across the room, a swift, silent shadow, lost again in darkness near the door.

"Come where?"

"You know the answer to that." And he did. The factory.

"Why should I go with you, there or anywhere else?"

"Because you want answers." And he did, so he went.

A station wagon was waiting outside. Carl Ross was driving. Samuels got into the back with Wheaton, while Haynes slipped silently into the front.

"Where's Olson?"

"He'll be waiting. There was an errand to be run."

Ross pressed the accelerator and Samuels settled back thoughtfully.

They pulled off onto the shoulder on an unlighted stretch of road not far from the factory. Before Samuels could ask any questions, he spotted Olson moving toward them. The one time watchman was carrying a large, brass bound steamer trunk balanced on his shoulder, showing no sign of strain. No one said anything while it was being loaded into the rear. Olson slid in beside Samuels without speaking.

The two policemen at Eblis glanced at each other uneasily, but they both knew Samuels and at least nominally accepted that the people with him were a team of specialists who'd been called in to examine the murder scene. Wheaton stayed in the shadows to avoid being recognized, and Olson and Ross made a major production of carrying the trunk of "equipment", even though Samuels was quite certain either of them could have managed alone.

The atmosphere inside was different; he realized that immediately. The cold, neutral machinery appeared unaltered, but there was an underlying sense of animation, hidden movement, the flow of blood under metallic skin, the touch of unseen eyes on his own flesh. The air was in motion, not a breeze exactly, but rather a slow crawling like the shallow, labored breath of some colossal beast.

"Why are we here? Are you going to kill me like the others...like you were killed? Turn me into one of you?"

Wheaton shook her head. "Our god rewards only those who join him of their own volition."

"Your god?"

"According to the number of thy cities are thy gods, O Judah." It was Haynes who answered, his voice deep, gravelly, solemn. They came to a stop in the press department, where the air tasted of static electricity.

"You're devil worshippers?" Samuels glanced from one face to another, seeking confirmation.

"Our allegiance is not to your Christian god, if that's what you mean. Ours is an older, more potent deity. When Yahweh destroyed Baal and his other rivals, only our lord was wise enough to conceal himself, gather his strength, wait for a time when this so-called gentler god would become weak and complacent."

"Weak and complacent?"

"Does Yahweh reward his people as does Moloch? Our rebirth left behind drug dependency, illness, and other frailties of the old flesh. Will your god free you of those weakening eyes, the growing pain in your hip, the scars of a lifetime?"

"You still haven't told me why I'm here."

"We require the assistance of someone who has not yet made the transition, someone influential. Obviously we can't hope to return to our old lives and need to establish new identities."

"Why can't your...god...conjure something up for you? Why do you need me?"

"Unlike Yahweh, Moloch does not claim to be the only god. And all the gods are jealous ones. Even gods need to be cautious at times."

"And what would stop me from promising you anything you want, and betraying you the moment I'm free."

"The wrath of any god is a terrible thing, but we will require a further binding."

As she spoke, Haynes and Olson unlatched the trunk and lifted the lid. A young girl was curled up inside, just barely a teenager, and small for her age. Her eyes were open but unfocused, her wrists and ankles bound, mouth covered by tape.

Samuels let his eyes speak the question.

"There's a drum of kerosene behind you." Wheaton gestured toward the shadows.

"A fire alarm will attract an awful lot of attention, don't you think?"

"There will be no alarm. Our lord is near. Can't you feel his presence?"

And he did feel something, coiled power quiescent but expectant, volition in solid form. There was another being in the factory with them. No, not just in the factory but manifest within the walls and floors and machinery itself. Moloch was the factory; the factory was Moloch.

"In times past, people gave their children willingly to the god. There will come a time when they will do so again, so many that their lines will stretch for miles. Moloch's hunger is insatiable and he has not fed for thousands of years, Captain."

Samuels stepped closer to the trunk, as though ready to comply. For the first time in his career, he regretted not carrying a weapon. It would have made things so much simpler.

Ross was the closest at that point, standing just beyond the trunk. Samuels drove his fist into the young man's chest and ripped out his heart, letting it fall to the floor in front of its owner's unbelieving eyes. Haynes was next, because he chose to leap toward his enemy, confident of the power of his new body. Samuels felt the flesh of both arms split as he emerged from within himself, the old mortal pains swept away by the transformation.

Claws raked Haynes from throat to groin and he fell to his knees, still not comprehending his own death. His second death.

Samuels could feel the god's rage all around him. The air thrummed with tension, the temperature had risen sharply, and some of the machines had begun to function even though no hand had touched them.

The two survivors attacked together, catching him in the midst of full emergence, and Wheaton slammed her fist past his guard and into the lower ribs. But the bones were already bending aside as his real body shook free of its cocoon, and he shrugged off the blow.

Wheaton turned to flee as Olson was torn apart, victim of Samuels' exhilarating sense of his own power. He caught her near the door, wrapping her struggling body within his great, leathery wings and slowly crushing the life from her new body.

This time, there'd be no resurrection.

With his enemies dead, the creature that had once been Evan Samuels returned to the press room, still vibrant with the god's presence, but muted now, uncertain. He approached the trunk, glanced inside, saw that the young girl was conscious now. Her eyes widened in shock when she caught sight of his face, horns and serpent hair and a flickering, bifurcated tongue.

"You've been absent from this world too long, Moloch," he said aloud, addressing the factory at large. "Your methods are clumsy, your tools weak and unreliable, and worst of all, you are ignorant and ill informed. Yahweh was clever but never strong enough to triumph. It is Baal who rules this world."

Samuels, or that which had once thought of itself as Samuels, felt the rage gathering on every side. He reached down into the trunk, lifted the bound girl out by her hair, held her dangling from one outstretched arm.

"By this gift to the one true god of this world, I cast you out of your own temple, Moloch." And with that, he severed the girl's head from her body with a single claw tipped finger.

A silent shriek of rage rose and faded, and the factory was once again no more evil or dangerous than usual.

And the world went on as it had been.

THE GUEST HOUSE

In the early morning of her second night in Managansett, Kim woke to her dead husband's touch.

It was a dream, of course, phantom memories of a sensation she'd never experience again, wish fulfillment. She realized the truth immediately but it was still unsettling. The pressure of his knee against the inside of her thighs, raspy chin lightly brushing her shoulder.

"I'm so sorry, Sam."

She rolled out of bed and turned on the nightlight. It was a low wattage bulb and emphasized rather than dispersed the gloomy shadows. Kim wrapped herself in a terrycloth robe and went downstairs to the kitchen.

Almost four thirty; she ought to sleep another two hours, rest thoroughly for her meeting at Eblis Manufacturing. Technically she didn't start work until the following Monday, but it was simple courtesy to introduce herself. Nicholson and his management staff would resent her, as they would any "spy" sent by corporate headquarters, but there was no sense aggravating an already tense situation.

"That'll come soon enough," she whispered softly, the sound swallowed up by the room.

She made a pot of coffee, stronger than she preferred, out of habit derived from Sam's love of caffeine. While it was brewing, she prowled the ground floor of the company guest house.

It was bigger than she had expected, four bedrooms and two baths upstairs, kitchen, library, and an oversized dining room below. Eblis had owned the property for years, used it for company functions, visiting dignitaries, and other purposes. Kim expected to remain in Managansett for at least three months, with periodic visits thereafter while the systems at Eblis were fine tuned to interface with corporate standards.

There was a muffled thud from the second floor.

Kim froze at the foot of the stairs, waiting for a recurrence. Had something fallen? Was there an animal in the house? Squirrels had watched disapprovingly while she'd carried in her bags the day before, and the house was certainly old enough to have breaches in its defenses.

After a brief search, she found the switch that turned on the fixture over the staircase, then cautiously investigated. Her hairbrush lay on the floor of the bathroom, but there was no other sign of disturbance. She set it down on the counter, several inches from the edge, and returned to her coffee.

The preliminary meeting had been even worse than expected. Nicholson was openly hostile and as Superintendent of Operations he'd be setting the tone for most of his subordinates. Jennison, the inventory manager, made no effort to conceal his interest in her legs, and she decided to forego skirts in favor of suits for the duration of her visit, hot weather or not.

"You have to realize, Miss Belk, that just because our systems are different doesn't mean they're wrong." Fox, the programmer, was an aloof, patronizing man who wouldn't meet her eyes.

"I never thought they were, Mr. Fox. But ADI uses a uniform reporting system for all of its transactions."

"If you give me the specs, I could write a back end conversion program..."

"The reporting itself is only part of the issue." Despite her good intentions, Kim felt her temper rising, decided to show a bit of steel below the gaudy hilt. "Standardization will make it easier for someone to take over in the event that you or anyone at this site becomes unavailable." She paused to let that sink in, then sheathed her sword. "We depend on the existing management team to implement the changes. My role is primarily advisory; I'll answer questions as they arise and help in any way that I can."

The message seemed to have been received, but it didn't add to her popularity. She wasn't even invited to lunch.

Kim spent the afternoon stocking the kitchen and bathroom. Managansett was a sleepy, mostly residential town that seemed to have stepped out of the timestream - no fast food restaurants, no video rentals, not even a shopping plaza. There was an IGA in the center of town, an independent drug store adjacent, but she ended up driving to Foodworld out by the interstate before crossing the last item off her list. Then she got lost on the way back, took the wrong turn off Reservoir Road, and finally arrived at the house in a mood composed of blind fury and despair.

She drank entirely too much wine with her supper and fell asleep on the couch.

"Kim? C'mon, honey, let's go up to bed." A hand gently gripped her shoulder.

"Hmmmm?" She moved her head, regretted it. The muscles in her neck were stiff and someone had glued her eyelids shut. Squinting, she stood with considerable difficulty, and only made it upstairs by holding onto the mahogany handrail. In the bedroom, she kicked off her shoes and fell face forward, still not bothering to undress.

The window fan had picked up a flutter, a regular disruption of its normal hum. Kim tried to sink back into unconsciousness but the intrusive noise interfered and she grew more rather than less alert.

She remembered the hand on her shoulder as she'd slumped on the couch.

"My God!"

Kneeling beside the toilet moments later, waiting to see if her stomach was finally empty, Kim wondered if she'd ever stop missing Sam, his touch, his voice, his habits, if she'd ever stop feeling guilty because she escaped the inferno that had been their car while he lay trapped inside.

The house was in order by Friday morning except that the air conditioning was largely ineffective. Kim considered visiting Eblis, decided against it. Instead, she reviewed the implementation plan, made some minor changes, and took an extended walk. The neighborhood was an older one, the houses surrounded by trees, and except for brief glimpses through windows, she saw nothing of her neighbors.

An hour later, the sky began to cloud over, so Kim returned to the house, let herself in through the front door, and bolted it behind her.

Something was wrong.

She prowled the ground floor for several minutes, returning to rooms she'd already inspected, convinced that something had changed while she was out. The sky rumbled distantly and darkened, but no rain fell.

"All right, let's do this systematically." Standing in the center of the living room, she turned slowly, cataloguing every item, checking its current location against her memory. Pillows in place on the couch, magazines in a fan across the coffee table, box of tissues beside the lamp. Lightning flashed brilliantly and she glanced out the front window just as the wind began to bluster.

The curtains were open, not all the way, but enough to provide a view of the front yard. They'd been tightly closed when she'd left. Or had they? Kim couldn't remember opening them, but perhaps she'd done it without thinking. The back door was bolted and she'd locked the front. All of the ground floor windows were secured. It didn't seem possible that anyone could have come in while she was gone.

There was absolutely nothing she could point to as the cause of her concern, but her nerves were on edge for the rest of the day.

The storm continued throughout the night, torrential rain, spectacular lightning, ragged thunder that jolted her from sleep on several occasions. The humidity rose steadily and she tossed off first the sheet, then her nightgown, letting the fan's feathery touch play across her back. The flutter became intermittent, which was even worse. Now she found herself listening, waiting for it to recur.

Hopelessly awake, she got out of bed shortly before sunrise, took a leisurely bath. The warm water was soothing and she let her head fall back, drifted off to sleep until a thunderclap jolted her awake. Momentarily disoriented, she flailed about, half rose, then fell, banging her forehead against the wall of the shower stall. Panicking, she threw herself over the side of the tub, lay panting on the bathroom floor.

"Get a grip, girl!" She closed her eyes and willed herself calm, then carefully stood, wincing at the throbbing in her forehead. The mirror revealed an already darkening bruise, but the skin remained unbroken. Kim put her hands on the sides of the sink, let her head fall forward. Tears ran down both cheeks, tears unconnected with any physical pain.

Several minutes passed before she ran some cold water, splashed it onto her face. Kim opened the faucet further, used her hand to rinse the sink, flush away the short black hairs sprinkled across the white porcelain. He'd never learn, she realized. For as long as he lived, Sam would leave the toilet seat up, throw rolled socks into the laundry, and forget to wash out the sink after he shaved.

For as long as he lived.

But Sam was gone, had died six months ago.

Kim jerked her hands away, fled the bathroom, ran downstairs and had the front door open before she realized she was about to run naked into a torrential downpour.

She sat in the kitchen with all the lights on until the sun finally broken through the clouds three hours later.

Kim thought about calling the police, discarded the idea. None of the short black hairs remained when she finally summoned the strength to investigate. It was an old sink; perhaps some previous guest had washed the evidence of his shaving up under the rim and she'd disturbed them somehow. That's what the police would think, anyway, if they didn't just decide she was hysterical.

She locked all of the second story windows, even removed the window fan in her bedroom. At night, while she was sleeping, she'd replace it.

The rest of the weekend passed uneventfully, and she arrived for her first official day at Eblis prepared for the worst. The worst was waiting. The "office" set aside for her was a desk in the typing pool. Zawicki, the office manager, ignored her demand for more privacy until she threatened to go over his head, then remembered a small, barely acceptable office not far from data processing.

Fox referred her to his assistant, a pleasant but browbeaten young woman who apologized with almost every sentence. "I'm sorry he's not available, but we're right in middle of our quarterly reporting cycle." Could Kim have a copy of the general ledger? "I don't know, I mean, I'm not authorized to give you one. I'm really sorry but you'll have to talk to Mr. Fox or Mrs. Raleigh."

Mrs. Raleigh, head bookkeeper, wouldn't release any information without Nicholson's authorization. Nicholson's secretary didn't expect him to be free at all today. "I can get you an appointment for tomorrow afternoon if you'd like."

Surprisingly, Jennison came to the rescue, loaning her his copy of the bill of materials and the inventory transaction records for the past fiscal year. Kim was in the process of upgrading her opinion of the man when he glanced around conspiratorially.

"You're not very popular around here, you know. Most of the staff were outraged when the announcement was made, and none of them likes changing things except Nicholson. And he only supports changes that increase his authority."

"I understand the resentment, but I have a job to do."

Jennison waved his hands. "Oh, you don't have to tell me. I'm on your side. Our systems are antiquated and ineffective. Unfortunately, the same is true of most of the staff." He leaned toward her, let his voice drop to a near whisper. "If you're having trouble, let me know. I can pull a few strings."

The week passed quickly. Kim's initial survey was disheartening; things were even worse than she'd feared. There'd been inventory shortfalls for the past six quarters, but the auditing procedure was so inadequate she couldn't tell whether it was pilferage, unrecorded scrap, over-shipments, or poor receiving records.

Jennison became her second shadow and, despite his obsequious manner, she almost looked forward to seeing him, even went to lunch with him once. When he offered to share his oversized office with her, she accepted after only a brief hesitation. Her assigned cubbyhole was impossibly small. Everyone else remained aloof at best, and open hostility was not uncommon. Thursday she had a shouting match with Fox when he insisted that ADI's order tracking system was inferior to the one he'd written from scratch, and Friday Nicholson called her over an internal phone line.

"I understand there's been some conflict with my staff."

"We've had a few disagreements, and the heat makes tempers short, but I don't have any real complaints." Actually, she had several, but voicing them now would only make matters worse.

"Perhaps you don't, but I certainly have."

Kim bit her lip, hoping that Nicholson would not make an issue of this and reprimand his subordinates. She needed their help, not just their cooperation.

"We're entering our busiest time of year, Miss Belk. I can't have you upsetting key people. If you can't find a more diplomatic way to do your job, I'm going to have to talk to your superiors back in Philadelphia."

For a moment, Kim thought she must have misunderstood. Then blind fury washed away her professional calm. "Be my guest, Nicholson. Here's Bob Satterfield's private line." She spit out the numbers. "Tell him I'm working on that inventory shrinkage he was asking about."

"I don't think I care for your tone, Miss Belk."

"Deal with it." She hung up, her hand shaking so badly she almost missed.

She worked late Friday evening. It was nearly dark when she pulled out of the parking lot, waving to the guard as she did so. He stared at her without returning the gesture. Christ, she thought, is there anyone in this place who doesn't hate me?

The house was dark when she arrived, and the air conditioning seemed to have died completely. "Probably needs freon." She made a mental note to look up the Purchasing Manager at Eblis on Monday. Fortunately, it had cooled off enough that she could survive with just the fan.

Kim was making up a salad for supper when she sensed that she was no longer alone in the house. There were no overt clues, just a tickling on the back of her neck, sounds so low they weren't consciously heard. She'd been slicing radish, stopped, turned with the paring knife still in her hand and walked out into the living room.

Thump.

She heard it clearly, moved to the foot of the stairs, had one foot raised to ascend when a series of metallic bangs shocked her into retreat. They ended almost immediately, but were replaced by a rushing sound that Kim finally recognized.

Someone had turned on the shower.

As silently as possible, she backed into the kitchen, fumbled behind her back and found the wall phone. She dialed 911 with trembling fingers. A woman answered.

"There's a prowler in my house!" Kim tried to keep her voice low and calm, but it sounded too loud, hoarse and crackling with tension.

"Your name, please."

"Kimberly Belk. I'm at 414 Waverly Road."

"I'm dispatching a car now, Miss Belk. Could you please describe your situation. Are you in any immediate danger?"

"I...I don't think so. I'm in the kitchen. He's upstairs, in the bathroom I think."

"Can you get out of the house safely?"

There was a back door from the kitchen. "Yes."

"Then leave immediately. Stay with a neighbor if possible. Don't come back until the officers are there, do you understand?"

She waited under a streetlight for only a moment before they arrived, two policemen her own age. They asked her to sit in their vehicle while they checked out the house, vanished inside without waiting to see if she complied. She didn't, instead walked aimlessly back and forth until one of them reappeared, gestured for her to approach.

"Well, ma'am, there's no sign of a break in and no one appears to be in the house now."

"The bathroom? I heard the shower."

"The shower was running when we got there, ma'am. We turned it off. Could you have left it on this morning?"

"Of course not. Besides, I heard it start. The pipes were knocking like crazy just before."

The second officer joined them. "Could be something wrong with the plumbing then."

Kim opened her mouth, realized she was about to shout at them, and held her peace. She was under a lot of strain; maybe the shower HAD been running all day, and she'd only noticed it when the pipes began knocking.

"I guess that must be it. Thank you, officers. I'm sorry I bothered you."

"That's what we're here for, ma'am." He didn't sound sincere.

The house was silent again when she returned, watching the police drive off before closing the front door. With self imposed deliberation, she climbed to the second floor, walked down the corridor to the bath adjoining the master bedroom. The shower curtain was still shedding drops of water, the tub hadn't quite drained, and the air was thick with steam.

The mirror over the sink was completely obscured except for three crudely drawn letters.

KIM

She used a towel to wipe them off, scoured the entire mirror. Had the police seen her name scrawled there? How could they have missed it? Or had it been written after they'd already descended?

Kim searched the entire house herself, found no one. But she sensed that someone was there.

Watching her.

"I've been thinking about taking an apartment."

Jennison looked up from his coffee. "Something wrong with the company place?"

"No, not exactly. It's just kind of big for me is all."

"But it's free." That seemed to settle the issue for Jennison. "Nicholson would never spring for rent."

"I could pay for it myself."

"There's nothing local, just a couple of rat traps the Kaplan woman runs out on the east end. You'd have to go into Providence. Forty minute commute, on a good day." He was staring at her chest again, she noticed.

"What's the story with that house anyway?"

"Story? The Waverly property you mean?"

"Yes." God, the man was obtuse at times. "Why has Eblis hung onto it so long? How often does it get used?"

"Rarely. It'd been empty for over a year when you came."

"Then why not sell it, pick up some cash, avoid the upkeep and taxes?"

"Oh, it's been for sale off and on for years. No one's interested. Bad reputation."

"What kind of bad reputation? Murder, suicide, drug peddlers, prostitution?"

"None of the above. Not that I ever heard of anyway. People just don't like the place. I grew up in Managansett, you know. When I was a kid back in the 1960s, it seemed like there was always a For Sale sign out front, and it was empty a lot of the time. We used to say it was haunted, and some of the kids claimed to have broken in and seen ghosts, but you know how kids are. The stories were always different so none of them really stuck."

"So how did Eblis come to buy it?"

"Didn't. They got it as part of the settlement of a lawsuit. But by then, no one wanted the property. They leased it a few times, but there was a lot of trouble with the tenants and they finally just stopped."

Later that day, Jennison contrived to brush his thigh against hers as they walked between offices. He kept his face averted but she knew it had been deliberate.

Kim woke up in the darkness, disoriented. "Sam?" No, no Sam. How long before her subconscious accepted the truth? The weather had turned unexpectedly hot and muggy again, and she'd forgotten to have the air conditioning serviced.

The lamp beside her bed remained dark when she turned the switch. Light bulbs, she thought. I forgot to buy light bulbs.

She slipped out of bed, searched fruitlessly for her second slipper, finally discarded the one she'd found and stumbled across to the bathroom.

No lights there either. The power then. She'd been down in the basement exactly once, couldn't remember seeing the fuse box. But it had to be there somewhere. No flashlight, no matches.

She made it out of her bedroom without incident, found the handrail for the stairs. The ground floor was a pit of ink. Kim considered her options.

"The hell with it."

She was turning back to the bedroom when a sudden, hot breeze swept in through the window. The door slammed shut, striking her outstretched hand as it did so. She stumbled back, grabbed for the handrail, and fell to one knee, nursing her bruised fingers.

When she tried the knob, it turned, but the door itself would not budge. There was no lock on it, but the humidity must have made the wood swell enough that it was jammed solidly in place.

The bed in the adjacent room was made up, so Kim felt her way carefully along the wall until she reached the doorjamb. She half expected this door to resist as well, but it opened easily and she was inside, closing it behind her.

The outline of the bed and dresser beyond were indistinct but visible. Kim shuffled forward, careful not to trip over anything, and was right next to the bed when a bolt of lightning illuminated the entire room.

There was a man lying in the bed, covered with just a sheet, one armed draped across his averted face. She saw him clearly in the glaring light, saw also the tattoo on his left forearm. A snake devouring its own tail, Ouroboros.

"It's a metaphor for the human condition," Sam always insisted. "We survive by devouring ourselves. Life and death are a continuum, not distinct events."

Kim found it impossible to breathe, backed away one step, then another as darkness returned. A long roll of thunder followed, then silence, a silence in which she heard the man move, the rustle of sheets, and then a whisper. "Kim?"

She whirled around, ran for the doorway and something solid and unsympathetic interposed itself. She fell to the floor, slumped against the solid wood of the door, and began sobbing. A few seconds later she fainted, or fell asleep, and it was morning when she next opened her eyes.

"Are you dating again?"

Startled and offended, Kim stared across the room at Jennison. "I beg your pardon?"

"Sorry." He didn't sound it. "Don't mean to pry. I just wondered if the accident was, you know, long enough ago that you might be willing to let me take you to dinner sometime."

"How did you find out about the accident?" She felt entirely disproportionate anger.

"Nicholson mentioned it at a staff meeting back before you showed up. Said we should make allowances if you seemed irrational at times because you were probably still grieving for your husband. I'm sorry, I didn't mean to bring up bad memories. Hope you're not mad at me."

"I'm not." A lie. "But I'm not ready for that kind of social life yet." The truth.

"Sam? Are you there?"

Kim felt ridiculous, sitting on the bed with just a single flickering candle for light. She didn't believe in ghosts, not really, but if there was just a chance that she was wrong, that sometimes love was strong enough to leave some lingering trace behind, then she had to act as though she did. Maybe there was some quality about this house that made it possible, an attenuation of the border between life and death.

How do you call a ghost anyway? She'd been sitting here for an hour, willing him to appear. Perhaps she needed a reverse exorcist. Tempted to laugh, she clamped down tightly, afraid she'd be unable to stop.

Her legs were cramped and she realized how utterly frustrated she'd been feeling. Fox was fighting her every byte of the way as she imposed the new programming standards on Eblis, Nicholson made veiled threats about her "drain on vital resources", her investigations into the inventory problem were hampered by inaccurate and missing paperwork, and Jennison had started touching her inappropriately, a nudge with a shoulder, a brief hand on her knee. She'd have to do something about him, and soon, but despite his offensive behavior, he was the closest thing she had to an ally and she was reluctant to alienate him.

"The hell with it. Get real, girl. You're working too hard and imagining things." Annoyed with herself, she turned on the lamp and blew out the candle. She felt silly and hungry, found both slippers this time and descended for a late night snack, two ice cream sandwiches from the freezer.

On her way back upstairs she paused. There was a faint scent in the air, sweet, almost familiar. A cologne of some sort. She wasn't very good at distinguishing different smells; childhood pneumonia had left her with diminished olfactory sensitivity. It had taken years for her to be able to recognize Sam's invariable Old Spice Aftershave. This was similar, and she'd run into it before, but couldn't place it.

The back of one hand was covering her yawn when she entered the bedroom. The lamp was still lit, its puddle of light warring with the darkness. Within its aura, a tiny candle flame flickered weakly. The candle she'd extinguished.

"Do you believe in ghosts, Dan?"

Jennison shook his head. "Of course not. If they were real, we'd know about it, wouldn't we? All that crap about flying saucers and bigfoot and ghosts, it's all nonsense. I mean, I've got an open mind, but not so open my brains fall out, right?"

He seemed unusually edgy today, and Kim had a feeling she knew why. After failing to reconcile inventories from internal sources, Kim had requested an accounting from several major suppliers. There were noticeable discrepancies in some of the split shipments, where the carrier dropped off part of a load at the plant and the rest at the Eblis warehouse in Scituate. It appeared that some of the partial shipments were received but never transferred into work in process. Compensating adjustments were made later so that re-orders were placed, adjustments originating in Jennison's office.

"Why do you ask?"

"What? Oh, just making conversation. I was remembering you said people used to think the Waverly house was haunted."

"You haven't seen anything, have you? No spooks, no clanking chains?"

He was sweating, despite the air conditioning, and Kim wondered if he knew how close she was to discovering the truth. She was already morally certain he was stealing from the company, and she expected to have proof shortly.

"No, nothing like that."

She sensed something, glanced up from her work to discover that he'd risen and come over to stand at her shoulder.

"It's almost lunchtime. Interested?"

Grimacing, Kim shook her head. "Another limp sandwich from Gimpy's? No thanks. I'll get something later."

"I can do better than that. I don't live far from here and I could whip up some pretty good stir fry." He let his hand fall on her shoulder.

It was a positive act of will not to wrench herself free. Instead, Kim slowly stood, turned to face him, and deliberately stepped back so that his hand fell away. Jennison moved closer and caught both of her arms.

"I'm very attracted to you, Kim. And I think you've grown to like me as well."

Calmly she raised her arms inside the circle of his embrace and pushed him away. "I don't think so, Mr. Jennison." Her voice was marvelously cool.

For a moment, it seemed he would pursue the matter but instead, he simply shrugged and turned away. "You don't know what you're missing."

But she'd learned something else. Jennison was wearing the same cologne she'd smelled in her bedroom.

It took several minutes to find the maintenance manager's office. The man who answered her knock was grey haired, his eyes bloodshot, and his skin a rich tan. "Yes, can I help you?"

Kim identified herself.

"Oh, the corporate spy. Come in, why don't you?"

The office was cluttered but surprisingly clean. "I'm Jake Reynolds. What can I do for you Ms Belk?"

"I'm staying at the house on Waverly, and I have a problem."

"The air conditioner? I wanted to replace that before you moved in, but Nicholson said to leave it as it was."

She wasn't surprised. "Actually, I've lost my house key and wondered if you had a spare."

"That's easy enough to cure." He opened a large, flat metal cabinet mounted on a wall beside his desk and extracted a key from one of several dozen hooks. "Here you go. If it happens again, just drop by and take one. They're on position thirty-one. I've got a couple left and my office is always unlocked."

Which answered the question she'd been hesitant to ask. Jennison could have acquired a spare key to the Waverly house at any time, and without anyone knowing about it.

She needed to catch him in the act.

Kim made her preparations carefully. On the assumption that he was watching the house, she kept to her routine, undressed and climbed into bed at ten. She left the light on for half an hour while she read, then set the book aside and turned it off. But instead of curling up in bed, she slid out from under the sheets, donned a pair of jeans and a halter top, and quietly left her bedroom.

When the front door swung quietly open just past midnight, she was watching from inside the hall closet.

As she'd suspected, the intruder was Dan Jennison. She waited until he'd closed and locked the door behind him before revealing herself.

"What an expected pleasure, Mr. Jennison." She turned on the overhead lights.

Startled, he staggered back, bumping a floor lamp with one arm. It rocked back and forth a few times before settling on its base.

"Kim, I was worried about you and I decided to stop by..."

His voice trailed away hopelessly.

"And what? Light another candle for me? Write on my mirror? Whisper names in the dark?"

Jennison's face twisted in confusion. "What the hell are you talking about?"

"Too late to play innocent, Jennison. I smelled your cologne the other day. I know you've been here before, just like I know how you've been diverting raw brass and copper to scrapyards and pocketing the proceeds." Actually, that was just an educated guess, but she read confirmation in his face.

"All right, yes, I've been here once before. I wanted to go through your notes and see just what you'd uncovered. The candle was childish, but I couldn't resist. Look, there's a lot of money involved here. How much would it take to keep this between the two of us?"

Kim should have been more cautious, but her contempt for Jennison overflowed when she realized that even now, even as he admitted she held his future in her hands, he was undressing her with his eyes.

"More than you've got, Jennison. Now get out of here before I call the police."

He hesitated and his face hardened. "No. No, I don't think so, not just yet. I was careless, but I'm not stupid. Did you know we've been sleeping together, you and I? No? Well, everyone at Eblis believes it, and several of them have heard bits and pieces of our pillow talk as well. It was your idea, really, the haunted house bit. I've asked them to be kind. After all, the death of your husband was particularly horrible. Burned to death, wasn't he, and after you were thrown clear. How much had you had to drink that night, Ms Belk? Were you fit to drive?"

Rage made it difficult to talk but Kim managed. "Get out of here, you asshole! I won't tell you again!"

"You won't tell anyone anything. I'm going to do you a service tonight; I'm going to reunite you with your husband."

And he lunged for her.

Somehow she slipped under his arms and away, but Jennison was right behind her as she ran into the hall. No time to think. She was on the stairs, climbing, hoping to lock herself in the bathroom, gain time to think.

He caught her at the top of the landing, brought her crashing to the floor under his greater bulk.

"I don't suppose you have any sleeping pills." He giggled nervously.

"You bastard!" She tried to kick free but he held on.

"No? Well, then I'm afraid you're going to have to write a suicide not on your laptop and then hang yourself."

Kim twisted to one side and jammed her elbow back into his groin. Jennison moaned and she slid out from under his body, but before she could stand he recovered enough to drive his fist into the side of her head. She fell back against the opposite wall, stunned.

"Bitch!" He stood up painfully and reached for her.

The bedroom door flew open with a crash and a chill, damp wind blew through the house. The lights from downstairs faded and died.

"What the hell?"

Jennison turned his head and, a second later, Kim followed his gaze.

Someone was standing in the hall, a tall, dark figure, anonymous in the shadows.

"Sam?"

Jennison laughed. "Don't you wish?" But they were the last words he ever spoke. The dark shape rushed toward him, Jennison instinctively retreated, lost his footing, and fell backwards down the staircase. When he came to rest at the bottom, his neck was twisted at an impossible angle.

"Sam? Is that you?" Kim struggled to her feet. The night was full of distant thunder.

"Kim." It was his voice, or at least his whisper. She felt a rush of sudden passion and sorrow, so intense that her head bowed forward, eyes shut to hold back a flood of tears. It was true; Sam's love was strong enough to transcend death. Strong even though it had been her fault that he'd died in the first place. There'd been a few too many drinks, she'd insisted on driving despite his objection, and then she'd felt compelled to drive faster than usual to prove her alertness.

The suggestion of hands touched her wrists, an electric sensation that made the small hairs rise along her forearms.

"You've forgiven me, haven't you, Sam?"

She lifted her head, eyes opening, her need for him so intense it was painful. The face lowered toward her as lightning flashed once more, and she read his expression despite the empty eye sockets, the skull from which the flesh had been boiled away by the intense heat of the fire, and knew that he had not and never would.

And that he would haunt her for the rest of her life.

PUPPETS

The house was filled with puppets, mounted on the walls, lying in rows on the otherwise empty bookshelves, thrown into drawers and corners. There was even a bucket full under the sink.

"Fuckin' old lady's nuts," Nelson muttered darkly, his voice low even though the house was empty. "So where's the fuckin' money?"

He'd found finding nothing worth stealing so far, but Old Lady Markas always paid for everything in cash and never went to the bank. Nelson knew because he'd been casing this house for weeks.

It had to be on the second floor. He checked his watch. She wouldn't be back for another half hour, plenty of time.

Up the stairs and into her bedroom. Tiny closet, more puppets, nailed to the wall, stuffed under the bed. No cash. No obvious place where it might be hidden. "You're pissing me off, lady."

He stopped suddenly back in the hall. Sounds from downstairs, low, metallic, the touch of key to lock. Nelson turned catlike, moved to the top of the stairs, saw the front door swing open.

The old bitch was back early!

Nelson crouched, fighting panic. What could she do? She must be at least seventy, wrinkled skin, white hair, always moved slowly. He disliked violence, but she wasn't playing fair, came back early, hid the money too well.

She closed the door, shifting her groceries from one arm to the other, then walked toward the kitchen.

He didn't have any choice. Couldn't get out without going downstairs and she might see him. His red hair was distinctive. A quick look and she might even recognize him. It was her own fault.

He quietly descended to the kitchen.

She was moving her purchases from bag to shelf, one at a time, each movement slow and deliberate. Tall, almost six feet, but not strong enough to resist him. Nelson picked up a frying pan from the table, not wanting to touch her wrinkled flesh.

The impact of metal against her skull made his forearm sting.

She moved toward him and Nelson stumbled back, almost tripping over his own feet, pan raised in defense now. He retreated as she advanced, tried for another strike at her head. Success! Despite a minor deflection caused by outstretched arms, he flattened her nose. She had to go down now!

She didn't. Old Lady Markas shrugged off the blow and moved with unexpected speed, her openhanded slap was like a thunderclap, knocking him back against the wall, so stunned he slipped down to a sitting position, unable to move.

For a few seconds, she stood over him and he half expected her to kick him to death while he lay in a stupor. But instead she turned and, incredibly enough, began to take off her dress.

Was the old bitch going to rape him?

Wrinkled flesh, pale white, shriveled and ghastly, and then the scar running up her back, not fresh but still livid, swollen, gross. If Nelson had been in control of himself, he would have retched uncontrollably at the sight.

And then the scar opened and the thing that lived inside the shell of Old Lady Markas emerged, all spindly limbs, parchment white and dry despite the once human husk that now fell unattended to the floor.

"Ruined it is," said a quavering voice as the thread thin body moved across the room to the knife rack. It reached up and selected a black handled carving knife. "Time for a new one."

"Fucking puppets," Nelson whispered, just before he started to scream.

AMY'S PUPIL

It seemed like such an innocuous request at the time, Amy Brooks never realized that it was anything other than casual curiosity. She was sitting on one of the painted wooden benches in the grounds of the Sheffield estate, long abandoned and recently seized by the town council in lieu of back taxes. The ornamental gardens had gone wild over the course of years of neglect, but the riot of color still made it one of the brighter spots in town.

She came here frequently and usually had the area to herself; the town's children seemed far more interested in playing in the sprawling cemetery or at the construction site for the new housing project. Consequently, she was startled when a voice spoke from quite close at hand.

"Whatcha doing?"

Amy glanced up from her work, blinking, confused, forced herself to smile when she saw Kevin Driscoll standing just out of reach. "Oh, hello Kevin. I didn't see you coming."

"What is that?" He raised a chubby arm and pointed at the knitting in her lap.

"This? Well, I don't know just yet what it's going to be. A sweater, probably." She lifted her work, only about eight inches square, and stretched it out for him to see the detail.
"How do you like it so far?"

Kevin moved closer, small dark eyes peering closely at the pattern. Amy found herself feeling pity for the child's unattractiveness, not for the first time either; she'd encountered him before while substitute teaching at the local elementary school. There were other children just as overweight as Kevin, and many others who'd never work for modeling agencies. But the gestalt effect in Kevin's case was unrivalled. His ears were too large and were bent slightly forward, his nose broadened coarsely at the nostrils, which were rimmed with tiny black hairs, and his eyebrows were unbalanced. The boy's teeth were uneven and his face had an odd, slightly asymmetrical cast that was unnerving until one got used to it. His hair was rarely combed and unevenly cut, probably by his mother, and he didn't bathe frequently enough. What's more, although he was only a few months past ten years old, he was already losing the war against acne, although it seemed more likely he'd just abandoned the field of battle.

"Well?" She prompted, unsettled by his startlingly intense examination.

"S'Okay, I guess. Can I watch?"

The last thing Amy wanted was an audience. Her knitting was a form of therapy, had no real practical application. The death of her husband and son in a car crash two years previously had faded from a stabbing, inescapable pain to a numb feeling of pointlessness, and she found repetitious, comparatively mindless activities like knitting or working in her garden helped to shut out the memories she couldn't face. It never occurred to her that the fact that she had never actually finished knitting an entire piece, nor the elaborately laid out garden plan she had designed, indicated a neurotic tendency to avoid endings.

"If you want to." Amy told herself that it was necessary to be extra nice to people like Kevin, who seemed to have no friends his own age, whose parents would have been in jail if verbal abuse and simple neglect were criminal offenses. Even the full time teachers in the school had little good to say about Kevin, whom they considered uncooperative, disruptive, inattentive, and possibly even "emotionally retarded", whatever that might mean.

She slid over on the bench to make room for him, but he remained standing. For a few seconds, Amy quite forgot how to knit, so unnerved was she by the prospect of an audience. But old habits moved her fingers even when her mind refused to function, and she was soon completing another row of intertwined red and yellow strands.

"Looks easy to me."

Amy felt a small flush of anger at what she interpreted as impertinence, but when she looked up from the knitting, Kevin's eyes seemed as guileless as ever. He was simply stating a fact as he saw it, with no implication of criticism.

"Would you like to try?" She was surprised when those words came out of her mouth, but there was no way to take them back even if she'd wanted to. And she didn't. Kevin's eyes had widened with such an obvious degree of interest, she felt the small thrill of joy that came all too infrequently to teachers, when a child actually demonstrated the desire to learn. It did briefly occur to her that she might be doing the boy no real favor by teaching him what would hardly be considered an appropriate skill for a young boy, particularly in as provincial a place as Managansett, Rhode Island, but Kevin was such a social pariah already, she probably couldn't do anything to increase his ostracism.

Kevin sat beside her and took the spare set of needles she handed him. "What color would you like?" She nodded toward her yarn basket.

The boy stared at the array of skeins and balls for several seconds before using the end of one needle to point out a lime green. Amy nodded to herself; personally she found the color too garish and never had understood the impulse that had caused her to buy it in the first place. With practiced skill she knit a small starter square and handed it to him.

Kevin's pudgy fingers moved awkwardly as he tried to imitate her movements. He seemed to have no difficulty catching the yarn with the point of the needle, but his coordination fell short after that. "That's all right, you'll get the hang of it. Relax a little; you're holding your hands too tightly."

An hour later, Amy was bored and searching for a tactful way to leave, but she was also impressed with the boy's determination to learn. He'd mastered the basics well enough to add row after row, but when she'd tried to get him to work in a second color, he shook his head vigorously.

"No, I like it this way."

She waited patiently until the last of the lime yarn was gone before setting aside her own work. "You've done very well, Kevin. Some people take days to get that far."

Indeed, the boy had produced a quite respectable rectangle.

"I want to make it bigger."

Amy tried not to frown, but didn't completely succeed. If Kevin noticed her displeasure, he ignored it.

"Well, I might have some more in here you could use, but I have to be getting home now, Kevin. It's getting late."

He stared at her with eyes that seemed brimful of hope. Amy felt her resolve collapsing under the pressure and hastily cut her losses. "Look, you can borrow that set of needles for a while if you want. I've got plenty. Pick out the yarn you want and you can take it home." Or wherever you go to be by yourself, she added mentally. Bill Driscoll would have a fit if he saw his son knitting, she suspected, and his wife Edna wouldn't be much happier.

There was, however, no more lime green, and Kevin wouldn't accept any other color.

"I just don't have any more, Kevin. It's not a color I use much."

The boy shrugged. "Can you get some?"

Amy began to wonder just what she'd gotten herself into. "I suppose I could buy some, Kevin, but why don't you just use one of these others? Some of them are very nice."

Kevin carefully folded his knitted rectangle and held it with the two needles in one hand, while the other plunged into the side pocket of his jeans. It emerged a second later with some loose coins and two tightly folded dollar bills. "I can pay you for it."

Amy thought about it, then shook her head. "I'll tell you what. I have to go to the store tomorrow morning anyway. I'll pick up one skein for you, my treat. But after that, you pay for your own." She was half convinced that she'd never see Kevin again, at least not with knitting needles in hand, and she didn't want to accept his money and then have to chase him down to return it.

"Okay," he agreed easily, hiding the money back in his pocket. "I'll come over your house after lunch."

She was still considering that when he disappeared along the path that wound through the thicket separating them from Reservoir Road.

Her expectations were wrong, and Amy found herself alternating between pleasure and dismay when Kevin showed up the following afternoon and ensconced himself on her back porch to knit, still adding lime green rows to his previous day's efforts. Amy excused herself and left him to it, but her conscience caused her to check back frequently, once with freshly made lemonade and cookies which she left beside his chair. An hour later, she returned to find him working as industriously as ever, her refreshments untouched.

This time when he offered to pay for another skein of yarn, she accepted his money.

And so the pattern was established. Kevin seemed perfectly willing to come by every afternoon, but Amy ignored his obvious disappointment and insisted that she had other things to do with her summer. He took on a paper route and seemed determined to spend every cent he made on lime green yarn, and she reluctantly brought him by the store so that he could make his own purchases. She also showed him the instruction books and patterns that were available, but Kevin seemed uninterested. Although he'd started new pieces in her presence, they all seemed to be repetitions of his first effort, a featureless rectangle, although the stitching was much tighter and more professional looking in his more recent efforts.

Toward the end of the summer, Kevin's visits dropped off and finally died away entirely, and Amy felt occasional twinges of regret. As unpersonable as Kevin was, he did share one of her rare enthusiasms. At first she thought he'd lost interest and turned to more typically boyish pursuits, but the clerk at the linen goods store mentioned that he was still coming in once a week to pick up more yarn. "We have an open order for the color he's using now," she confided in Amy. "He must be working on a quilt big enough to cover the whole town. He was very upset when the latest shipment didn't quite match the color he'd been using. I tried to explain the problems with different dye lots but he didn't seem interested in an explanation."

The leaves were already well turned when school started in September. The insurance and her husband's investments provided a more than adequate income, but Amy arranged to be on the list of substitute teachers once again, telling herself it was important that she do something active to occupy her time, ignoring the fact that she could have had a full time position almost for the asking.

Although she occasionally saw Kevin Driscoll walking through the corridors, he seemed much the same as always, answering her cheery greetings with monosyllables, and she was never called upon to substitute for a class that included him.

It was during the first week of October that she next had an actual conversation with Kevin.

It was an unseasonably warm night and she'd been having one of her less restful evenings. Everything she looked at in the house carried memories of her missing family. Finally she decided to go for a walk, hoping to tire herself out and bring on the anesthesia of sleep. She walked down to Main Street, then turned and followed it westward, past the silent shops and offices of downtown Managansett. It was only eight o'clock, but already most of the town was dark and silent, only the small diner and a convenience store still open.

She passed the high school, then crossed to the back side of the cemetery, taking advantage of the new halogen lights that had just been installed. She'd come a good three or four miles already and would have nearly as far to go on the return trip, but the exercise made her feel good even if her calves were a bit sore.

On her way past the Sheffield estate, she spotted a light moving out past the building.

There were two good reasons for her to walk on. First of all, whatever was happening was none of her business. Second, Amy was not a particularly strong woman, and although there was surprisingly little violent crime in Managansett, it was not unknown, and discretion dictated that she move on as quickly as possible. And so she might have done, had she not heard a voice that was almost certainly that of Kevin Driscoll.

She entered past the stone posts that once held a massive gate, crossed the small parking area and followed the gravel path toward the rear. "That's it. Come on now." This time there was no question; Kevin's voice was low but warbled a bit, as though the premature adolescence of his complexion was striking at his vocal cords as well.

Closer now, she could see the light, motionless, and identified it as a gas lantern set on one end of a wooden bench. Kevin sat just beside it, holding a large glass bottle in his lap.

"Kevin! What are you doing here?"

The light was uneven and flickered, but even so she thought the look he directed toward her was a blend of surprise and fear. She blinked and her vision wavered and when she focused it again, he appeared no more than his usual ambivalent self.

"Hello, Miss Brooks." He made no effort to answer her question, however.

She came closer, noticed that the bottle held something that flew back and forth, beating its wings against the glass as it attempted to escape. A moth, and a fairly good sized one.

"What are you doing out at this time of night, Kevin? Do you know how late it is?"

"Yes," he answered simply. "My bed time's not till nine."

"Well don't you think you should be heading home then? Won't your parents worry about you?"

He considered this for a second. "Nope." And she wasn't certain which question the boy was answering. Perhaps both.

She took another step forward just as Kevin turned his face slightly, eyes suddenly alert. His left arm shot out so suddenly that Amy was startled, drew it back almost immediately. He lifted the lid of the jar and pushed something inside, replacing the cover to prevent its escape. Now there were two moths imprisoned.

"Are you collecting moths?"

Kevin paused for a second, considering this. "Nope."

Amy shook her head, not understanding. "Then what *are* you doing?"

"Just catching them."

His tone was so matter of fact that Amy suddenly felt very uneasy, as though something clear and important hovered just beyond the reach of her understanding. Involuntarily, she took a step backward. "Well, make sure you head home soon then. I'll be seeing you."

The boy made no reply.

Amy was almost back to the road when she heard Kevin calling to the moths again and she stopped, still bothered by the encounter. Slowly she turned, trying to convince herself to mind her own business and go home, but curiosity was too compelling. Moving as quietly as she could, she skirted a row of unruly privet hedge and moved to a vantage point where she could spy on the boy without being caught at it.

She watched while he caught two more moths, then told herself it was time to go, convinced that she was letting her imagination run out of control. But before determination could turn to action, the situation changed. Several meters away but close enough for every detail to be visible, Kevin opened the lid of his jar and reached inside.

Amy watched in horror as he methodically placed each of the captured moths into his mouth and gulped them down.

She managed to get back to the road and almost two blocks away before turning to vomit into the bushes that bordered Caterall's Travel Agency.

Amy Brooks went out of her way to avoid Kevin Driscoll after that evening; she even began purchasing her yarn at a store on the Providence line rather than chance running into him. Twice she was called to substitute for his grade and twice she pleaded illness even though it was by no means certain that Kevin would be in any of the classes she'd be covering.

As fall faded toward winter, only one more incident involving Kevin impinged on her life in any way, although in this case, she did not make the connection until much later. One Monday morning, the manager of Cresswell's Grocery arrived at work to find that someone had broken a window and removed what was estimated to be several hundred dollars worth of assorted foods, mostly canned meats, peanut butter and jelly, soft drinks and assorted junk foods including beef sticks, pretzels, potato chips, and boxes of cookies and crackers. The store' alarm system had mysteriously failed.

The police department asked a lot of questions, but never turned up any fruitful information.

November passed and December roared in with a fierce but short lived snowstorm that melted away in a couple of days. Christmas lights were up all over town and school was winding down toward the holiday vacation. This was a bad time of year for Amy; Christmas always reminded her of how lonely she was. Her own parents had died years before, and she was not close to any of her living relatives. She volunteered most of her free time to charitable organizations, soliciting contributions for the homeless, delivering donated presents to the needy, and similar projects. Several friends asked her to spend Christmas day with them, but she declined all such invitations, not wanting to accept what she perceived as charity.

Three days before Christmas, Kevin Driscoll disappeared. Or at least, that's when he was reported missing. Amy knew one of the local police officers quite well, and he told her confidentially that there was reason to believe that the boy had actually skipped out three days before his absence was reported, that the parents had figured he'd get cold and discouraged and come back home without their raising a hue and cry.

Kevin left a note saying he was going to Providence to sneak aboard a train for California, so search efforts were concentrated in that area. Despite a widely publicized campaign, no one came forward to admit giving the boy a ride to Providence and by the middle of February hope had pretty much been abandoned.

Spring came early. The first week of March was sprinkled with sixty degree days, although the brisk wind made it feel cooler than that. Amy hated the cold and had remained cooped up in her house throughout the winter months, so she bundled up in a sweater and hat and resumed her habitual evening walks as soon as the weather permitted.

It was on Thursday night that she lost her hat. The breeze had died down that afternoon, so she was completely taken by surprise when it rushed up suddenly just as she was passing the Sheffield estate. She swore softly and uncharacteristically and raced to retrieve the hat, but no sooner did it land on the unruly grass than a fresh gust snatched it up and carried it off.

Although it was dusk, there was still sufficient light to see and she followed along the side of the building only to watch in exasperation as the hat was grabbed by an updraft and whisked over the nearest line of mock oranges and barberries to land in a patch of lilacs well beyond easy reach.

There was no way she could climb through the barberry without doing substantial damage to her clothing, to say nothing of her skin. But she was loathe to let her property go without making some effort to rescue it, so she slowly walked around the periphery of the thicket until she found the first of several narrow paths that led into its depths.

Happily, she was able to reach the base of the lilac without too great an effort, but despite vigorous shaking, the shrub would not relinquish its grip. Amy, however, was more determined than ever, and an adjacent oak tree seemed to offer a solution. By climbing carefully up to the first fork and extending her body along one of its lower branches, she was able to just reach the brim of the hat, capture it between two extended fingers, and tug it free. But in her moment of triumph, she saw something else as well, a small patch of bright color just visible from her vantage point in one of the denser parts of the thicket.

It was a familiar lime green.

Amy climbed down, drawn irresistibly to investigate further. At ground level, she could no longer see the swatch of color, but she retained a pretty good idea of its location. Some rapid investigation revealed no path that was likely to help, but she was able to slide under an uprooted birch tree and find a relatively traversable bit of ground that led in the right direction, and a few minutes later, she was able to stand fully erect in a small, cathedral like expanse of open space completely enclosed by densely grown foliage.

A rope had been run from the fork of an oak tree to a slightly lower one in a maple. Hanging from the rope was a very large mass of knitted, lime green yarn, roughly in the shape of an oversized cocoon. The ground below it was littered with plastic bags, empty soda cans, opened tins of meat, and other debris.

Amy approached cautiously, already convinced that she knew what she'd find. Kevin Driscoll, unhappy with family and school, a loner, had knitted himself a place to hide and live where no one else could bother him. She moved cautiously, steeling herself for a tragedy. There's no way Kevin could have survived the winter in such flimsy quarters, she told herself; his thawing body was probably lodged somewhere inside his handiwork.

But when she peeled back the flap and looked inside, all she found was more trash, a good sized store of untouched food, and a set of clothing appropriate for a young, overweight boy.

Later that spring, Amy's own life began to heal. She found it a little easier to mix socially, and toward the beginning of summer, even met someone she liked well enough to date. His name was Kenneth Dodd, he appeared to be a year or two younger than she, and admitted that like her he had no family to speak of. What's more, Kenneth was a strikingly attractive man, the kind who posed for cigarette ads, rugged and competent, but quiet, so reserved in fact that Amy found herself dominating conversations for the first time in her life. And he seemed to find her irresistible.

They went out together several times, kissed a bit tentatively at first, with more enthusiasm later. On their eighth date, Amy hinted that she might be willing to be invited back to his place. On their ninth date, Kenneth took her up on the offer.

He had a small apartment on the far side of town which he'd moved into only a few months earlier. On the drive over, he spent most of the time apologizing for what she'd see, explaining that he hadn't been working long enough to afford much in the way of furniture. But when she first walked through his front door, it wasn't the lack of furniture that caught her attention. It was the walls.

They were all painted a very bright lime green. "Kevin," she whispered softly, remembering.

And from behind her heard, "Yes."

ANIMATION

It all started with marshmallow bunny rabbits. It was Easter and Maddie was not quite three years old. She was a precocious child, quick to learn, alert to changes in mood in the house, and clever at solving the kinds of problems that face kids that age. She wasn't talking much though, and even though the doctors had told us there was no evidence of any physical or mental impairment, Peg and I were getting a little worried.

"Maybe she just doesn't have anything to say," suggested one doctor. But we knew that wasn't true. She just chose ways other than language to make her feelings and wishes known.

Not that she didn't speak. She had said "mommy" and "daddy" right on schedule, and intermittently ever since. She'd learned the dreaded "no" early, but usually relied on an agitated shake of the head to express denial. But she hadn't said a full sentence of more than two words yet, and I could probably have written her entire spoken vocabulary on a single sheet of paper. I wasn't worried exactly, but I was concerned.

Anyway, it was Easter weekend and even though Peg and I are no longer practicing Christians, we celebrated the holidays for Maddie's sake. There was supposed to be a neighborhood Easter Egg hunt, which she had somehow heard about and wanted to participate in even though she was too young, and she'd talked about "eater yegs" and the "eater bunny" once or twice, which behavior we were trying to reinforce, even though the "eater bunny" sounded distinctly unpleasant to me.

So that morning there were marshmallow bunnies decorating the breakfast table, one yellow, one pink, and one white, arranged in a semicircle so that they all faced Maddie's plate. She beamed when she spotted them, which made me feel good, and climbed up into her seat while Peg cut up pancakes into bite sized pieces.

"Good morning, Maddie," I said quietly.

She looked up at me and beamed.

"I hope you're hungry this morning. Mommy made extra pancakes."

Maddie nodded solemnly to indicate she was indeed hungry.

I reached across the table and pointed at the three animal shaped confections. "Do you know what these are, Maddie?"

She blinked once and nodded, first at them and then at me.

"I think you're fooling me. You don't really know what they are, do you?"

Her head went up and down more vigorously, and this time she crossed her heart.

"Why don't you tell Daddy what they are, Maddie?" There was a note of anxiety in Peg's voice that annoyed me. Maddie was even more sensitive than I to mood and she could certainly tell that this was more than an idle question. But Peg was home with her all the time, and I think the prolonged silences were beginning to bother her.

Maddie sighed and let her head fall forward, and I thought we'd blown it again, but just as I was about to turn back to my own breakfast, I heard just the faintest whisper.

"What was that, Maddie? Did you say something?"

"Eater bunnies," she said again, the whisper only slightly louder.

"That's right. They're Easter bunnies." I smiled as broadly as I could without feeling as though I was overdoing it and patted her lightly on the head.

"Good girl," added Peg, turning away hastily so that neither of us could see her expression.

We told Maddie she could eat one of the bunnies each day but only one because too much sugar was bad for her. It didn't matter, though, because she didn't want to eat any of them. She'd adopted them into her family of friends, the various stuffed animals that decorated her bedroom. She set her head stubbornly when Peg told her she couldn't take them to her room.

"You'll get bugs. The bugs will come to your room and try to eat the Easter bunnies if you take them there. But they'll be perfectly safe here until you're ready to eat them yourself."

Maddie glanced in my direction, as if hoping I'd intervene, but Peg and I had long since agreed not to reverse each other's decisions in front of Maddie. So the bunnies stayed on the kitchen table, under the glass dome of the cheese server, when Maddie went to bed that night.

But they weren't there in the morning. They were in her bedroom, sitting side by side on the shelf above her bed, and when Peg accused her of taking them, she shook her head back and forth with such animation that we knew something unusual had taken place. We thought it was Maddie's first lie, but we were wrong.

It was less than a month before the second incident. The three of us had driven over to Managansett to tour the newly opened topiary gardens behind the old Sheffield Library. Maddie was fascinated by fake animals – cartoons, statues, paintings, puppets – every representation she encountered. Oddly enough, she wasn't particularly enamored of the real thing, expressed no desire to have a pet, and was clearly bored at the zoo, at least until we got to the souvenir shop. So the topiary garden seemed a logical place to visit.

She was just as fascinated as expected, ran back and forth pointing at the various shapes, quietly demanding that we nod and assure her that we thought they were equally wonderful. It wasn't very crowded, but the mazelike passages were a bit confusing, and despite our insistence that she stay close, we hadn't been there more fifteen minutes before we lost her.

There's a kind of panic that sets in when you can't locate your child that is quite unlike any other. We separated and rushed back and forth frantically for a while, calling her name and occasionally asking other people if they'd seen a small girl come running by. No one had and we were getting pretty desperate when we were paged from the ticket booth and found our daughter sitting calmly on a folding chair.

"She walked right up and said she was lost and that her name was Madeleine Cortland," said the cashier. That was probably more than she'd said to the two of us combined all day.

Peg knelt down to check Maddie over, brushing a tiny forest of twigs and other debris from her clothing. "Where have you been, young lady, and how did you get so dirty so quickly?" Maddie just shrugged.

"How did you find your way back?" I asked quietly. It had taken Peg and I a couple of tries ourselves. The maze was surprisingly large and complex.

"Elfant showed me."

"An elephant showed you," I translated. "I don't remember seeing any elephant."

"There's one at the far end," the cashier volunteered. "It hasn't grown in completely yet, but you can tell what it is if you stand back a ways and look."

"Did someone near the elephant show you the way back?" asked Peg.

"No!" Maddie insisted. "Elfant showed me. Elfant! Elfant!"

I wanted Maddie to become more verbal, but not in the form of temper tantrums. I lied and said we believed her and we called it a day.

The third incident was exactly one week later. We were home, Peg and I cleaning house while Maddie played in the side yard. One or both of us looked out the window every few minutes to check on her. The yard was fenced and the gate closed and locked, but we both knew better than to believe that any containment system was completely childproof. We had bought a set of ceramic farm animals for the yard, sturdy enough that Maddie couldn't break them easily but light enough that she could move them around. She never seemed to grow tired of playing with them, and often fussed because we wouldn't let her bring them into the house.

We were in the midst of a major reorganization that weekend so we lost track of time, and it was two in the afternoon before we realized that we hadn't done anything about lunch. Peg rushed out to the kitchen to get things started and I went to retrieve Maddy and get her washed up.

She was sitting on the grass, surrounded by her unresponsive friends, and I wondered what was going on in that convoluted mind of hers. She rarely spoke to her toys just as she rarely spoke to her parents, and I was never able to make any real sense out of the games she played even after watching them for hours. I was wondering the same thing this time as I walked toward her, but when I drew close, I frowned.

"Where did that come from?" I pointed at a wrought iron rooster that leaned drunkenly against the side of a ceramic pig.

Maddie blinked at me then slowly raised her arm and pointed at the roof. I looked up, following her finger, but could see nothing except the unadorned chimney. Frowning, I was about to look away when I realized that something wasn't right. Something was missing.

The weather vane was gone.

My head snapped around and, sure enough, there it was, still leaning against the pig.

"Now how did that get down here?" I caught myself scratching my head and laughed at myself. Obviously it must have fallen off. We were just lucky that no one had been hurt when it fell.

But Maddie took my questions seriously. "Flew."

I normally humored my daughter's fantasies but I was distracted this time. "No, honey. It's not a real bird. It can't fly."

She frowned and shook her head. "Flew," she said again. "Flew to me."

"Of course it did," I said this time, and she smiled and let me take her inside.

There were no omens or warnings on the day of the accident. Peg had to work all day that Saturday so Maddie and I were on our own. I hadn't planned anything so I asked her what she wanted to do. "We could go to the zoo or a movie or even the beach."

"Muttonjeff." She said it all as one word, but I knew what she meant. About an hour's drive away, at the west end of Cape Cod, stood a large gothic style bed and breakfast on the crest of a low hill set well back from Route 6A. There was a long winding driveway flanked by two very large stone lions at the street side end. We'd passed it one day while visiting antique shops and I'd called them "Heckle and Jeckle" but Maddie had insisted they were "Mutt and Jeff" because she'd been watching that particular cartoon recently. So Mutt and Jeff they were.

We packed up a picnic lunch and got in the car and set off down Route 13 to Interstate 95 and then Interstate 195 toward the Cape. It was a nice clear day but it was cool, and since the season was well over, there wasn't much traffic. We got off the highway in Wareham and started along Route 6A, slowing whenever I saw something that might interest Maddie. She actually spoke almost a dozen words during the first hour, which was almost a record.

The problem started because I wasn't paying enough attention. I swerved slightly across the median line just as a car full of teenaged boys came around the corner in the other direction. The driver over-reacted, swerved off the road, and churned up a lot of dirt and dead leaves before returning to the roadway. I glanced into my rear view mirror and was relieved that they hadn't hit anything. I was less relieved when they turned around and came after us.

If I'd been alone, I might have acted differently. I'm not a small man, and I can often physically dominate others in a confrontational situation. But I had Maddie with me and I wasn't going to take any chances. I pressed down on the gas.

They chased me for at least a couple of miles while I frantically tried to remember where the local police stations were situated. I realized that we were about to pass Mutt and Jeff and even though we were traveling far too quickly, I called to Maddie to watch out, that Mutt and Jeff were coming up. I didn't slow down because I didn't know that our pursuers had abandoned the chase just seconds earlier.

Technically I was speeding, but not excessively. Charles Ordway, however, had a blood alcohol level three times the legal limit and was moving faster than seventy miles per hour when he rounded the curve and came toward us. I saw him, of course, and tried to brake, but I don't think he ever noticed us at all. He sideswiped my Honda, sheering off most of the driver's side and we began to spin clockwise as we were thrown to the right. Most of the impact was on the passenger's side, but we rolled completely over onto the roof before we hit the maple tree. I think that's when Maddie was thrown clear, but I'll never know for certain. The trunk stopped our roll, but the wood was rotted and it split vertically. A very large portion of the maple fell on top of the car.

I blacked out for at least a few seconds. When I opened my eyes, I was hanging upside down, and my seatbelt had somehow twisted so that I could only move one of my arms, and that just barely. Everything seemed very, very quiet and I could hear the dripping of gasoline from my ruptured tank. And then the sound of the flames from Ordway's Ford. He'd been smoking and his cigarette had fallen into the puddle of liquor on the floor of his car. I couldn't see it but I could smell the fire.

"Daddy?" It was Maddie, and corny as it sounds, my heart leaped when I heard her voice.

"Honey, are you all right?"

"Head hurts." She sounded rueful. I was trying to think of what to say next when she moved into my line of sight. Even upside down, with dirt stained coveralls and a smudged face, she looked beautiful to me.

"Maddie, listen to me. Stay away from the cars, do you understand? I want you to walk down the street, careful like Mommy and I showed you, and find a house. Tell them you were in an accident and bring them back here. Can you do all that?"

"Get help."

"That's right. I want you to get help. Can you do that for Daddy?"

"Mutt and Jeff can help."

"No, honey, I'm afraid not. This is people work. You need to find some people to help." I waited, there was no answer, and I realized she had gone. Then I tried to move and there was this incredible pain shooting through the side of my head, and that's all I remember about the accident.

I woke up in the hospital the following afternoon, in considerable pain. A nurse demanded to know how I felt and I demanded to know what had happened to my daughter. She didn't seem to know and repeated her question, but I insisted that she find out immediately unless she wanted me to rip the tubes out of my arm and get out of bed. She didn't know whether to look concerned, angry, or frightened, and ended up with a blend of the three, but she told me to wait a moment and disappeared through the door.

I doubt she was gone for long but it seemed like eternity and I was seriously considering following through on my threat when she returned, followed by an older woman whose nametag identified her as Doctor Thorne.

"I understand you've been causing some trouble, Mr. Cortland."

"I want to know about my daughter," I said as evenly as I could. "She was with me in the car."

"Yes, I know. Please don't agitate yourself. She's perfectly all right. She has a nasty looking bump on her head, not nearly as large as yours, but she's resting quietly now and there's not likely to be any permanent damage. Your wife went down to the cafeteria a few minutes ago. I've sent one of the orderlies to find her."

"Maddie's all right then?"

"Perfectly. There are a few scratches and bruises, but children her age are much more resilient than the rest of us. Now lie back and let me take a look at you."

That's pretty much it except, as they say, for the punch line. I spent two days in the hospital, and went home sore and confused. The soreness was predictable. The confusion was not. I was confused because a police detective came to see me a few hours before I was discharged, a polite, distant man named Everson who looked as though he was perpetually on the verge of a sneeze, knew it, and was very unhappy about it.

He was also unhappy about my accident.

"You didn't see anyone else in the area, before the crash or afterward?"

"Not a soul beforehand. When the other car came around the curve, I just had time to register what was going to happen before he hit us. And afterward, my field of vision was pretty limited."

He looked, if possible, even less happy than when he'd arrived, and I asked him if there was a problem. "Well, yes, there is. You see, according to your report, you were pinned under your car, but your little girl wasn't."

"No, she was thrown clear fortunately."

"And you somehow crawled free before the car burned?"

"I must have. I don't remember much about it, but she couldn't have dragged me out on her own. She's only three and I'm not a small man. Why is this important?"

He sighed and combed his hair with his fingers. "It probably isn't anything. Just an odd loose end. You see, Mr. Cortland, the seatbelt in your car wasn't released, it was ripped open. And according to your statement, your car was resting on its roof at the end, but when we arrived at the scene, it was lying on its side and there were strange marks on it."

"Marks?"

"Scratches. Deep scratches. Long parallel cuts right into the metal, as though someone grabbed it with some big metal claw and pulled it up on its side to get at you."

"But that's impossible," I said, and meant it.

"It's not impossible if it happened." He sighed and closed the notebook in which he'd been writing. "But I suppose it doesn't really matter. The other driver, Ordway, was clearly at fault, and if he'd survived the crash, he'd be facing serious charges." He stood up. "As it is, let me wish you a speedy recovery, Mr. Cortland. And say hello to your daughter for me. I met her the day of the accident and she's a real charmer."

Two days after I was released from the hospital, I asked Peggy to drive me out to the accident site. There were still odd pieces of wreckage strewn through the underbrush, but that wasn't what interested me. I wasn't there for any such morbid reason. I wanted to see the statues.

They were there, of course. Mutt was exactly as I remembered. I almost missed the change in Jeff, but when I looked more closely, I noticed that he was now sitting with one forepaw draped across the other. Maybe the bump on the head had addled my memories, but I was quite sure that before the night of the accident, Jeff had squatted solemnly with his forepaws arranged side by side.

Did Maddie somehow bring Jeff to life to save me? I don't know. I'll never know. After the accident, she began to pick up language normally and nothing unusual has happened in the two years since. Maybe the bump on her head changed something or maybe she just grew out of it. I told Peg what I suspected a while back and she very obviously humored me but didn't believe a word of it.

"Does it bother you to think that Maddie's isn't special?" she asked.

"But she IS special," I answered. "And always will be."

FOLLOWING ORDERS

I still have nightmares about my experiences during the war in Viet Nam, but it wasn't the war that you saw on television and in the newspapers that scarred me. It was another war entirely.

Like a lot of young men of my generation, I considered running off to Canada, or allowing myself to be sent to jail as a draft dodger, or contriving to do something during basic training that would get me thrown out of the army. I did none of these things, not because I believed in what we were doing, or because I was staunchly patriotic, but simply because it was easier to do what I was told.

I was a pretty good mechanic even then and I made sure people knew about it, so when I got shipped off to Asia, it was no surprise that my orders assigned me to a motor pool. I'd have been perfectly happy to have spent the year repairing jeeps and armored personnel carriers so long as no one was shooting at me. They flew me up to Phu Hiep, a village on the coast, where a helicopter unit and an infantry battalion sat side by side behind a wall of barbed wire and minefields. It only took about a week to realize that the redundancy factor was at work; we had enough mechanics to handle a fleet two or three times as big as the one we were servicing. Which meant that some of us spent a lot of time sitting around waiting for something to do. Which isn't a good thing in the army.

A few of us started getting tapped for field work, including myself. I'm a pretty big guy and I look kind of fierce even when I don't feel that way, so about once a week they sent me over to the operations office with a full pack and my M16 and I was off with a half dozen other poor souls to make a security pass through Phu Hiep or one of the outlying villages, just to make sure Charlie wasn't preparing anything unpleasant for us. We never found anything and since our search schedule was on a regular rotation and very predictable, I would have been surprised if we had.

That's not entirely true. We stumbled on something all right, but it wasn't what we'd been sent out to find.

We were on our way to Tuy Do, a tiny little village whose residents clearly resented our visits even though we always brought chocolate bars and other small presents when we passed that way. It was hot that day – it was always hot but it was particularly bad because the humidity had spiked – and Hale, the squad leader, told us to take five but not to drink too much water. We all knew better but he always had to say it anyway. It had become a ritual.

Anyway, I decided to take a leak and slipped off into the jungle, eyes searching the ground for tripwires, when I came across the body. The first body. One of the other guys found the other two after I'd shouted – screamed is more like it – and they all came running. I'd never seen anyone dead before and even if I had, I don't think I would have reacted much differently. The body was all messed up. All the parts seemed to be there, and I didn't look closely enough to discover otherwise, but they weren't quite right. One arm was attached lower than the other, below the breastbone, and both eyes were on the same side of the nose. One hand had seven fingers, the other three. The only thing normal was the spear shaft sticking out of the chest. It looked like just what it was, except the shaft was all carved with odd squiggles and symbols.

I believe it was Gomez who found the other two. My body was a male, I think; I never looked. He had one of each. When I finally felt that I could move without throwing up, I went to join the rest of the squad, who were clustered unwisely close together a few meters away. The two bodies lay under a tree, both naked; my corpse had been dressed in familiar village style. The woman's face looked almost normal, except that her ears were mounted too high on her head. The rest of her body was bizarre. She had two small breasts, but they were low on her back. Her sexual organs had replaced them on her chest. One leg ended in a stump; the other was bifurcated and had two normal looking feet. The guy next to her looked more like a snail. His neck came out of his chest rather than rising above the shoulders and his arms and legs were all set low on his body, as though he'd moved around on all fours. Both of them had elaborately carved spears thrust through their bodies.

"What the fuck?" said Portman, echoing all our thoughts. Chabert knelt down and poked at the woman's body until Hale ordered him to stop.

Portman broke out the radio but Hale shook his head and told him not to break radio silence. "Do a tight sweep along there," he waved to indicate a section of the perimeter. "But stay in sight of one another. Just make sure we're secure here. These bodies are fresh."

I took the left wing with Appleby and Mitchell, while Chabert, Gomez, and Hewitt went right. We were lucky because the terrain wasn't bad and it didn't take long to clear the arc of jungle. For the moment at least, we appeared to have the area to ourselves. We used hand signals to tell Hale we hadn't found anything and he signed for us to return. My group had no trouble at all, but when Chabert and Hewitt arrived, they were by themselves.

"Where's Gomez?" barked Hale.

The other two exchanged puzzled looks. "He was right behind me a minute ago," said Hewitt.

"No he wasn't." Chabert shook his head. "That was me. He must have been in front of you."

Hewitt giggled. It was a nervous habit that drove me crazy. "No, you were in front of me. I'd recognize that fat backside anywhere."

They might have argued further but Hale told them to shut up. "Okay, let's go find him. And this time buddy up. No one goes off on his own."

We swept the area carefully and thoroughly and there was no sign of Gomez. He was a big guy, tough as nails. I couldn't imagine anyone taking him out without making a sound. But he was gone. Hale was furious. I could hear it in his voice even though his words were measured. He ordered us back to the clearing where the bodies lay and this time we all got back safely.

Except the bodies weren't there anymore.

Now even if you believe my story so far, and I wouldn't blame you if you didn't, you might not accept what happened next. First of all, there is absolutely no possibility that we hadn't returned to our starting point. There were several unique features and even if there hadn't been, we could still see the cigarette butt that Portman had ground out on an exposed rock. But the bodies were gone, which suggested that we were not alone after all.

Hale was biting his lip furiously. He did not want to lose a man, particularly this way. He told Portman to call it in, but it turned out our radio wasn't working. Nothing but some weird kind of static. The thing about Hale is that the madder he gets, the quieter he is, and he was almost whispering when he told us we were aborting and returning to base. I liked Gomez and I hated just going off and leaving him, but I was seriously spooked by now and so was everyone else. Mitchell had found one of the spears lying under some ferns. He hadn't wanted to touch it because there were bloodstains but I picked it up, I guess because it was the only physical proof I had that this hadn't all been some kind of dream.

We should only have been about ten steps from the trail we'd been following, but when we went that way, it just wasn't there. See? I said you wouldn't believe it. Neither could we at the time. We knew that our base was directly southeast so we broke out compasses, but we got three different readings for north, none of them even close to one another.

"What the fuck is going on?" It was Appleby this time, and Appleby never swore. It was almost as shocking as the bodies had been.

We had no idea which way to go but there was no point in staying where we were. Hale looked around for a while, then apparently decided to take the path of least resistance. We started down a gradual slope. There was a lot of brush and we couldn't travel in a straight line, but we made decent time. Sooner or later, Hale told us, we'd cross a trail or find cultivated rice paddies or something. The sun was almost directly overhead so it was hard to use that to choose a direction, but we figured that would change as the day progressed and that we could always adjust if we were headed the wrong way.

We walked for over three hours. We never talked much on patrol; it wasn't smart to attract attention. But we were even quieter during that trek. I'm not sure how long we would have gone without saying a word if we hadn't suddenly recognized where we were.

We were back at the clearing where we'd found the bodies. Where the bodies had disappeared. Except that one of them was back now. Except that it wasn't one of the bodies we'd found before. It was Gomez. At least, I think that's who it was.

The body lay prone and it was dressed in fatigues and when Hale rolled it to one side we saw the nametag. Someone swore. It might have been me. But it didn't really look like Gomez. There was no mouth, for one thing, unless it was hidden somewhere under the fatigues. And the ears grew out of the cheeks and the hips were twisted ninety degrees so that his legs were askew and I didn't look any more after that. A carved spear shaft stuck straight up out of his back, the twin of the one I was still carrying.

Portman was looking a little sick. He sat down on a rock and looked up at the sky. "Guys," he said quietly. "Why hasn't the sun started to go down?"

No one tried to answer him.

We had a little bit of food with us, but we weren't supposed to spend the night away from camp and presumably they'd send a chopper to look for us when we didn't report back before dark. On the other hand, it looked to us like it never was going to get dark. Hale posted sentries and told the rest of us to try to get some sleep. I didn't expect to, but since I'd been in the army I'd acquired the ability to doze on command and I drifted off for awhile.

I came to when Hale nudged my shoulder. He looked scared and that scared me. Hale wasn't the kind to show fear. He was a little guy, so short that I don't think the army would have let him in if they hadn't been so desperate for manpower. I knew he was from Newark and that his family had been poor and I guessed he'd had a rough life, but he'd thrived in the army, made corporal in near record time, and I'd never heard anyone give him any lip.

"Goodrich! Wake up! We have a problem."

I shook off the last vestiges of sleep and looked around. Everything seemed quiet. "What's wrong?"

"Mitchell and Chabert are both missing. They were supposed to be standing guard but when I went to check on them, they were gone."

"Maybe they switched off with some of the other guys." I knew that was unlikely even as I said it.

Hale shook his head. "When I got back, Hewitt and Appleby were gone too. I can't find anyone but you."

I did a roll call in my head. "What about Portman?"

Hale caught his breath. "He's here." He hesitated. "At least I think he is."

Hale led me over to an oversized tree where I'd last seen Portman sitting with his back against the trunk, his legs splayed out in front of him, eyes closed and breathing regular. His legs were still splayed out from the trunk, but his body wasn't there anymore; his hips seemed to have melded into a gnarly bole. Even worse, his flesh was warm and I think one of his knees flexed slightly while we were standing there."

"No sign of the others?" I asked.

Hale shook his head. "It's just you and me and I'm not so sure about me."

I thought he was just joking, but his face was very serious. "I mean it, Goodrich. I feel peculiar."

"Maybe it's shock," I suggested. "I'm not feeling any too steady myself."

"No, it's more than that. I feel like there's something wrong with my body. I reach for something and it's as if my arm is moving at the wrong angle, or the wrong muscles are tensing and relaxing."

"Just nerves," I told him, but I'm not sure which of us I was trying to reassure. "We can't stay here." Actually here was likely as good as anyplace else but I had a sudden aversion to the clearing.

Hale nodded. "All right. Let's follow the sun." He glanced up and laughed at his joke. The sun was directly overhead.

I gathered my things, including my souvenir spear. Portman's pack was still where he'd dropped it and I spotted an M16 propped against a rock. Hale retrieved his stuff but uncharacteristically let me take the lead. On a whim, I set off directly away from where the trail was, or where it had been.

We were moving mostly uphill at first and the going was tough. There were vines dangling everywhere and the ground cover snatched at our ankles and turned slippery under our boots. The heat was relentless and we hadn't seen fresh water in a while so we only took sips from our canteens. Then we passed a gentle crest and started downhill and that was a little easier although there was still no path. And then, at last, there was.

It wasn't much and I almost missed it and kept going, but I noticed the narrow band of harder packed earth and pointed it out to Hale who considered then nodded. Neither of us said that things couldn't get worse because we all know how that works out, but we were probably both thinking it.

The ground got rockier and the foliage began to thin and in half an hour or so – my watch had stopped – we found ourselves walking along a crumbling ledge on the side of a very steep defile. At first we couldn't see much peering over the edge except the tops of trees and elaborate webs of vines and brush, but then we spotted a fast moving stream weaving through the landscape which gradually turned into a narrow gorge. The water looked inviting because we were running pretty low but there was no obvious way down so we continued to follow the path, which ran roughly parallel.

The gorge made a sharp curve and opened up slightly. We saw a tumbled pile of rock where part of one cliff face had collapsed, and there were at least three dark cavities which we assumed must be caves. Neither of us had spoken much at that point, but Hale seemed to have recovered some of his self confidence.

"We have to get down there."

I was less than optimistic. The wall was very steep on this side, but it was sandstone and treacherously unstable. If we'd had a rope, I might have been more willing, but we didn't and I wasn't about to risk breaking a leg, or worse. Hale started to argue the point, but then the situation changed.

Two men emerged from the center cave mouth and walked down to the stream. They were both wearing fatigues but they were still pretty far away and they didn't look up at us. One of them might have been Chabert or Hewitt, and the other was definitely Appleby. He'd lost his headgear and his V shaped Mohawk was unmistakable.

Hale called to them but they never even glanced in our direction.

I won't try to describe our descent, which was tedious, uncomfortable, and often scary. Footholds collapsed under our weight and a couple of times we had to climb back up in order to find a safer way down. But at last, somehow, we managed to reach the floor of the gorge. By then Appleby and his companion had disappeared, presumably back into the cave.

We drank our fill and splashed across the stream to the opposite side. I was all for storming up to the cave mouth and demanding answers, but Hale was more cautious and he insisted that we proceed carefully, making use of whatever cover we could find. "We'll call to them when we're close enough."

But we didn't have to. I don't know where Mitchell had been hiding, but he came out of nowhere and touched me on the arm. I spun around, bringing my weapon up, and Mitchell was staring right at me. His face was perfectly recognizable. But Mitchell had been short and chunky and this Mitchell was tall and lean and he had a V shaped Mohawk. Which meant it hadn't been Appleby after all. Or at least not completely.

I said his name, making it a question, and stepped back. Hale came up beside me and raised his weapon, but there was something odd about his posture and I realized that one of his arms had an extra joint and the other was short and withered. I think I shouted something and moved away, intending to bring my own weapon up but instead somehow I got confused, dropped the M16, and raised the spear instead.

That probably saved my life.

Other figures had emerged from the cave and were walking toward us, including a foreshortened Portman whose head was half sunken into his body and a four armed version of Chabert who had no eyes but easily picked his way across the broken ground. Only Hale still carried a weapon. I brandished my spear even as I wondered if I could really use it against my friends. Or were these my friends any longer?

It didn't matter. The choice was taken from me. I watched without understanding as the Mitchell thing jerked and then fell headlong, the shaft of another spear protruding from his back. Things flew through the air and more bodies dropped and the most vivid memory I have is that there was absolute silence. The spitted bodies made no outcry as they fell and the ones launching the spears gave no war cries or shouts of satisfaction. It all happened very quickly. I was aware that several men wearing elaborate markings on their bodies – and little else – had emerged from the nearby trees and brush. If I had been paying more attention I think I would have noticed that the symbols on their chests and thighs and foreheads were the same as those on the spears, but I didn't really look at them and now I'll never know. At least two of them examined me carefully without coming within arm's length and they apparently decided I was all right because they ignored me after that. They checked each of the prostrate forms, but did not remove the spears, then disappeared back into the jungle.

They had not spoken a single word. I looked after them, but could not see any sign of their passage because it was so dark. The sun was going down at last.

I found a trail the next day and reached a small marine encampment within a few hours. I told them the truth, but not all of it. I said that I'd become separated from the rest of my patrol and gotten lost, that I had no idea what had happened to them, and no, I had not heard any gunfire. They sent a chopper to take me back to Phu Hiep. Hale and the rest were listed as missing in action. Their bodies have never been found.

So how did I manage to avoid the same fate? Well, I've thought about it a great deal during the past three decades and I have a theory. A couple of theories, actually. Carrying the inscribed spear might have made me somehow immune to whatever was affecting the others. It was stolen from my hooch shortly after I returned to duty, but I'd spent some time copying down the symbols carved along the shaft and after I became a civilian again I looked at them every once in a while and finally I took them to Brown University and found a professor who was willing to try translating them. He got back to me a few days later and asked again where I'd first seen them – I had invented a story about finding some ruins in the jungle – because they were an interesting variation of some old Chinese myth.

The ancient Chinese believed that before there was a universe there was Hundun, that is, Chaos. Hundun and the Universe had a kind of mutual hate thing going on, and the Order vs Chaos dichotomy isn't unique to Asia. Anyway, the Universe supplanted Hundun but it didn't destroy it. This continuing tension was the source of demons, dragons, magic, and other supernatural phenomenon. Hundun made a good fight of it for awhile, but it turns out that Order is more stable than Chaos – no surprise there – so Hundun's influence faded with the passage of time. Faded, but never quite went away.

Now that might explain what happened to the other members of my squad, but it doesn't enlighten us about how I escaped. Or does it? If we had all been changed, then the results of our contact with Hundun would have been invariable, and invariability is Order. So by sparing me, Hundun validated itself. It sounds logical to me, but then again, Chaos isn't subject to logic.

But did I escape or just receive a temporary reprieve? I'm not sure any longer, because it might just be that this has been preying on me for so long that I'm losing my reason. You see, I'm right handed, so I'm writing this down with my right hand. But it's hot tonight and I'm also drinking a nice cold beer and when I took the last sip I realized that I was holding the can in my right hand.

My other right hand.

IMPULSIVE BEHAVIOR

Did you ever notice how sometimes the most trivial impulse takes on a life of its own? One guy climbs a hill and flies a kite, and the next day there are a dozen. The potential must have been dormant in all of those other people until it was nudged into action. We talk about inspiring political speeches, but there's never anything new or original in the words themselves. There's some other agency at work which pushes us from resigned acceptance to active protest.

I first met Brad Long in Mona's basement on a rainy Friday night. Her place had become one of my favorite hangouts since I'd returned for my sophomore year. Dave Hartley had introduced me to Mona and her friends and I didn't feel quite as uncomfortable with them as I did with the heavy drinking fraternity types, the deadly serious business majors, or any of the other social groups on campus. Not that I blended into this crowd very easily either. I invariably wore traditional, dull shirts and pants, shaved daily, and there was neither a bead nor a sandal anywhere in my wardrobe. This made me somewhat suspect in their eyes, but I was tolerated because my politics were acceptable and Dave was my friend. "Mouse" Brewster used to tease me occasionally for wearing the "uniform of the oppressing class", but it always seemed to me that beads and shawls and beards and sandals were just another kind of uniform.

Anyway, sometimes Dave and I came together, sometimes I came alone. This was one of the latter times. Mona lived in an "apartment" that consisted of one third of an unfinished basement, her space marked by blankets and sheets hanging from the ceiling. She had decorated with the usual furniture – a mattress lying on the floor over a sheet of plastic to keep the damp out, book shelves consisting of planks and cinder blocks, candles stuck in wine bottles so covered with melted wax that you could no longer read the labels, psychedelic black light posters, a stack of tomato boxes to hold her clothing. The basement smelled of pot, cheap wine, and urine, and the narrow windows and hanging blankets ensured a perpetual dusk. When I arrived, the Beatles were singing the praises of Rita the meter maid somewhere in the background.

Mona actually had another apartment, a very nice one in fact. Her mother had died when she was an infant but her father was a wealthy construction manager who apparently wasn't home very much. She was the archetypal rebellious teenager when she wasn't being the doting daughter. The only time she stayed at her nice place was when her father was visiting, and we were all warned to steer clear. Mona might detest daddy's politics, lifestyle, and poor parenting skills, but she liked knowing the money was there even while she was ranting against the evil capitalists. On the other hand, she had more spending money than the rest of us combined, and she was always amply supplied with pot, wine, and munchies when we got together.

She was already pretty drunk when I got there that evening. Mona was indifferent to pot, but she soaked up sweet wines like a sponge. When I came down through the bulkhead door, she was half sitting, half lying on the mattress, wearing a tight dress slit to her waist on both sides. The dress had ridden up and not much was left to the imagination. Like the other three guys present, I pretended not to notice. Caley, a quasi-anorexic blonde with stringy hair, oversized glasses, and pinched features that made her face look caved in, was watching avidly. Dave had gotten drunk one night and made a pass at Caley and her response, which he wouldn't describe, had convinced him that she wasn't interested in guys, which for some reason made all of us guys more interested in her.

Anyway, Mona gave me a tipsy greeting and turned back to her conversation with Randy. Randy had recently begun illustrating his solidarity with Native Americans by buying peyote from a Pakistani grad student and wearing a genuine Navajo shawl, made in Japan. Randy was obviously in lust with Mona, but as far as I knew she had never allowed anyone to touch what she frequently displayed. The remaining two people sat on upended orange crates in front of the wooden cable spool that served as Mona's table. I recognized George Pike right away. George was tall and thin, cadaverous, with thick dark eyebrows and unkempt black hair. George bubbled with nervous energy, which seemed to confuse him as well as elude his control. He was perpetually unhappy, so quick to become outraged at some social or political ill that he could no longer discriminate between major and minor issues. He had shrugged off the announcement of the use of napalm in Cambodia, but had flown into a frothing rage when told that minority enrollment at the university was slightly lower than proportionate to the state's racial makeup.

George was relatively calm now, sitting with his hands folded in his lap. He had a tic in one eye that was firing like crazy and he kept wetting his lips, but he seemed completely captivated by his companion, whom I'd never seen before. The stranger didn't look like he belonged here, any more than I did, I suppose. He was wearing dark, sharply pressed slacks and a white shirt, open at the collar, with a sports coat that looked expensive. His hair was thick and dark and precisely combed and shaped. He was, I suspect, good looking though his face was a bit thin and his eyes were set so deep that they seemed to be peering at the world out of a dark well. I instinctively disliked him, perhaps because I felt he was trespassing on my prerogatives. I was the token straight in this group and intended to stay that way.

As if he could read my mind, the newcomer turned and gave me a frankly appraising look. "Hi. I'm Brad. Brad Long."

"Dan," I answered reluctantly. "Dan Kramer. "

"Pleased to meet you, Dan."

That was a blatant lie. Even George felt the sudden tension, and for the first and only time during our acquaintance he tried to be the peacemaker. "Brad's a mole inside the YAF. He's been telling us all their plans."

George was paranoid about the Young Americans for Freedom, convinced that they were a tool of the conspiracy that secretly controlled the government. As a freshman, he'd joined the Students for a Democratic Society, but they weren't radical enough for him. He'd gone from one fringe group to another, was thrown out of the Marxist Club, and most recently had founded the Che Guevera Society. He'd recruited three other members initially, but had expelled them as insufficiently Marxist.

"Is that so?" I sat down cross legged on a straw mat, since all of the "chairs" were taken. There was a half bottle of sherry on the table and some paper cups. I poured myself some, trying to decide if I was curious enough about Brad to engage him in conversation, or repelled enough to ignore him. He didn't allow me the choice.

"Know thy enemy," he said quietly. I noticed that he wasn't drinking, or smoking, and wondered just what he was doing in Mona's basement.

"That's not always as easy as it sounds," I answered, trying to sound sophisticated, failing miserably. I don't honestly remember if he said anything else that day. I got into a conversation with Caley, who usually only spoke at length when she was ranting against the establishment, the war, conformity, or any of her other causes and obsessions, and the next thing I knew, Brad was gone.

The following morning, George broke into the Political Science Department offices and trashed their files, then set a fire. He was arrested, expelled, and sentenced to four years in prison, in that order. I never saw him again.

Aside the First. I've never understood why people embrace organized religion. It's not that I object to religion as such, but churches have no appeal for me. They're created by mortals, not any theoretical supernatural Creator, and as such they're imperfect, inconsistent, and sometimes actively evil. My own beliefs are rather more nebulous. I think that within each of us there exists an impulse toward greatness and that the utmost service we can provide to our theoretical Creator is to do everything within our power to realize our potential. But there are other impulses as well – the need to reproduce, to be accepted by our fellows – and still others not so admirable – cruelty, the thirst for power, the attractiveness of violence. Most people have difficulty finding a balance. Including me.

The next time I noticed Brad Long it was only in passing. While still a freshman, I'd become fascinated with the art crowd, who considered their lifestyle Bohemian rather than hippie, a distinction not obvious to the unenlightened. There was one corner of the Student Union Grille which they called their own. They drank mostly coffee – no booze allowed - but occasionally someone brought a funny looking cigarette that got passed surreptitiously around the table. Smoking wasn't allowed either, but most of the staff were students and they didn't care.

I had fallen into orbit around them a couple of weeks after arriving on campus, fascinated by their discussions of cubism, Dali's hidden symbolism, and other arcane subjects. My infatuation lasted until I got frustrated at being unable to contribute, retired to the campus library during my free time for a couple of weeks to educate myself, only to return and discover they didn't know what the hell they were talking about. Welcome to the real world, Dan Kramer.

On this particular day I craved caffeine and had stopped for a quick fix. There were half a dozen people in the art corner, only a couple of whom I recognized. I would have walked right past except that seated directly in the middle, like Christ at the Last Supper, was Brad Long. He was dressed very much as he had been the last time I'd seen him; in fact, they might have been the exact same clothes. I hesitated, moved a bit closer, trying not to act interested.

"You can't separate art from reality!" I recognized the speaker, Terry something, a fairly skilled caricaturist who had also produced some of the ugliest paintings I'd ever seen. The last I knew he'd embraced Dadaism, was railing against bourgeois values and trying to become Marcel Duchamps.

Brad's voice was unmistakable. He almost purred. "No, of course not. But you can use art to transform the world. The artist distills his environment and creates the catalyst for change. The ultimate achievement is to use reality as a canvas, to arrange the elements in a way that makes truth obvious, no, inescapable."

It sounded like the same crap that had fascinated me in my ignorance and I turned away, probably sneering, and got my coffee. Two days later, Terry was taken to the local hospital in an ambulance, but they were unable to save his life. He had piled all of his belongings in the middle of his room and turned three of the four walls into a panorama of a massacre scene in Vietnam. There were mutilated bodies everywhere, most of them very bloody, and he had used his own blood. He had passed out just as he was starting the final wall.

Aside the Second. Perhaps the most insidious flaw in the human race is the impulse toward self-destruction. At its most extreme, we have suicides and martyrs, but it is in its less obvious form that it causes the most widespread damage. We acknowledge the bad effects of activities that we know are dangerous or debilitating – cigarettes, speeding, heavy drinking – but that doesn't stop us from indulging in them. Even more subtle are the little things we do to ourselves that aren't as logically dubious, that we may even try to believe aren't harmful at all. We choose careers that demand higher pay rather than those which are more fulfilling. We vote for politicians because of their rhetoric or affiliation rather than their character or agenda. We marry for status, or to spite our parents. At times, we even derive perverse pleasure from our own misery. But we rarely do anything about it. For most of us, compromise is the solution and we achieve a reasonable degree of contentment. Not everyone is that lucky.

One of the reasons I was never fully accepted into Mona's crowd was that I wouldn't smoke pot. I drank alcohol, which was probably just as bad, but I'd resisted the temptation to get high. At first, my reluctance was just nerves. It was, after all, against the law. That wore off quickly, but by then I had become increasingly annoyed with the constant pressure to conform from among the supposed nonconformists. Eventually people stopped offering me a toke.

Dave Hartley had been my roommate for a while, but he'd moved off campus before I'd done the same, and frankly, as much as I liked Dave, I didn't want to share quarters with him again. His idea of doing the laundry was to start drawing clothing from the bottom of the hamper, perhaps theorizing that they couldn't possibly still be dirty after so much time had passed. We stopped being roommates, but we were still friends, and when Paula dumped me and I got depressed, I went over to see him.

His place wasn't much more than a closet. He had to sit on the bed to leave enough room for me to squat on the floor. Dave wanted to tell me all about his most recent trip – he'd discovered LSD – but I cut him off. I was already regretting the impulse that had brought me there and I knew I'd have to act quickly or I'd change my mind. "Are you holding?"

His eyebrows went up. "No one's going to bust us here."

"That's not what I meant. I want to get high."

Dave was a true convert. He was always at his happiest when he was turning other people on. Unfortunately for my plans, my timing was less than optimal. He'd spent all his spare money on acid and the cupboard was bare.

"But I know where we can get some."

So I followed Dave to yet another dingy room, occupied by a nervous looking type who called himself Mole. But Mole had been sick and had missed his weekly connection. "Try Caley," he suggested.

So we walked to Caley's place, even though the wind had picked up and distant lightning flickered in the darkness. I hadn't seen much of Caley lately. She'd found a new friend, a quiet, almost furtive girl named Milly who always looked as though she was terrified, and they were off someplace together. My second thoughts were evolving into third and fourth thoughts by then, but Dave convinced me to try "just one more place."

"Maybe we should just wait until a better time."

"No, this is cool. There's a party at Bill Calderall's tonight and someone will be carrying."

It was spitting rain by the time we arrived and thundering ominously. Calderall and two friends had rented an entire house. They were all seniors. I'd met Calderall once and hadn't liked him. I didn't like his house much either. It was in a rundown neighborhood, and all the lights were off. I would have thought that no one was home except that Buffy St. Marie was singing about Sir Patrick Spens somewhere on the second floor. I told Dave I didn't think this was such a good idea but he wasn't about to let me off the hook after he had played the line for so long. He grabbed my arm and led me inside.

It took a minute for my eyes to adjust to the dark. There was one candle burning on the mantle a t the far end of the room, but it was guttering. I could smell incense, sweet and cloying and far too strong. There were people in the room as well, three or four sitting in chairs in the dark, no one speaking. Another was standing beside one of the chairs, and a passing car's headlights provided a snapshot of what was happening. Bill Calderall was sitting with his eyes closed. A cord had been wrapped around his bare arm and the standing figure was injecting something with a hypodermic. It was Brad Long.

"C'mon, upstairs." Dave led me to the second floor quickly, before I could mount any resistance. There were perhaps a dozen people sitting on the floor, each with his or her own candle flickering between crossed thighs, and the atmosphere was tinged with smoke. "Just give me a minute," said Dave, who had already spotted a friend. But at that very moment, lights started to flash outside the windows and someone shouted "We're busted!" I barely managed to stay on my feet as the crowd rushed toward the stairway.

There was a great deal of confusion. Someone was using a loudspeaker, but I couldn't tell what he was saying. Someone else screamed and several someones were swearing. Dave and I were suddenly alone on the second floor, and I thought the world was coming to an end. Fortunately, Dave's survival instincts were better than mine. "This way, quick!"

He led me out onto the fire escape, which didn't seem to me much of an improvement. The yard was enclosed by a tall stockade fence and helmeted figures had already moved to cover the side door. "We'll have to jump!"

For a second or two, I thought Dave meant for us to leap down into the yard, but then I saw what he actually intended, and that seemed even worse. The house next to us, just beyond the fence, had a fire escape matching ours, facing toward us. There was a short landing where we stood and Dave retreated to the far end, bolted forward and jumped, landing neatly on both feet. He made it look easy.

I was scared green, but the thought of being arrested was even scarier. I stepped back to the far end, gathered what passed for courage, and ran forward. I made it, but not as picturesquely. I landed sprawling, tore my pants, bloodied my knee, and sprained my wrist. Dave helped me up and we climbed down and made our escape.

Calderall and four others were sent to prison. One of the guests died of an overdose. Another nine people were arrested on minor charges. Brad Long was not among them. I never did try pot.

Aside the Third: I'm not sure why the urge to self destruction persists in the human race. At first glance, natural selection should have bred it out of the species long ago. That can only mean that – for the race if not the individual – self destruction has some survival value. Those first few water breathing creatures that emerged into the air must have died, but they kept on coming even when their instinct for survival must have told them to stay right where they were. But what was the mechanism that triggered their actions?

Final exams took up a lot of my time for the next few days. I was having particular trouble with Russian, which I had unwisely chosen as my foreign language on the theory that it was so different from the romance languages that it would be easier to learn. Somewhere along the way, I did look up Brad Long in the student directory, only to discover that there was no listing under that name. That surprised me, but I assumed it was either a mistake or that he'd transferred in after the directory was printed. It wasn't until much later that I attached any significance to the fact.

The trimester ended and I accepted an invitation from Mona to go with her on a trip home to Flint. Caley came as well, but Milly had insisted she needed to visit her family in Grand Rapids. Dave came with us, and Randy, of course, since he was the only one with wheels, a Volkswagen minibus with predictable psychedelic flowers and political slogans painted on the sides. We were halfway there before I began to wonder how Mona's dad was going to react to a van full of hippies, but I needn't have worried. He was away on a business trip, which was the only reason Mona had invited us along.

The house was impressive in an antiseptic, institutional sort of way. There were two kitchens, a half dozen bedrooms, and a common area that could have hosted a political convention. The furnishings were minimalist, some rooms containing only a table and chairs, and the bedrooms had recessed dressers and wardrobes that could be concealed behind sliding panels, leaving just a bed.

"How many people live here?" asked Dave.

Mona shrugged. "Just Daddy and me. When I'm home. When he's home."

"Typical capitalist wastefulness," muttered Randy, but I could tell that he was impressed by his intimate contact with obvious wealth. I tracked down Randy on the internet many years later. He's a stockbroker.

There were plenty of beds, obviously, but Randy staked out a chaise lounge by the pool (heated, indoor, floodlit, and more than Olympic sized). Dave made a diffident approach to Caley, was efficiently rebuffed, and wandered off to get high. I put my bag in one of the guest bedrooms, then wandered down to the TV room (we'd call it a home theater today), and stretched out on the couch. Much to my surprise, Caley showed up a few minutes later, nudged my leg with her knee, and told me to move over.

She obviously wasn't interested in the television – some routine private eye series – so I pretended to follow what was happening on the screen while surreptitiously watching her. I had visions of kinky sex, cast myself in the role of the guy who converted the gal from her lesbian yearnings, and was rehearsing scenarios in my mind when she shattered my illusions.

"I miss Milly."

I didn't answer right away. My fantasies evaporated, taking my voice with them. I shifted position, drawing further away from her. "It's only for a few days. She'll be back before classes start."

"Maybe."

I hadn't considered this scenario and felt confused as well as frustrated. "Her grades are okay, aren't they? She's not flunking out or anything?"

Caley shook her head. "She didn't go home."

"But she told Mona…"

"She lied. She lied to all of us. I got a call from her mother this morning. They're in Europe and she was apologizing that they couldn't get together for term break." Caley's voice was lifeless, brittle, desiccated.

"Then where is she?"

"I think she's with a guy." She made it sound obscene. That's probably how she thought of it.

"What guy?" It was none of my business, but the question came out all by itself.

"That Brad guy. You know, the pretty boy who used to hang out at Mona's. I saw them talking together."

Indeed, I knew who she meant. I think that was the point at which I realized how strong an antipathy I felt toward Brad Long. I hadn't thought myself capable of actually hating a person on such a deep, personal level, but Milly seemed so fragile that she might be broken by a strong breeze or a harsh word and the thought of them together made me furious and fearful.

We both lapsed into silence. The detective show ended but I never did find out who murdered the librarian. When I emerged from my thoughts, Caley had curled up at her end of the couch and was asleep. She looked like a child. I found a spare blanket in the bedroom I'd chosen and draped it over her, then went to bed myself. It took a long time to get to sleep.

We didn't talk about Milly again. Classes started and there was no Milly. A week passed and her parents showed up, worried because they hadn't heard from her. It was another week before they found her body. She'd lurked in a patch of woods near the railroad tracks, jumped in front of a passing train at the last moment. The engineer had never seen her and the body was thrown into dense undergrowth where it was hidden from casual view.

There was a suicide note pinned to her blouse. It was a catalogue of all the disappointments and difficulties in Milly's life, most of which seemed pretty trivial. The last line read: "Carrie showed me what I have to do." No one ever figured out who Carrie was.

Aside the Fourth. If we accept that the survival instinct is primary, and logic suggests that is the case, then it must require a very powerful counterbalancing influence, perhaps encountered at a precise and crucial moment in time, to alter human behavior. A suicide bomber does not just decide one day that it would be a good idea to blow up a bunch of strangers. College students do not switch from art history to business economics on a sudden whim. A woman does not casually accept that her husband has become abusive. There has to be another factor in the mix. There must be an external trigger.

I only encountered Brad Long one more time. Spring term was coming to a close and the war in Vietnam was hotter than ever. Most graduating students were about to lose their deferments, and even the relatively safe underclassmen were feeling both frustration that their voices were not being heard and anxiety that the hated war would still be going on when their personal respites expired. So there was a demonstration on campus.

It was well organized, at least during the planning stages. I helped distribute fliers encouraging students to participate, outlining our goals, and emphasizing that there was to be no violence, no property destruction, no direct confrontation with the police. The Kent State shootings were still a few months in the future, but there was no love lost between the anti-war movement and the local National Guard, many of whom were in the same age group but not

the same socio-economic class. The organizers didn't want any
incidents.

Unfortunately, all radical movements attract extremists. The
troublemakers on campus were well known to the demonstrators and
plans had been made to contain them, but for some reason this
particular protest drew a lot of people from outside the area. There
were strangers camping out on the banks of the Red Cedar River.
The campus and local cops weren't chasing them off even though
they didn't have student IDs. Then came the rumor that student
deferments were going to be suspended, and a sudden wave of new
recruits overwhelmed the bare bones structure that had been erected
to manage things. A lot of the original organizers, myself included,
quit in disgust and began advising people to wait for another day.
Some even listened, but not enough.

I did show up on the day of the demonstration, but I carefully
stood among the spectators. Somewhere between three and five
hundred protestors were milling about near the administration
building with more arriving in an intermittent stream. A line of
police officers and National Guardsmen stood in a semicircle in front
of the building, brandishing batons and looking alternately nervous
and angry. It had also turned unseasonably hot, and tempers were
fraying.

I spotted Brad almost immediately. He was not, as I might
have suspected, egging on the demonstrators. Instead he stood with a
cluster of uniformed men. He was talking quietly, not arguing, and
they were nodding their heads. After a moment, he moved away,
hovered near another cluster, and started talking again. Perhaps a
minute passed, their heads nodded, and Brad moved to the next
group.

I had to know what he was saying to them. I picked my way
around the perimeter of the area so that I could approach the line of
uniforms from the rear, where clusters of school officials, plains
clothes police officers, and journalists had positioned themselves to
watch what was happening. A couple of suspicious looks came my
way, but my clothing and demeanor must have reassured them
because no one challenged me.

Brad was just to my right, half turned away. His voice was
low and I had to concentrate to understand what he was saying. "Go
for the couples. If you call the girl a bitch, the guy'll have to do

something and then you'll have an excuse to use force." The heads began to nod and Brad smiled and moved on to the next group.

I didn't see the ignition point. I heard shouting from somewhere out of my line of sight, and then the entire line of uniforms moved forward. The protestors began shouting en masse, some demanding an end to the war, others the removal of the "pigs" from the campus. Someone with a bullhorn shouted orders and the advancing line came to a halt. The university president stepped forward to address the protestors, but he never had a chance to speak. I saw one of the Guardsmen point his baton at a girl with long, wheat colored hair. He must have spoken, because the guy she was with stepped in front of her and said something back. The baton waved, he tried to grab it, and a handful of Guardsmen surged forward. The collision spread rapidly in both directions and everything after that was chaos.

Two dozen arrests, scores of injuries. But I didn't see any of that firsthand.

Aside the Last. We rarely have trouble finding someone else to blame for our mistakes. God's will is done, the government is controlling us, aliens guide human history, our parents have high expectations, our friends would be disappointed, violence on television affects our kids, the teachers aren't doing their jobs, it's too much to ask, we're only human. It's comforting to think that we're not responsible, that we were influenced by an irresistible external force.

Nature is neither kind nor cruel. Individuals who survive do so because they are better adapted to their environment than those who perish. To a certain extent, modern civilization has circumvented this process because we believe that all life – all human life, that is, and sometimes only those human lives of which we approve – deserves to be protected. The mechanisms of a process that powerful may be circumvented, but the process itself cannot. The process evolves right along with us. It's up each individual to find the strength to survive.

Brad Long left as soon as the violence started. I'd been watching him and when he turned and walked past the admin building into the parking lot, I found myself following him even though I'd never made a conscious decision to do so. Although I kept my distance, it was probably unnecessary since he never once looked back. He led me down toward the Red Cedar River and I quickened my pace to avoid losing him as the path twisted and turned through the trees and bushes.

Now here's the part you're not going to believe. There's one sharp bend in the river where the path is completely obscured by densely packed vines, then splits into two separate paths. I saw Brad disappear into the curve and hesitated, waiting to see which branch he would take. A few seconds passed and a young woman emerged from the bend, average build, wearing white jeans and one of those green plastic raincoats that were so popular that year. No sign of Brad.

Impulsively, I hurried down the path into the bend. There was no one there, and there was no way that he could have slipped away through the briar. I ran down one of the emerging paths for a few yards, then turned back and followed the one the young woman had taken. When I reached the field behind dormitory row, I could still see her in the distance. There was no one else even close to us.

I picked up the pace and was only a few steps behind when we reached Akers Hall, one of the new high-rise dorms at this end of the campus. I wasn't sure what I was going to do. Could I ask her if she'd seen Brad back by the river without sounding like a jerk? Probably not. Frustrated, I discarded that idea but I was too stubborn to just walk away. I stayed on her trail, threading my way through groups of students who were oblivious to the drama taking place at the admin building.

My quarry approached a mixed group of half a dozen people sitting under a tree. I heard her introduce herself as "Carrie" and ask if she could join them. They all had the same text book open so it had to be some kind of informal study session. Carrie sat down with them, opening her copy of the same book. I would have sworn that her hands were empty while I'd been following her. I had a paperback novel with me, so I found a shady spot nearby and sat down, pretending to read.

I was close enough to hear bits and pieces of their conversation, and key words like "cognitive development" and "gestalt" told me it was a psych course they were discussing. Ten minutes of eavesdropping made me feel pretty silly and I was about to get up and go about my own business when a crisp voice spoke up. "You know, it's really too nice a day for this. Why don't we go over to the grill?" Three people agreed and stood up, the others insisted that Monday's test was too important and that they needed to study.

The sudden change caught me by surprise, particularly since the defectors were coming right toward me. I tried to act casual as I got to my feet, but as they passed, I glanced toward Carrie. She was looking directly at me out of eyes that seemed set so deeply into her face that it was as though she was peering out of a dark pit. I'd seen those eyes before.

They were Brad's eyes.

CAT EYES

"What do you suppose she's looking at?"

Janice rolled over, squinting because Kyle insisted on opening the curtains as soon as he was awake.

"What do I suppose who's looking at?"

"Tara. She's watching something."

"So ask her what's she's watching." Janice closed her eyes and tried to summon sleep, but knew it was a waste of time. Once actually awake in a lighted room, there was no going back.

"I took French in college, not catspeak. C'mon, look at this. It's weird. She's following something across the room."

"It's probably just a bug."

"No, there's nothing there. Nothing I can see anyway. Look at her, will you?"

Janice sat up abruptly, leaned forward in an exaggerated pose, stared at the bemused cat which was indeed moving its head slowly from left to right, eyes fixed on an invisible focal point.

"There! And I don't see anything either. Satisfied?"

It was an innocuous conversation, forgotten before she finished her shower.

"What in the world are you doing?" Janice let the front door close behind her, stared down at her husband. Kyle was on all fours, his face hovering just a few inches away from Tara, who hadn't even glanced in Janice's direction.

"Quiet!" He whispered intensely. "Don't break her concentration."

"Oh for Christ's sake." Shaking her head, Janice wandered out to the kitchen where, as usual, Kyle had dirtied twice as many dishes as necessary to prepare his lunch, and had failed to clean any of them. On her better days, she dismissed his untidiness as artistic temperament, but increasingly of late she found herself thinking the word "sloppy".

"How's the new painting going?" She plugged the sink and started the hot water, squirting a dollop of liquid soap into the churning water.

"Okay." Even filtered by distance, Kyle's voice had faltered.

"Can I take a look?"

"If you want." Kyle never assumed the stereotypical pose of the artist reluctant to reveal works in progress. But he'd become increasingly defensive since the disastrous show in Boston had failed to stimulate new interest in his paintings, and Janice was treading carefully.

Once the dirty dishes were in to soak, she dried her hands, then walked casually down the back hall and upstairs to the semi-finished attic Kyle used as his studio. She had to turn sideways to get past the neatly stacked, unsold canvases, some of which were already coated with a dusty film.

It's just a phase, she told herself firmly. Tastes fluctuate but work of real value always finds its audience. It was a litany she'd rehearsed so often it had become a mantra to ward off evil thoughts.

Kyle's current project was mounted on an easel under the skylight. She hadn't been up here in almost a week and there was evident progress, but not as much as she'd expected and there was no glitter of still wet paint. Kyle hadn't touched it recently.

Superficially it was the quintessential Kyle Langston masterpiece. A surreal landscape where trees weren't always anchored to the ground, and their branches created intricate and even suggestive patterns. A translucent church was the central focus, its placement reinforced by the asymmetrical downward sweep of bracketing storm clouds. A half dozen almost human figures had been sketched in the foreground, a woman with spiderlike legs, a man with a dorsal fin, four children whose bodies were joined at kneecap and elbow like paper dolls.

They were familiar figures, too familiar. Although the arrangement was different, each element in the painting was a reprise of an old theme. Kyle rarely spoke about his declining popularity, but Janice sensed his disillusionment, his worry that he'd lost what he often called his "twisted vision". Financially, they were secure even if he never sold another piece and could live quite well on their investments. Her modest annual salary from Eblis Manufacturing covered most of their routine living expenses and the interest on their investments was significant. But the money had always been secondary for Kyle, who'd been known to make presents of some of his best work to particularly admiring fans.

He was sitting on the couch when she came back downstairs,

but his eyes were still on Tara, who'd abandoned her invisible prey in favor of the scratching post.

"I've got some time off coming. Feel like getting out of Managansett for a while? We could make reservations up in Keene."

At first he was so unresponsive that she thought Kyle hadn't heard, but then he shook his head. "Have to get some work done first. I'm running behind schedule. Do you suppose she's lonely?"

Janice blinked, completely disoriented. "Do I suppose who's lonely?"

"Tara. I mean, we never let her out, and she hasn't seen another cat since we bought her from Mrs. Howe."

"I don't know. Maybe." The unfocused conversation was unsettling. When Kyle failed to respond, Janice sighed and drifted back to the kitchen, resolving to bring up the subject of a vacation another time, when Kyle was more himself.

There was a surprise waiting for Janice when she came home the following evening.

"Another cat? That better not be a male, Kyle Langston, or we're going to have a serious discussion about the decision making process in this house."

He shook his head, hardly glancing in her direction. "No, Misty's female. Beautiful, isn't she?"

"If you're into cats, I suppose." It hadn't been a good day. Production was lagging behind schedule, a couple of key orders were in jeopardy, and the departmental profitability statement for the previous quarter had been less than scintillating.

Janice ignored her husband and his new friend and went directly to the kitchen, where Tara was already sulking under the table. To her surprise, there was only a single dirty plate, although several empty cans of cat food sat on the counter less than a meter from the garbage bin.

"You're going to make them fat if you keep feeding them like this." She counted six cans, swept them all into the trash.

"Cats know when to stop. It's instinctive with them."

"Yeah, right." But she whispered it on her way out to the pantry to consider meal options. There were two cases of cat food in the corner, and a large box of catnip sat on a shelf.

Janice opened her eyes, aware that something was wrong. She wasn't alarmed, exactly, but apprehensive. Kyle's side of the bed was empty and when she tested the sheets with her hand, cool.

The house was silent, but there was a light on in the front room. Robed and slippered, she moved in that direction, tempted to call Kyle's name but oddly reluctant to break the silence.

He was lying on the rug in his pajama bottoms, no top. He often slept that way during the warm weather, but invariably put on a robe while out of bed, even just to visit the adjoining bathroom.

Tara had apparently gotten over her pique because she was co-existing quite happily with Misty now, had even condescended to allow the newcomer to lick her fur clean. Kyle lay silently, his chin supported on folded arms, so motionless that Janice thought he'd fallen asleep. She was considering going back for a blanket with which to cover him, when his head moved closer to Misty, bobbed for a second, then drew back to its original position.

If she hadn't known better, she'd have sworn he had licked her fur.

"It's not an hallucination or a waking dream," he told her over breakfast a few days later. "I've confirmed that much. They both see whatever it is that they see."

By now, Janice no longer even blinked at the sudden interjection of odd comments into their conversations, particularly since Kyle's obsession had become clearer. And obsession it was, so demanding that she was beginning to be alarmed.

"I don't understand why this is so important to you, Kyle. They're just cats. Who knows why they do the things they do?"

"But it's not the cats that I'm interested in, Janice. Don't you see..." He paused, wet his lips with his tongue, visibly searching for words. "They have a kind of vision that we don't. They can look at the real world, see things that are invisible to us. It has to be...I don't know...some kind of self imposed blindness. Maybe as we became civilized, we shed some of our instinctive abilities in order to make room for rationality and creativeness and things like that. It was a tradeoff that we made and forgot."

Mentally, Janice drew a deep breath. "Okay, let's say you're right. What's the point of crying over spilt milk, particularly if we've gained so much in its place?"

He shook his head and gestured nervously with raised hands. "I'm not convinced that we've actually lost it. Maybe we've just forgotten how to really look at things. We've circumscribed our own vision to concentrate only on what directly affects us. Who knows how much of what's really out there we never see?"

Janice closed her eyes, marshalling her thoughts. "Kyle, we're talking fantasy here."

He blinked, and his face grew calmer as he reached across the table and touched her arm. "Hey, kid, I'm not spacing out on you, honest. Maybe I'm making this sound like a bigger deal than it really is. I mean, I don't really expect to suddenly find myself staring at a whole new world, you know. It's more like a change in perspective. The cats, well, they're a way of channeling my concentration. Maybe you're right; maybe what they see is just some kind of waking dream, a shared hallucination. But even if that's the explanation, then maybe I can achieve the same thing, and if I can translate that to my work..." He let the sentence trail off.

It sounded more like the Kyle Langston she'd met and married fifteen years earlier. Janice smiled, leaned across the table to kiss her husband. "I'm sorry, Kyle. I guess I'm letting the stress from Eblis distort things."

"You could quit. We don't really need the money."

"I know. But I'd be bored and I'd bother you while you were working. Besides, I don't want the bastards to think they've driven me out. I fought hard enough to get a management position in Macholand and I intend to rub their noses in it for as long as I can."

Their conversation drifted to other topics as they finished breakfast, and Janice told herself everything was all right, that she'd been letting her imagination run away from her. Kyle was Kyle, oddly preoccupied at times but perfectly normal.

Except that he played with his food so long that it was cold by the time he finally ate it.

That evening, she threw eight empty cat food cans into the garbage, then dragged the overfull bag out to the heavy duty trashcan in the garage. When she lifted the lid, she found a rolled canvas jammed inside. Curious, she opened it far enough to identify the translucent church.

For the first time since she'd known him, Kyle had

abandoned a work unfinished.

"I can almost see it," he told her. "I haven't figured out how to translate it to the canvas yet, but I'm moving in that direction. C'mon up and take a look."

Janice dropped her purse on the couch. "Kyle, I just got home, it's been a rough day..."

"C'mon, c'mon. You have to see this." He was ignoring her and she felt a flash of sudden anger, but it vanished quickly. Kyle hadn't been this enthusiastic about anything he'd done in a long time, and his mood was contagious.

"All right, all right!" She followed him as he led the way to his studio.

"You've moved the easel?"

"Yeah. The light was wrong where it was. It was too bright and...straight. So what do you think?"

At first, she couldn't quite take in what he'd done. It was rough work, just a preliminary sketch so far, but already its overall shape was emerging. Or not emerging. Silently she moved back and forth, examining the tentative lines from different angles. Kyle had ignored several of the rules he'd enumerated for her in the past. There was no central focal point, and the individual artifacts were randomly distributed, without balance but still following some undefined pattern. Somehow he'd simulated holographic effects because she could actually see around the trunks of the trees, although they were drawn in solid, assertive lines.

It hurt to look at them. Literally. She blinked as her eyes strained to trace the patterns.

"Don't try so hard," he cautioned. "It works better if you let your eyes blur a little. Softens the discontinuities."

"It's a really bizarre effect. How did you manage it?" There was a longstanding rule between them; Janice never lied about her reaction to his work, although sometimes she carefully avoided expressing an opinion. This time she really wasn't sure about her reaction.

"I'm finally starting to get the hang of looking at things the way the cats do. They watch with their whole bodies, not just their eyes, you know. There are all sorts of somatic interactions I never suspected before."

Her face stiffened very slightly, imperceptible to anyone who didn't have Kyle's sensitivity to visual cues.

"Okay, no more about the cats right now. But what do you think of the results?"

Janice answered honestly. "I'm not sure. It's disconcerting at first, a little bit jarring. But it *is* eye catching, and I've never seen anything remotely like it before. I can't say I like it, exactly, but I don't dislike it either."

"I've only sketched in the major features so far. I think once I've added texture and lighting, the effect will be much stronger."

"Not too much stronger, I hope." She averted her eyes, suddenly aware of an ache in her forehead. Stress, she thought, but wondered. "You're onto something though, Kyle; I'm sure of it."

"Then let's celebrate."

The headache was already receding. "Fine with me. Adesso's or Chinese?"

That night, they made love with rather more passion than either had demonstrated in months. Janice recovered her breath and settled down to sleep with her chin pressed tightly against Kyle's sweaty chest.

"You smell funny. Something sweet."

He wrapped his arm around her shoulders. "Probably catnip."

"Catnip?" She raised her head.

"Yeah. I put some in an old sock for the cats this morning and they dragged it across the living room rug."

"They'll smell up the whole house that way."

"Yeah. I'll have to watch them closer."

By the time it occurred to Janice to wonder how Kyle could have picked up such a strong odor of catnip from the living room rug unless he'd rolled in it himself, he was snoring, and by morning she'd forgotten all about it.

"Did you buy another cat while I wasn't looking?"

Kyle looked up from the evening paper. "No, of course not."

"Well, we're certainly going through the cat food like wildfire. I think you're overfeeding them."

"They don't look fat to me."

"No, they don't, do they." She was suddenly thoughtful.

"Tara's a lot more active now that Misty's here. I suppose

they're both burning off a lot of calories."

"Yeah, that must be it."

In the days that followed, Janice began to wonder if there was something wrong with her. Kyle was working again, and obviously happy about it, even though he still spent a lot of time watching the cats, still talked about the strange insight he'd gotten by studying them. By every reasonable standard, she should have been relieved and happy. But she wasn't.

Something was wrong. Not overtly wrong, but perhaps more disturbing for precisely that reason. The first clue was Kyle's insistence that she stay out of his studio.

"Just for a few days, until I have the new painting finished. The final effect is going to be really stunning, but I need for you to see it with virgin eyes, so to speak. Trust me on this one."

Janice was hurt by the announcement, but hid it as well as she could. If Kyle noticed, he didn't let on.

The other changes were less subtle. Kyle stopped showering. He was still clean, washed himself carefully every day. But he apparently used the sink and a facecloth and never stepped in the tub, as though reluctant to immerse himself in water. And his sleeping schedule was strange. He no longer slept through the night but instead took frequent naps, night and day. Catnaps.

They continued to buy cat food by the case. And more frequently.

Then Kyle disappeared one evening.

The darkness was coming earlier every day now as autumn edged its way toward winter. The thermostat clicked on and off through the night and sometimes the day as well. Kyle insisted that the painting was progressing although he couldn't spend as much time on it as he liked.

"The light goes so fast, and I can only hold the vision within very narrow limits so far. I just don't understand enough yet."

Sometimes Janice woke at night, muscles rigid with formless panic.

It was a Friday night following a strenuous week. After twisting arms at work, she'd accomplished her main objective, addition of a temporary partial second shift to get production back on schedule. As a reward, she'd picked up the new Stephen King novel on her way home, and planned to spend the evening with her legs curled up beneath her on the couch.

Kyle had played with the cats for a while after supper, then retreated to the bedroom for a nap.

Two hours after she sat down, Janice slipped a bookmark between the pages and stood up, wincing as her cramped legs protested the change. She went into the bedroom to change into a nightgown.

Kyle wasn't there.

In itself, that wasn't alarming. He could have gone up to his studio without her having noticed, but the stairway lights were off and that didn't seem likely. She stood at the bottom, head tilted upward and called his name.

No answer.

Could he have gone out? The back door was latched from the inside and they almost never used it. The novel was engrossing, but not so much so that Kyle could have walked past her unseen. The bathroom was empty, as was the small den, the kitchen, and the dining room.

"Kyle?" She called his name loudly now, concerned, then began a second circuit of the house.

She was opening the door to the dark and silent studio when he answered from the first floor.

"Janice?"

His voice didn't sound right. Janice came down the stairs so quickly she almost missed a step.

"Kyle? Where the hell have you been?"

"In the bedroom." He was almost whispering.

Janice reached up, touched his forehead. It was damp with perspiration. "Where? Under the bed? You scared the Shit out of me." She didn't know whether to feel relieved or angry.

"I did it, Janice. I saw what the cats see. Not just its shadow, but a real look."

"What are you talking about?" Panic fluttered beneath her diaphragm. Kyle sounded frightened; he was shivering and not because of the cool air.

"It's not like I thought it would be. The colors are loud, and the shapes smell bad, and things move except not in straight lines..." His voice trailed off.

"What are you talking about, Kyle?"

"I didn't understand." It was as if he wasn't speaking to her at all but to himself. "Maybe it wasn't a tradeoff. Maybe there was a good reason for blinding ourselves."

Janice felt the sting of imminent tears, fought to suppress them. "You've been working too hard, that's all. Why don't you just lie down, close your eyes, try to sleep. In the morning, you'll feel a lot better."

She wasn't sure he'd been listening, but he nodded. "Yes, close my eyes. I should do that."

She guided him into the bedroom, helped him undress and slip under the covers. Then she sat in a chair within reach, listening to him breathe, wondering what had happened, what she could do. That's where she fell asleep.

Janice woke up in bed, fully dressed, in the middle of the morning. At first she felt guilty about sleeping so late, then remembered the strange events of the previous evening.

Kyle was sitting in the living room, drinking coffee, staring out the bay window toward the reservoir.

"Are you all right?"

"Yeah, I'm fine."

"Really?"

"I think so. There's coffee ready."

Actually, there was less than a cup left in the percolator. Janice started a new pot, then decided to feed the cats while she was waiting. Except that she couldn't find their bowls, and there was an empty shelf in the pantry.

"Are we out of cat food?"

"I threw it out."

"Threw it out? Why in the world...?"

"I hope you aren't going to be upset, but Misty and Tara are gone."

"Gone?"

"I took them to the shelter first thing this morning. It was nice of you to pretend, but I knew you never really liked them."

"I never minded..."

He cut her off. "They're gone. Let's leave it at that."

Life returned to normal, or a close approximation, a situation that lasted almost two full weeks. Kyle disappeared into his studio for much of the day, but his sleeping schedule returned to normal, he showered every morning, and the smell of cat began to recede from the house. Janice took some of her accumulated vacation time so she could stay home and on more than one occasion she found her husband staring off into the distance, although viewing vistas invisible to her.

"You're still seeing things, aren't you?" She hadn't wanted to bring the subject up, but it was harder to pretend not to know what was happening. "Do you want to talk about it?"

"You don't want to know. I made a terrible mistake, Janice. I only hope I realized it in time."

"It's over with," she reassured him, hoping this wasn't one of her rare lies.

"What you can't see can't hurt you," he said quietly. "But if you can see..."

"Ssshhhh!" She placed a finger on his lips. "It's all in the past now. Let's just forget it."

The bedroom was dark, but there was enough light from the street lamp outside to illuminate Kyle's profile as he sat on the edge of the bed, silent, motionless.

"Are you all right?"

"I can see it, Janice. I've tried not to, but once you know how, it's impossible to stop. Even with my eyes shut, sometimes, I know it's there."

She sat up, trying to shed sleepiness quickly enough to deal with the situation. "Kyle, it's just your imagination."

"No," he answered quietly. "It knows I'm here and it's coming for me. I've known for some time, but there's nothing I can do about it. I close my eyes and tell myself I'm imagining things. Then I open them and try not to look, but I can't be on the guard all the time and sometimes I see it out of the corner of my eye, and it's always closer. I know why the cats watch so closely, Janice. What you can't see can't hurt you but what I can see can hurt me."

There was such obvious pain in his voice that she leaned forward, reached out to touch his arm, but he pulled away, stood up and stepped away from the bed.

"Goodbye, Janice. I love you, but I can't stand this anymore. I have to know. I have to see." And then he moved, ever so slightly, and the shadows seemed to twist at the foot of the bed, a distortion that reminded her somehow of Kyle's last, unfinished painting. She thought she heard him cry out as though from a great distance, but the sound was cut off so quickly that she wondered afterwards if it had just been her imagination.

"Kyle?" But he didn't answer, and when she turned on the lights, the bedroom was empty.

She filed a missing persons report, but the detective assigned to the case seemed resigned to failure and his optimistic promises lacked sincerity. Janice called once or twice before throwing his card away, and never heard from him again.

Misty had already been claimed, but she managed to rescue Tara from the shelter. It was an impulsive act; as Kyle had suggested, she'd never felt any particular attachment to either cat, but now that he was gone, she was desperate to atone for any imagined lack of empathy she might have demonstrated in the past. She even resigned her position at Eblis to spend more time at the house, moved restlessly from room to room as if anticipating his return at any moment, a step back from the limbo into which he'd disappeared.

Winter passed. Tara had somehow become pregnant at the shelter and bore a litter of eight kittens. Janice found herself spending more and more time with them, teasing the feistier ones with bits of yarn, nursing the weaker until they were strong enough to eat on their own. Occasionally she'd catch them staring attentively into empty space, watching something she couldn't see, and whenever that happened, bitter tears undermined her carefully maintained composure.

"Do you see him, Tara? Do you see Kyle?"

And she'd try to focus on whatever they were staring at, and once or twice she thought she detected something, not a shape or a motion, but a hint of shape or a breath of motion, and whenever that happened, she looked away immediately, usually left the room, hating herself for her cowardice but unable to remain.

Because as much as she wanted to see Kyle step out from wherever he'd disappeared and back into her life, she was afraid that

she might see something else entirely.
    Something considerably less welcome.

NEXT DOOR NEIGHBOR

"She's put a curse on my dad and I've got to make her stop!"

Kevin rolled his eyes dramatically and shook his head. "Give it a rest, Luce. There's no such thing as witches. And what are you going to do, burn her at the stake?"

The thirteen year old dropped her eyes, but her voice was just as firm as ever. "I don't know exactly, but I have to do something. And I need you to help."

"Whoa!" Kevin backed away from the couch with his hands raised protectively. "No way I'm getting mixed up in this. You want to sneak into Old Lady Brackford's house, then go right ahead. I won't tell anyone, but I'm not going with you."

Lucy unfolded her legs and stood up, meeting her friend's eyes steadily. "I'm not asking you to go with me. All I want you to do is call the next time she comes into your father's store. That way I'll know she's going to be out of the house long enough for me to look around without getting caught."

Kevin bit his lip, dubious but unable to find a good reason to refuse. "If Dad finds out..."

"He won't. I promise."

The phone rang while she was eating lunch with her mother the following Saturday.

"I'll get it." Lucy pushed back from the table and snagged the phone off the wall before her mother could react. Her father was upstairs in bed, still suffering from the mysterious illness that had bothered him ever since he had argued with Mrs. Brackford about the condition of her yard. The neighbors had never been on good terms; Mrs. Brackford rarely came outside, left the house only once a week to do her shopping, and hadn't spoken a hundred words to Lucy's parents during the three years they'd lived in Managansett.

"Luce? It's Kevin. She's here."

Lucy blinked, glanced nervously toward her mother, who was staring out the kitchen window, face drawn with tension. "In the store?"

"Yes, of course in the store. What do you think, we invited her over for tea?"

Lucy cupped her hand around the mouthpiece, forced herself to speak casually. "Okay, thanks a lot. I'm on my way." She hung up.

"That was Kevin," she volunteered. "He wants to know if I can help him with some deliveries."

Her mother glanced up, her expression puzzled for the few seconds it took her to replay the words in her mind. "If you want. Finish your lunch first."

"I'll take it with me." Lucy snatched the remains of her sandwich from the table, but her appetite had vanished.

There was a crumbling stone wall surrounding Mrs. Brackford's property, but Lucy knew half a dozen places where she could climb over without difficulty. She chose one as far from the road as possible. It wouldn't do to be seen; Mrs. Brackford didn't tolerate children on her property. Three years earlier, Kevin's parents had been forced to retrieve him from the police after he'd indulged a ten year old's curiosity and dropped down inside the wall from an overhanging branch.

The yard was so thickly overgrown that Lucy barely had to crouch to remain concealed as she made her way to the back porch. The grass was up to her waist, and a riot of mock orange, forsythia, and lilac, all tied together with tethers of wisteria and bullbriar, screened her from the street. Beyond the rear wall was the dirt access road to the reservoir, and on the opposite side, the Nettletons had put up a ten foot stockade fence to cut off all sight of their reclusive neighbor's property.

The back door was latched, but the adjacent window was wide open, lacked a screen, and was just the right size for climbing through.

Lucy found herself in a pantry. The room was long and narrow, dimly illuminated, and lined with shelves. Most of the items stored there were recognizable, familiar brands of canned goods, bags of flour and salt, boxes of cereal, bottles of fruit juice and soda. There were also two rows of mason jars with handwritten labels, but the scrawl was illegible and the contents amorphous and unidentifiable.

A door at one end opened into the kitchen.

Kevin hung up the phone and hurried back out to the store. There were still two more aisles of groceries to restock before his father would let him go for the day, and he wanted to take the bus to Providence with some of his friends. The surreptitious phone call was no big deal, but he felt nervous anyway. What if Lucy was right? What if Old Lady Brackford really was a witch and somehow knew magically what he'd done?

He looked around nervously. There weren't many people in the store; business had been bad ever since the big shopping plaza had opened just outside of town. Kevin walked to the front, crossed the head of each aisle, puzzled at first, then mildly alarmed.

"Are you lost, young man?"

Startled, Kevin looked behind him. His father was standing there with his hands on his hips.

"Hi, Dad. Just needed a stretch. Almost done."

"Well hurry it up. People can't buy what they can't see."

"Yeah. Hey, Dad, didn't I just see Old L...Mrs. Brackford come in?"

His father frowned. "Came and went. Spent three bucks. I think she's taking her trade over to Foodworld now. That's one customer I don't mind losing. Now get cracking if you want the afternoon off."

Kevin went back to work, briefly considered trying to call Lucy. "Too late for that," he whispered.

The kitchen was worse than the yard outside. The sink was filled with dirty dishes and pans, which spilled over onto the counters. There were so many piles of them on the floor, Lucy had to pick her way carefully. Open packages of food were interspersed with the crockery, many of them sporting thick coats of fuzzy green mold.

The smell was so overwhelming that Lucy's eyes stung, and she almost turned around and fled back the way she'd come. Instead she passed through to the door beyond.

The front room was less repulsive, though just as neglected. A layer of dust covered most of the visible surfaces, and small clouds plumed from the rug with each step. There was very little light; heavy drapes cloaked the windows.

A narrow staircase led to the second floor. Lucy licked her lips, aware that her heart was beating frantically, but refused to turn back now. Her father's life might be at stake.

There was a narrow hall at the top, with two doors on either side. The first two rooms were cluttered with old furniture, piles of clothing and blankets, and other household odds and ends. It looked as though neither had been disturbed for years. The third was quite obviously where Mrs. Brackford slept. It was marginally cleaner than the rest of the house, but piles of dirty clothing had accumulated in every corner and under the bed, which was not made, and even in the dim light Lucy could tell that the sheets were heavily stained. There was a small adjoining bathroom, similarly cluttered and unsanitary, the counter and floor littered with a forest of broken grey hairs. She poked around briefly, opening each of the bureau drawers, but found nothing of interest.

The last room was very different.

Margery Dodge extracted four envelopes from the mailbox, three of them bills. She sighed. If Ed didn't get better soon and go back to work, they were going to be in serious difficulties. The doctors were hinting that it was psychological, but she knew better than that. Ed had always been so enthusiastic about life, it was hard to recognize him in the tired, dispirited, weak willed body that lay upstairs.

She glanced up to see their neighbor, Mrs. Brackford, unlocking her front gate, a small paper bag tucked under one arm. Margery grimaced with distaste. The kids called her a witch, and she figured they were only one letter wrong.

Amazingly enough, the last room was immaculate. The walls were clean and bare except for a pair of woven tapestries whose subject matter seemed to be the sufferings of the damned in the nethermost regions of Hell. There was a work table in the center of the room and a curtained alcove at the far end. When Lucy brushed the curtains aside, she found herself facing what appeared to be a small altar, flanked by two elaborate pewter candelabras fitted with black candles. There was a reddish brown stain covering parts of the altar and such a rancid, unpleasant smell, she backed away, letting the curtains fall back into place.

There was a doll on the table.

It was Ken, Barbie's companion, twin to the one now tucked at the very back of Lucy's closet, wearing a poorly cut shirt and no pants. She picked the doll up tentatively, then dropped it when something pricked her fingers. More cautiously, she turned it over, saw that the buttocks were coated with grime of some sort. She squinted and raised it close to her face. Hair, lots of short hairs like those her father left on the sink when he shaved in the morning. And little semicircles that must be nail clippings.

Lucy gasped. She recognized the shirt as well; it was cut from the same material as one of her father's favorites - the one he had reluctantly thrown away a while back when he wore through one elbow. This was it; this was her proof that Old Lady Brackford was a witch. Clutching the doll tightly, she turned to leave.

That's when she heard the front door open and shut downstairs.

Ruth Brackford carried her small package through to the kitchen, removed the syrup of ipecac and tossed the bag aside without looking to see where it fell. There were a few other things she needed and she began gathering them from where they lay within the chaos.

She shivered slightly. The afternoon was growing chill and she was more sensitive to the cold lately. The pantry window was broken and wouldn't close properly, and she'd been putting off getting it fixed, so she simply closed the pantry door, cutting off the draft.

The lock clicked as it engaged.

Lucy's first thought was to escape and she was actually halfway to the stairs before she hesitated. To have come this far without accomplishing anything was unbearable. She stopped, thinking furiously. She would have the doll, of course, but no one would believe her, or if they did, would dismiss it as an old woman's self delusion. And it would only provide her father a brief respite; Old Lady Brackford would not admit defeat so easily.

Lucy turned and quietly walked back down the hall, then slipped into the bedroom and bathroom beyond. She had to hurry.

Ruth Brackford started the laborious journey upstairs. The climb seemed to require more effort every day. She thought idly of having her bed moved downstairs. There was an oubliette off the kitchen that would serve as a bathroom, and the pantry could be redone to meet her other, more special needs. But that would involve bringing strangers into her house; she couldn't possibly move the furniture herself. No, she thought, I'll just have to make do.

Edward Dodge's effigy lay where she had left it. She set down the small bowl she was carrying and leaned forward, regaining her breath. "No hurry is there, neighbor? You'll be happy to wait for me."

When the stitch in her side subsided, she used a spoon to move a dollop of the noxious brew she'd concocted to the doll's face, smearing the plastic lips. "Tastes wonderful, doesn't it?" Her laugh was a thin crackle. "Ipecac and sour cream, mashed maggot and rotting meat, everything needed for a healthy lad like you."

Lucy watched from where she hid concealed by the altar curtain, terrified but elated when Old Lady Brackford's thin, ugly laughter changed tone. She began to gasp and raised one hand to her throat. Lucy hadn't been able to remove all the residue of her father's body from the doll, but she had managed to add a good number of discarded grey hairs to the sticky patch. Enough of them, it appeared.

Ruth Brackford gasped and bent forward, shoulders heaving as her stomach abruptly tried to empty itself. She maintained control, but swayed as she turned, lurching toward the door. When she was out of sight, Lucy emerged from her hiding place, snatched up the doll, and headed for the door.

"Clever girl, aren't you?" Mrs. Brackford was standing just out of reach, leaning against the wall. Lucy had expected her to go directly to the bathroom. She froze in the doorway, clutching the doll to her chest.

"Give that here, you little thief!" She held out a not too steady hand and Lucy realized she was still suffering the effects of the potion she'd inadvertently administered to herself as well as Edward Dodge.

"All right, take it." She held the doll out, just a few inches beyond the woman's reach. Old Lady Brackford's eyes glittered with hatred, but she pushed away from the wall, took an unsteady step forward.

And Lucy bolted past her, shuddering as she brushed against the woman's thigh.   She almost fell in her haste to get downstairs, recovered and continued at no less hectic a pace.

The front door had an old fashioned key lock and wouldn't budge. Lucy glanced up toward the head of the stairs. Ruth Brackford was leaning on the rail, her face split into an unpleasant smile. "Leaving so soon, child? I won't hear of it."

Lucy didn't even notice the kitchen's odor this time, masked as it was by the smell of her own fear, a fear which grew to absolute terror when she found the pantry exit also locked. There were no other kitchen windows big enough for her to escape through, so she ran back to the front of the house.

Old Lady Brackford had moved to the head of the stairs but hadn't descended yet. She had both hands pressed tightly against her stomach and her face was, if possible, even paler than it had been before. No wonder her father was so sick, Lucy realized, if even a small portion of the vile concoction could so affect someone.

"You've been a bad girl, you know." The voice was a bit less ragged and Mrs. Brackford descended a single step. The windows were larger in the front room, but multipaned, held together by a latticework of wood. She could smash one, given time, but there wasn't that much time left.

"I haven't had visitors in ever so long."

Lucy glanced up the staircase. Mrs. Brackford was three steps down now, one hand holding the rail. Desperately, Lucy held the doll out with one extended arm, closed her eyes, and began to turn in place.

She spun desperately, moving her feet as quickly as possible, trying to stay in the same spot. Twice she bumped into the back of a chair and once into an end table, but she kept her eyes shut, afraid to see how close her enemy might have come. But eventually she was overcome with dizziness and staggered to a stop, out of breath, leaned against an overstuffed chair while her breathing returned to normal.

There was no one on the staircase. Ruth Brackford lay crumpled at its foot.

Lucy found the key ring on the kitchen table and let herself out. She scrubbed the doll clean in a stream that ran through the woodlot separating the development from the reservoir, then buried it under a pine tree.

When she got home, her father was sitting in a chair in the living room, his color better than it had been for over a month.

"How are you feeling, Daddy?"

He smiled with considerable animation. "A lot better, squirt. Gave your mother quite a fright though."

Margery Dodge walked in from the kitchen. "Your father fell down in the bathroom. I thought he'd had a heart attack."

"Just dizzy for a minute or two," he said quietly. "But I feel a lot better now. As good as new, in fact."

BALANCING THE BOOKS

The dead were walking around inside Russell's head long before they actually began to rise from their graves.

It had felt strange coming back to Vietnam after forty years and he really hadn't known what to expect. He had not recognized Ho Chi Minh City, formerly Saigon, but that might have been the case even if it had not become so westernized in recent years. He had only visited Saigon twice during his tour, and he had been more interested in getting drunk and laid, in whatever order, than in taking in the sights.

The bus ride to Qui Nhon had been uneventful, although he had attracted curious looks from most of the other passengers, all of whom appeared to be Vietnamese. Most were too young to have been alive when he'd last visited their country, but there were a few older people and he wondered idly which side they had supported during the war, although his personal opinion was that most of the people in the country had never really understood what the conflict was all about and had simply applied or transferred their allegiances as each situation warranted.

In Qui Nhon he managed to rent a car, a Lambretta which had seen better days. The roads were acceptable and he'd retained enough pigeon French to find a shop that would sell him what passed for a road map. He highlighted the route to Phu Hiep, filled the gas tank, stored a basket full of provisions with his suitcase in the back, and set out to drive back into his own past.

Russell Dorner had been twenty years old when his number came up and he'd been drafted into the US Army. He had briefly considered running off to Canada but had dropped the idea. Dodging the draft would reshape the life he foresaw for himself. Of course, dying in Vietnam would do so even more drastically, but he had no intention of becoming a casualty.

Boot camp had horrified him. Although intellectually he understood that the abusive brow beating was designed to instill into recruits an instinct for obedience, that knowledge made the experience no less unpleasant. Nor was he able to find much solace in the companionship of his fellow sufferers. It was there that Russell had met Brandon Kirby, a tall, heavy set West Virginian who alone among his acquaintances seemed unimpressed with the screams and insults of the drill sergeants. Russell had admired Kirby's self assurance and took vicarious comfort from the other man's ability to make the sergeants, even the company commander, visibly uneasy.

Russell's disdain for the men in his barracks had gone unspoken but not unperceived and he had been the butt of several cruel jokes during his time at Fort Dix, culminating in an assault one evening that left him bruised and bloody behind the commissary. It had been a relief when his orders finally arrived transferring him to Advanced Infantry Training at Fort Lee, where he would receive instruction in supply management and small arms maintenance.

Fort Lee proved to be only marginally less horrible than Fort Dix. He was allowed some time to himself, the drill sergeants were slightly less abusive, and the weather was warmer. There were actually times when he didn't feel miserable, although once again he was isolated and friendless. It was during his fourth week there that he spotted Brandon Kirby walking across the battalion parade grounds. Although they'd barely spoken in basic training, Russell's loneliness had reached a point where it overwhelmed his shyness and he awkwardly started a conversation. Brandon hadn't said much, but he hadn't rebuffed the advance, and the two had become regular acquaintances if not friends.

The road to Phu Hiep was clearly marked on the map, not so clearly on the ground. Some of the "roads" were in fact dirt tracks, and at least one bridge was too narrow for even the Lambretta, necessitating a time consuming detour. The country here was more as he remembered it, flat and with relatively sparse vegetation this close to the coast.

Phu Hiep itself leaped into existence so suddenly it took his breath away. He had known that the old army base was still there, had stared at it for hours off and on using Google maps. But the image on the screen fell far short of the reality. The actual buildings were in better condition than he had expected; the Vietnamese were using them as warehouses now and kept them in reasonable repair.

The dead stirred in his memory. Phil Reynolds had killed himself after receiving a Dear John letter from his girlfriend. Bob

Maziarz had died in a helicopter crash. Milton Dionne had been shot by a sniper and Kalmer Melby had been knifed after making a pass at the wrong soldier. Russell had not actually seen their bodies at the time but he saw them now, stumbling blindly through his tormented memories, each mutely accusing him of having left a debt unpaid, not to them but to another, and perhaps to himself as well. The one body he had seen was John Chapman, a nice kid from Seattle, who had forgotten to stoop while deploying from a helicopter. The sagging but still spinning blades had neatly taken off the top of his head while Russell stood almost within reach. There'd been splatters of blood and brains on his uniform.

These were all the people he had known well who had died during his tour in Vietnam. All but one. The one remaining was Brandon Kirby and, to a lesser extent, the other members of Squad 2 of the 8th Recon Platoon.

At first it had seemed that they would part ways after their stint at Fort Lee. Both were going to Vietnam, of course, but Kirby was assigned to an infantry unit in Nha Trang and Russell had orders to report to a supply facility in Cam Ranh Bay. Kirby left as scheduled, but Russell's plans were changed after he had unwisely allowed Kirby to convince him to sneak off post for a final celebration. Russell had been caught, given a summary court martial for unauthorized absence, and served thirty days in the Fort Lee stockade. When his sentence was complete, he'd received new orders assigning him to the headquarters company of the 268th Combat Aviation Battalion in Phu Hiep, where he would be the S4 (supply) clerk and armorer.

He spotted Brandon Kirby less than an hour after arriving at his new post. Kirby was sporting corporal's stripes but even though his uniform was starched and proper, it somehow looked slovenly on him. It was more Kirby's manner than his clothing, a pronounced slouch and the hint of a smirk. Russell was less surprised than he should have been. He had been convinced for some time that there was a link between the two of them that not even the US Army or the Viet Cong could easily sever.

It took two days to complete his in-processing, and another to be briefed on his duties. "You won't have to worry about the supply side," Sergeant Grimes told him. "That's all consolidated at the group level now. And there's not much to do in the armory either. The troops are all responsible for their personal weapons and the heavy stuff is serviced by the air crews. But don't worry. I'll find something to occupy your time."

Russell hadn't been sure whether or not he should track down Kirby, but the decision was taken out of his hands. Kirby was waiting for him when he got back to his hooch that evening, an unfinished wooden building divided into rooms that held bunks and metal lockers and not much else.

"Howdy, friend. Didn't expect to see you again. Small world, isn't it?"

Kirby was sitting on Russell's bunk so that his back was against one wall. "My orders got changed. What about you? I thought you'd be out in the jungle slaughtering Vietcong by now."

Kirby shrugged. "Not yet. My unit is based here temporarily, protecting you candy asses." Russell hadn't noticed what Kirby was holding until the other man raised his arm and offered him the flask. "Have a sip."

Russell shook his head. "No thanks. I thought we weren't supposed to have any liquor outside the enlisted men's club."

Kirby shook his head. "There's rules, and then there's rules. Have a drink. I won't offer again."

"No, thanks anyway."

"Candy ass." Kirby took a long pull.

Russell was lucky. One of the local shopkeepers spoke fluent English. Nguyen Phuh had worked as a translator in Da Nang and talked about the war as casually as though it had been some memorable social occasion. He agreed to let Russell leave the rented car parked behind his shop, loaned him a bicycle, and provided suggestions about how he should proceed on his quest. His daughter, who wore the traditional ao dai, a long dress slit up to her hip, packed his provisions into a pair of panniers. Russell thanked him, paid a more than adequate fee, and promised a bonus on his return.

"You take care, Mr. Dorner. This is a dangerous place you visit. Number ten bad." The man seemed genuinely concerned.

"I know. I've been there before."

Russell hadn't ridden a bicycle for years and was unsteady at first, particularly after he'd left the hard packed road and set off through the fields. The foliage was thicker than he remembered, but otherwise it looked very much as it had forty years earlier. Memories of his last trek through the region hit him with an almost physical force and his head began to pound as the dead renewed their relentless march. You owe us, they insisted. If you pay your old debt, it will help us find rest.

He had never expected to end up as a grunt. Russell typed 80 words per minute, wore glasses, and had quickly lost the twenty pounds of muscle he'd gained in basic training. Although it was obvious that there really wasn't enough work for another clerk in the company, he had expected to be transferred to a similar support job. His judgment might have been correct except for two factors. First, the only category where there was a chronic shortage of manpower was in the field where enemy action, fatigue, drugs, and expiring enlistments constantly winnowed the ranks. The second factor was Brandon Kirby.

Kirby had a small circle of friends. No, that wasn't correct. He had a small circle of hangers on. They tended to be – or hoped to be – diminutive versions of their leader. Even the First Sergeant seemed mildly deferential to Kirby, who somehow never ended up on the list for KP, guard duty, latrine detail, or any of the other less desirable assignments. Russell wandered into their orbit on a few occasions and sometimes found himself being harassed until Kirby put an end to it.

"Leave the boy alone. He's got enough problems without you fellas adding to them."

Russell wasn't quite sure where he stood in Kirby's estimation. Not a friend, exactly. More like a pet.

But it didn't hurt to have an influential patron. When he had inadvertently offended one of the unit's doorgunners, a young firebrand from Arkansas, Russell had done everything he could to suggest he was part of Kirby's inner circle. It had apparently worked. The doorgunner ignored him thereafter.

Russell had almost decided that Vietnam wasn't so bad after all when he was reassigned.

Although Russell had been convinced that his last visit to this area had been burnt so deeply into his memory that he could never forget it, he soon discovered that memory and reality weren't always congruent. He was also forced to abandon his bicycle, chaining it to a tree that stood alone in the center of a small clearing, a spot he felt relatively confident he could find on his way back.

There were landmarks, but some of them were so overgrown with vines and moss that he had difficulty recognizing them. A couple were so well disguised that he never saw them at all. The heat was oppressive, the humidity even more so, and dragonflies and other insects buzzed around his face with audacity. The game trail was still there and the sight of a particularly twisted tree made him clench his hand into fists.

"There has to be a mistake, sergeant." Russell raised his eyes from his new orders, which he had already read a dozen times. "I'm a clerk."

"No, son, you're a soldier." Sergeant Grimes might have felt some sympathy but he was far too regular army to let it show. "We do what we're told, when we're told, and with a smile on our face."

Russell wasn't smiling. He'd been relieved of his duties and transferred to the 8th Reconnaissance Platoon, currently preparing to leave its station in Phu Hiep and move to a forward base camp twenty miles inland. The 8th Reconnaissance Platoon was, needless to say, Brandon Kirby's unit.

He knew he should have seen it coming. Two weeks earlier, during one of his periodic attempts to ingratiate himself with Kirby and his satellites, Russell had unwisely accepted the offer of a drink. It was not his first taste of alcohol, but it was his first prolonged drinking bout and he'd become quite uncharacteristically talkative and loud. The possibility that he was finally being accepted as an equal had goaded him into a more daring frame of mind and he'd been loudly and rather creatively commenting on the company commander's penchant for malapropisms and blunders when Captain Dowdell himself arrived on the scene. Russell and several others had received an Article 15 for drunkenness; somehow Kirby managed to avoid the same fate.

Reduced from Specialist Third Class to Private First Class, Russell had taken his place in Squad Two of the 8th Recon. The corporal leading that squad was Brandon Kirby.

Their very first patrol was along the same route that Russell would retrace forty years later.

He retraced it, however, with difficulty. Not only was the landscape heavily overgrown, but Russell was a bit overgrown himself. At forty he had started gaining weight and losing hair, and both trends had continued ever since. They had not followed the trail directly; that would invite an ambush. Nor could they directly parallel it within easy sight; that would invite a close encounter with a booby trap. Russell considered using the trail now, since it would be much easier, but he wasn't sure if he could recognize the point where they had turned away.

For a change, he spotted the next decision point easily. It was pretty obvious. The broken boulder ahead looked just as much like a yawning, toothy mouth now as it had in the 1960s. Russell felt vaguely cheered. It was as though he'd encountered an old friend. He turned to his right and climbed to the crest of a low ridge. They'd followed this relatively high ground for several minutes before walking into the trap.

Even after Kirby had removed about half of the contents of Russell's pack, it still felt crushingly heavy, partly because several additional ammo clips had replaced the ration packs that had been jettisoned. "You run short of food, you go hungry. You run short of ammo, you die." Kirby had slapped him on the back. "Cheer up, boy. This is going to be a cakewalk. Not much of a pucker factor at all."

There were eight men in the squad. None of the remaining six were happy about their new team member. "Goddamned newbie." Russell didn't flinch. He'd been called worse.

They set out at first light, their mission to follow an arc through the near jungle surrounding the base camp. Choppers had done aerial surveillance already and had not spotted anything, but you couldn't be sure unless you actually walked the ground, or so said Lieutenant McGarvey.

At first, Russell had jumped at every sudden sound, but nothing had happened and by mid-morning he was more concerned about the aches in his shoulders and calves than in any theoretical ambush. In fact, when the shooting actually started, it was a second or two before he realized what was happening. It was simply luck that he wasn't killed before he dropped to the ground.

The firing was sporadic from both sides after the initial burst. Russell could see that Private Adams was lying motionless out in the open, dead or unconscious. He had no idea until much later how the rest of the squad had fared, although at least four were returning fire and he heard Kirby shouting unintelligible instructions. The firing continued sporadically for a quarter hour. Russell had clutched his M-16 so tightly that his knuckles hurt, but he hadn't fire a round. He wondered how long it would be before air support arrived, then remembered that Adams carried the squad's only radio.

After a longer than usual hiatus he began to hope that the enemy had moved off. There was a rustling to his left and he brought his weapon around in a panic, but it was Kirby. "Where the hell is Adams?" he demanded in a hoarse whisper.

Russell pointed to the prostrate form.

"Shit! We need his radio. You're a smaller target than me, Dorner. Crawl out there and get it."

"No way!"

"That was an order, boy. I haven't got time to babysit you just now."

Russell had no idea what he might have said or done next because the jungle came alive at that moment, rounds slicing through the air all around them, chewing up leaves and bark and the ground itself.

Kirby turned and ran. Russell followed in his wake, making no effort to dodge or crouch. It was utter blind panic and it was utter blind luck that he survived the next few seconds. The rest of the squad died where they lay.

Russell was not nearly as physically fit as Kirby, but somehow he managed to stay right behind him during the next several minutes as they raced through the jungle, stumbling over roots and tufts of wirelike grass, brushing drooping branches and vines out of their way, leaping across small obstacles and climbing or bypassing large ones. They instinctively headed downhill and only began to slow when fatigue and the change in terrain made their previous speed impossible.

They had entered a stretch of marsh broken by isolated islands of solid soil. There was still gunfire behind them, but it was intermittent now. Although their progress had become more deliberate, they were still moving quickly, so quickly that they both ended up in the tarpit before either could warn the other.

As Russell walked along the ridge, he felt his pulse quicken. He could imagine Viet Cong lurking in the trees to either side, waiting for him to walk into range of their weapons. There were no Viet Cong any more, but Mr. Phuh had warned him that there were still bandits in the wilds. "Bad men live there. Very bad men."

Bad they might be, but there were worse things, things that walked around inside his head. Russell felt no fear, only excitement. And just in case, he had a very illegal handgun in his pack and a legal but nasty hunting knife on his belt.

He stopped next to a fallen tree. He wasn't quite sure of the spot where the ambush had taken place, but it couldn't have been far off. And he knew exactly what direction he had run. There was only one way down from here that was traversable now as it had been then. His excitement growing, he started toward the marsh.

Russell was not as deeply mired and his smaller body mass helped. Once he had shed his pack, which promptly sank out of sight, he was able to catch hold of firmer ground and slowly pull himself free of the clinging viscous mass. Even that short effort left him exhausted and it was a few seconds before he turned to see what had happened to Kirby.

The bigger man had not fared as well. He was unable to reach the perimeter of the pit and only his head, arms, and upper chest were still visible. "Get me out of here, Dorner! I'm sinking!"

Russell nodded, looked around. A few seconds searched turned up only one fallen branch long enough and sturdy enough to help, and it was so thickly wrapped with vines that he was unable to free it. Kirby had wisely stopped struggling, but he was still slowly sinking. Only the tops of his shoulders were above the surface now.

"Quit dicking around!" For the first time in Russell's experience, Kirby sounded uncertain of himself, even fearful. It gave him a profound sense of power. This was his chance to put Kirby deeply in his debt, to reverse their roles for perhaps the only time it would be possible. He attacked the fallen branch with renewed energy and finally wrested it free.

That's when he heard the voices. They were male, there were several of them, and they weren't speaking English.

The tarpit was easy enough to find. It had a distinct smell that he had forgotten. Russell slowed his pace and moved more carefully. It might be a dramatic end to his quest if he fell into the tarpit a second time, but he had no intention of doing so. He was here to banish a ghost, not become one.

It was very much as he remembered it. He found a fallen tree nearby and seated himself, looking out across the turgid surface. The dead were no longer marching around in his mind; they were running at full speed because they knew the end was near.

A few seconds was all it took to convince Russell that he could never drag Kirby to safety. The man was too heavy and the tarpit's grip too powerful. And time was a factor as well. He guessed that the other man had at best ten minutes to live. "I'm sorry, Kirby. I can't get you out."

"Yes you can!" Both men were whispering because the enemy was close.

"I'm not strong enough. I'm sorry." Russell dropped the branch and turned away.

"Get back here, private! You will get me out of here, because if you don't, I'm going to holler like hell and our friends up the hill there will come down to find out what all the fuss is. I'd rather be taken by the gooks than end up in here."

Russell had no doubt that Kirby would do just what he said. If their roles were reversed, he would probably do the same. "All right." He picked up the branch. "I think the ground's firmer behind you. Hold on a second."

He walked around the perimeter of the pit to a spot which was neither firmer nor closer to the foundering man, but which was out of his line of sight. Russell raised the branch, extended it out over the edge of the tarpit, hesitated for a second, then brought it down with all the strength he mustered onto Kirby's skull.

The blow neither killed him nor rendered him unconscious, but it did stun Kirby long enough for Russell to brace one end of the branch against the back of his neck, and then push downward. There was a low plopping sound and Brandon Kirby disappeared beneath the bubbling surface.

Russell hid himself in a stand of dense ferns and waited for the voices to go away.

Forty years later Russell was not alarmed when the surface of the tarpit began to churn, slowly at first but with increasing violence. The dead had been returning to life all over the world, a few at a time but with increasing frequency. He knew that bubbles of gas collected and occasionally rose to the surface, but as the seconds passed, he sensed that this was something more than that, and he rose from his seat and stepped back as though expecting the tarpit to explode.

In a sense, that's exactly what happened.

Figures began to emerge from the tar. They were animals although he could not identify them specifically because what remained of their flesh was black and shrunken. Some were clearly feral cats, others were monkeys and a few were birds. There was at least one long necked creature those limbs seemed to be a cross between feet and paddles and a snake as thick as a man's thigh. Their eyes were gone and they may have been blind, but they moved with a clear purpose, though none came toward Russell. Perhaps they were instinctively seeking their natural prey.

The revivified creatures moved in a slow and jerky fashion, so uncoordinated that Russell felt more wonder than fear. He had no idea what was happening, but it clearly had nothing to do with him.

But then at last it did.

A large figure groped its way up out of the tar and began pulling itself painfully toward solid land. Russell did not need to be able to read the nametag on the uniform to know that this was Brandon Kirby, somehow incredibly reborn to the world. And that did have something to do with him. And still he felt no fear. Instead he felt elation. Now, at last after all these years, he would be able to right a wrong, restore balance, banish the demons that had tormented him ever since the day he had watched this same man disappear into the tarpit.

The floundering form was at the edge of the pit now, slowly raising its body from the oozing mass. Russell calmly reached into his pack and took out the handgun. He stood up and moved to stand directly in the path of the thing from the pit. "There's a debt between us, Kirby," he said aloud, even though he didn't know if the man, or whatever it was, could hear him. "It's time that debt was paid."

He raised his arm and fired directly into the Kirby thing's face and it reeled back, waving its arm futilely. "That's for beating me up in basic training." He fired again. "And that's for bullying me into leaving base without permission in Virginia." The blurry figure staggered, part of its head missing now, but patiently reached forward and started to climb out again.

Russell stepped to one side, placed the muzzle of his weapon against the side of the deformed head, and fired a third time. "This one is for getting me drunk and transferred into the infantry." He shifted his aim and fired five more rounds into the chest and upper torso, in the general area of the heart, if the thing still had a heart. "And those are for leading us into an ambush and running off and leaving me."

The body collapsed this time and Russell thought it was all over but one arm flopped forward and then the other, and once more it began to heave itself toward dry land. Russell sighed and watched as it dragged its legs clear of the tarpit and began to struggle to its knees. "You always were a tiresome bastard," he said calmly and took the knife from his belt.

The severed limbs jerked and twisted for awhile, but eventually stopped moving. Russell tried to remove the head but he wasn't strong enough to sever the spinal column so he contented himself with finding a heavy rock and smashing the skull and its contents to a blackened mush. The torso continued to heave and spasm periodically for several minutes afterward, but eventually it stopped moving.

He kicked all of the various parts back into the tarpit, collected his pack, and started back the way he had come. Russell Dorner felt better than he had in decades.

The dead might continue to walk, but at least they wouldn't do so inside his head any longer.

THE LAST SUPPER

It's not easy being dead.

Jackie was discovering new difficulties with each passing day. It started when she got out of bed in the morning, or out of the trash bin, or the trunk of a wrecked car, or wherever she had chosen to sleep – or more likely simply collapsed – the night before. When she had been alive, she had always started off her day with a quick shower to wash off the night sweat, but now unless it was raining she had to do without. On the other hand, she didn't sweat anymore so she could deal with it.

Fortunately, she had never been a breakfast person, so she was able to ignore the craving for long enough to get her head together and plan the day. She did that while applying her makeup, and that was a major hassle. It took forever to add enough rouge to bring some color to her cheeks and she used up her cosmetics so quickly that she often had to take time out from hunting down the living in order to replenish her supply. It was getting harder than ever to find a proper mirror as well, although sometimes she was just as glad that the image was pretty fuzzy. The prospect of getting old had always frightened her a little, but she had discovered since that the alternative was worse, at least in terms of keeping her youthful looks.

Jackie took pride in her work. On more than one occasion she had been mistaken for a living and had been forced to defend herself from myopic or just desperate hunters. The classes in karate had been intended to keep her fit and trim, but the training had come in handy more than once. And her reflexes were still pretty good as well. Sometimes a particularly nimble living would be able to evade her, but usually if she got close enough that they realized she wasn't one of them, she had no trouble running them down. Of course, that meant she'd had to give up her heels, but barefoot was better anyway. For some reason the soles of her feet had retained more of their sensitivity than most of the rest of her body and when she was running barefoot she could almost imagine herself as still being alive.

Although she had abandoned shoes, she took special care with the rest of her clothing. Unfortunately, she had to change outfits daily and since there were no dry cleaners any more, she never got to wear anything more than once. Even if she didn't get bloodstains on them, they inevitably picked up her pungent aroma and the living picked up on that right away. She had tried masking it with perfume at first, but her own sense of smell was so acute now that it was actively painful and she had been forced to do without.

Once she felt ready to face the world, Jackie started making plans specific to the day. At first she had found it easy to make arrangements for brunch, but the situation had changed once the food supply had grown tighter. Now a late lunch was more likely and on a few occasions she had not eaten until mid-afternoon. The trend was definitely toward longer hunting periods and at the back of her mind, Jackie felt a mild concern that the progression did not bode well for the future. But Jackie had been pampered as a living and was not in the habit of thinking beyond the immediate future. Things would take care of themselves. They always did.

On this particular morning, she was more than ordinarily pleased with herself. She had spent the previous night in an actual bed in a posh apartment, alongside what remained of one of the original tenants of said posh apartment. There had even been enough left for a late night snack. Whoever had brought down this particular prey must have been confident that he or she could find more living without much difficulty. Most of her kind did not waste food; some even gnawed the bones. There had almost been enough tissue left for the body to rise and Jackie shook her head with annoyance. The city didn't need any more stomachs to feed.

It was a bright, dry day. Jackie nodded approvingly. When it was humid, she was more likely to attract flying insects and that was a dead giveaway, no pun intended, to the living. She had found a closet full of stylish clothing in the apartment and was wearing a bright red dress cut moderately low in front and immoderately so in back. Fall was well underway and she considered adding an expensive fur piece, but she decided that it would hamper her movements when she closed in for the kill, and when she examined herself in the mirror, she decided she was still sexy, mostly, so long as she wasn't too close to the observer.

The streets were quiet outside. A wary dog passed her by, growling softly. Jackie ignored it; dogs and cats were much too fast for her unless she had them cornered. The downtown was pretty well depleted so she started toward the suburbs, though somewhat reluctantly. She was a city girl, born and bred, and always felt out of place when surrounded by trees and shrubbery and too much open space. But a girl's gotta do what a girl's gotta do.

Jackie passed a few other hunters along the way. Most of them wandered aimlessly, and wouldn't find prey unless they were incredibly lucky. Some of them were moving so slowly that they probably would be unable to make a kill unless they happened upon a paraplegic, preferably a sleeping one. Two youngish looking men – she thought they were young but it was hard to tell because they had made no effort at all to keep up their appearance – had set up a reasonably clever trap. They had caught a young living and tied it to a streetlight where it alternately sobbed and screamed for help. The hunters were obviously hoping for a bigger kill, but Jackie figured they'd get hungry enough to eat their bait before much longer. Nice try though.

She was starting to feel a few pangs herself, nothing she couldn't ignore, but a warning that she didn't have all day to waste.

Jackie had been in the city morgue when she'd opened her eyes, aware of loud noises around her. She sat up before she was aware of where she was, and when the sheet had fallen away her initial reaction had been deep embarrassment. The sounds resolved themselves into several series of overlapping blows, which turned out to be others of her kind trying to escape the refrigerated drawers in which they'd been temporarily stored. Fortunately she had not been there long and had been scheduled for an autopsy. She had not expected to wake up, had not wanted to when she swallowed the handful of sleeping pills, but when she slid down off the table she experienced an exhilaration that had been missing ever since Jeff threw her over for Gloria. Even now she underwent a change in her body at the thought of those two that she suspected was as close to anger as she could still manage to feel.

She'd been looking around for something to wear when she found the technician hiding in a closet. It had been very fortunate.

The woman had been almost exactly Jackie's size and her uniform had fit perfectly. She had tasted pretty good too.

The first few days had been confusing but pleasantly so, with the living still running around trying to restore order, many of them refusing to believe that a five foot two woman could pose any threat to them until it was too late. Then they'd come with weapons and she'd been forced to become a little more perspicacious, holding back while others of her kind dragged them down, then darting in to pick off targets of opportunity.

After a few days the barricades had gone up and the hunt had taken on a new form. Mass attacks were not as successful against well organized defenders. Some of her kind had turned on one another; she'd tried a sample herself but it was like eating cardboard. Their numbers had dwindled considerably during assaults on the secured neighborhoods, but one by one the strongholds had started to fall until only a few remained. Jackie had done pretty well for herself hanging out on the fringes of these communities, picking off clandestine foragers. She could still manage to talk, although it took a conscious effort to squeeze her lungs to force air up her windpipe. The result was far from perfect, but she figured the husky result probably sounded sexy.

But today she was going to her special place. As far as she knew, no other hunters were aware of the colony of living who had moved into the old factory on Montage Road. They kept a low profile. There were no obvious barricades although the building was no doubt secured and guarded from within. Foraging was done quickly and efficiently by armed groups. She had watched them cut down and then incinerate a trio of hunters once and had wisely stayed out of sight. Fortunately, she had recently fed or the allure of their living flesh might have drawn her out into the open anyway.

She found a good vantage point at a second floor window in a furniture shop across the way and settled down to watch. Jackie had always been a patient person. Nothing in life had seemed worth getting excited about before she'd met Jeff. And after he'd left her, it had gotten even less interesting.

Shortly after mid-afternoon, she spotted six of them, four men and two women. Two of the men were heavily armed – shotguns and handguns – and the others carried knives and makeshift clubs. They moved cautiously and quickly down the street and

Jackie darted from window to window to keep track of them. It was soon obvious where they were heading. There was a small shopping mall two blocks further on.

They entered through one of the small shops on the perimeter that faced the street. Jackie did the same, but two stores away. Quickly making her way through racks of pet supplies, she spotted them through the front window. They had split up into two groups of three, one climbing the dead escalator to the second floor. One armed man and the other couple walked right past the store where she stood, but none of them looked in the window.

Jackie admired their system. The armed man stood in the open while the couple went inside, gathered whatever was on their shopping list, and carried it out to where he stood. They all moved on to the next store and repeated the process. She considered rushing the guard but knew that she wouldn't be able to cross the distance before he cut her down with the shotgun. One barrel probably wouldn't stop her permanently, but if he blew off her kneecap, she'd be effectively hobbled. Even so, she felt a stirring of the craving and staved off the urge to risk it anyway.

Someone else was less disciplined. Two shabbily dressed figures burst out of a gift shop and lunged toward the man. He raised his weapon and calmly shot the first one in the face. The body flew backward and landed awkwardly, arms and legs flailing. It continued to move but couldn't seem to coordinate itself enough to rise. The second shot wasn't wild but it only took out a shoulder and spun the attacker around. He had been a big man and he stayed on his feet, charging again after only a momentary hesitation.

The living switched to his handgun but Jackie knew when to take her cue. He never even heard her coming until she was on him.

The big man wasn't willing to share the kill. While the guard tried to crawl away, blood streaming from his torn throat, he swung awkwardly at Jackie, warning her off. She figured she could have taken him down, but it wasn't necessary. There were two more in the store. And besides, the other armed man was already coming down the escalator.

Jackie found the couple inside the drug store, cowering behind a display of cold remedies. She came up from behind. If she could subdue them quickly, the remaining armed man might not waste time trying to find them, assuming he killed the other hunter.

She picked up a large can of floor wax and hit the woman, who was closest, on the crown of her head. She fell forward without a sound.

The man spun around, an expression of shock on his face, and Jackie's martial arts training took over. She wasn't as fast as she had been when she was alive, but she didn't need to be. The man was awkward and defenseless and she chopped him down within seconds. It happened so fast that she didn't even recognize him until he'd slumped to the floor. It was Jeff. She'd wondered what had happened to him. With a sudden wave of elation, she rolled the woman over.

Gloria!

There was the roar of a shotgun, then silence, then a harsh male voice called out. "Get back here right now, guys! We're leaving!" Two other voices answered and they all shouted some more. Jackie waited for them to leave. It didn't take long and none of them came into the drug store. Once they were gone she went back to the pet shop and pulled down an armful of leashes.

Gloria woke up first, but Jackie had gagged her. She didn't want to hear anything that bitch had to say. It was all she could do to keep from tearing the woman's heart out immediately and wolfing it down. Gloria began to cry while Jackie ignored her. Jeff came to a little while later. She'd used twice as many leashes to secure him to his chair. There was no way he was going to get away from her this time, not unless she allowed him to.

His panic turned to shock when he saw her and his mouth opened. "Jackie? Is that you? I thought you must have been killed." He gasped. The light wasn't great in the drug store since the electricity was off, but there were outside windows and he could see well enough to know that she wasn't one of the living any more. "Oh God!" he said at last.

It took a few seconds before Jackie could get her lungs to move and her voice was threadier than ever. "Hello, Jeff. Did you miss me?"

It was possible that Jeff had never heard one of her kind speak before. He looked startled, then seemed to conclude that he might be able to reason with her. He'd always been able to talk her into doing whatever he wanted. "Thank God it's you. Yes, I've missed you very much." His effort to sound calm and sincere was not quite an abject failure, but it was pretty close.

"Liar."

There was a short silence. "What are you going to do with us?" His voice shook.

"What do you think?" She licked her lips with exaggerated care. Gloria gave a muffled squeal and renewed her struggles but Jeff seemed fascinated.

"Could you really do that to me? After all that we meant to each other?"

Jackie would have had trouble keeping a straight face except that her face stayed pretty straight now no matter how she felt. She summoned energy for another round of speech. "I'll make you a deal, Jeff. I'm not really hungry enough for a two course meal," her eyes switched back and forth between the two bound figures, "so I'll eat one of you and let the other go."

Jeff responded exactly as she'd hoped he would. "That sounds fair."

"And I'll let you decide who gets to go free." It was starting to get dark outside and she was having trouble seeing his face. Her eyes weren't quite as sharp as they had once been. Jackie had anticipated the problem and had gathered several boxes of candles. She began lighting them and setting them up in a circle around her two prisoners.

Jeff and Gloria exchanged panicky looks, but Jeff was no dummy. If Gloria thought he was going to sacrifice himself to save her, she was even dumber than Jackie thought she was. But the expression in her eyes proved otherwise. She knew what Jeff was going to say, in general if not exactly.

He turned to look at Gloria. "Sorry, darling. It was fun while it lasted."

Jackie thought she knew approximately what Gloria was shrieking through her gag. She wasn't pleading for her life. She was trying to tell Jeff exactly what she thought of him. Too bad, thought Jackie. Under other circumstances, we might have been friends. Then she tore Gloria's throat out.

After her immediate hunger was sated, Jackie began pulling out the tastier morsels of Gloria's body. Jeff alternately turned his head away in disgust, and turned back to watch in horrified fascination. The dismemberment didn't take long and a pile of steaming organs was slowly cooling on a hideous plastic tray she'd commandeered from housewares.

Jeff finally could wait no longer. "So what about it? Are you going to let me go or not?'

Her lungs were a bit more limber now that she'd eaten. "Oh, I'll let you go. I always kept my word, didn't I?"

Eager to please, Jeff nodded furiously. "Yes, you did." He squirmed a little. "I'd like to get back before it's full dark."

"Patience. There's one more thing we have to do first."

Suddenly Jeff looked anxious. "What one thing is that?"

She tried to smile, managed a pretty good imitation. "Nothing we haven't done before." She carried the tray over to where he sat and nodded toward the candles. "I thought we'd just have one more romantic meal together, for old time's sake. Would you prefer breast or thigh?

PAYMENT IN ARREARS

Derek smirked with secret knowledge as the eulogy droned on. The largest chamber of the Managansett Funeral Home was crammed to capacity, friends, neighbors, and relatives of the deceased gathered for their last glimpse, a few distraught with genuine grief, most merely uncomfortable, either because of the oppressive humidity or because they accepted the event as a social duty rather than as an expression of an actual sense of loss.

"Betty Sanderson was a true humanitarian," Mayor Korman's voice rose momentarily, then dropped to its previous, barely audible level. Only those closest to the front of the room would be able to make out the individual words, but since the mayor's speeches were notoriously low on content, the majority of his audience was undoubtedly silently grateful for the poor acoustics of the room.

Derek stood at the doorway, inches from the register wherein several hundred people had already ritually recorded their names, concrete evidence of their acquiescence to a custom Derek considered shallow and false. He had seen thousands of visitors come and go since Bill Garrett had hired him, and it was his considered opinion that the curious and the duty bound greatly outnumbered the truly grieving. Charade or not, the ceremonies of death served Derek's purposes admirably. If the societal urge to pay one's last respects had not existed, there would be no reason to restore their bodies to a condition so reminiscent of life. And then where would he be?

"Betty Sanderson was a devoted mother," Korman emphasized the topic sentence of each paragraph of his prepared text by raising his head and spearing the audience with his unfortunately shifty gaze. Surreptitiously, Derek allowed his own eyes to stray to the left, where a row of plush seats was customarily reserved for the immediate family. Ben Sanderson sat with head up, eyes bright, ostensibly listening carefully to every word that was spoken. As Town Manager, he theoretically reported to the Council, not the mayor, but everyone in Managansett knew that Korman dictated policy with a rigid, if invisible, hand. Even in this moment of tragedy, Ben Sanderson would strive to appear attentive. After all, life and career would continue after this day was nothing but a sad memory.

But Derek spared Ben only a brief glance, even less for the boy, Eric, thirteen years old, who twisted uncomfortably in his seat, clearly bored and anxious for an end to the entire affair. Next to him sat Shannon, his sister, her expression solemn, dark eyes downcast, hands clenched tightly in her lap, long white fingers contrasting sharply against the utter black of the mourning clothes. Shannon was reputedly a strange child, extremely close to her mother and with no real friends her own age. That was a shame, Derek realized, watching her face out of the corner of one eye, because Shannon was turning into quite an attractive young woman.

"Betty lived and died with dignity." Derek turned his attention back to the mayor, who seemed to be winding up his dissertation. Dignity? Derek scoffed silently. There's precious little dignity in having your internal organs scooped out and your veins filled with formaldehyde. He would like to have seen the expression on Korman's face if he had been present during the preparation of a corpse for viewing. The fat old fool would probably pass out or lose his lunch or something, and he sure as hell wouldn't be spouting off about the dignity of death.

Derek was amusing himself with an inventive fantasy along those general lines when he realized that people were filing past. Bill Garrett touched his shoulder.

"Wake up, Derek. I have to get out of here early. Marge'll have a fit if we don't show up at the Nicholsons' on time."

Derek struggled to reorient himself. "Yeah, sorry. Guess my mind was wandering."

But Garrett was already at the front door, nodding sympathetically while unobtrusively trying to move people along as expeditiously as possible.

Derek watched the Sanderson family as they rose, talking among themselves in terse whispers, preparing to leave. Young Eric appeared to be relieved, Shannon and Ben drawn and weary. He crossed the room, deliberately keeping his voice low, emotionless, as he addressed Ben, watching Shannon move at the edge of his peripheral vision.

"You could use the back door if you'd like."

Sanderson glanced up at him as though he'd sprung from the air itself.

"The back way to the parking lot," Derek explained. "If you want to avoid the crowd."

Sanderson blinked, then nodded. "Why, thank you. That's a good idea." He turned to his children, raising one arm as though to usher them onward. Derek led the way.

He stood watching as they climbed into a long, dark Lincoln, and was rewarded by a flash of white leg as Shannon seated herself. She certainly was turning out to be quite a sexy young woman, much like her mother, whose unexpected and instantly fatal stroke had precipitated this meeting.

"What is the matter with you tonight, Derek?" Garrett stood behind him.

"Oh, sorry." He closed the door. "What's up?"

"We have to get this place cleaned tonight. There's another showing tomorrow, from eight to ten, just before the funeral. I'll be in early to work on the Brierly boy, but I won't have time to help you in the morning so everything has to be done now."

Derek nodded. This was working out exactly as he'd hoped. "Look, Mr. Garrett. I don't have any plans for this evening and you do. Why don't you just let me take care of things? I'll stay as long as it takes."

Garrett stopped in mid-stride, turned toward the younger man, his expression uncertain. It wasn't the first time Derek had been left to lock up, but there was a considerable amount of work to do and Garrett felt a twinge of conscience. "I don't know..."

"There won't be any problem. I don't mind, really."

Garrett's face remained troubled, but Derek could tell he had already won the battle. "That's very thoughtful of you, Derek. We might actually arrive for dinner at a reasonable hour. I appreciate this; you're a good boy and I'll owe you a favor. Be sure that you've locked everything up, though; there have been some strange stories from over in Providence, bodies disappearing from funeral homes. Probably some teenagers playing around with satanism in a big way." Derek assured his employer that he would be careful and after receiving a few last minute instructions and the spare key to the front door, he watched Garrett depart in rare high spirits.

Derek attacked the work at hand with fervor, vacuuming, dusting, spritzing the flowers, removing limp petals and discolored leaves. He replaced one burnt out light bulb, swept the floors, emptied the waste baskets, checked the pens by the register, locked and doublechecked every window and door. When everything had been completed to his satisfaction, he returned to the chamber where lay the body of Betty Sanderson.

She had been a handsome woman, and the stroke which had claimed her life had not marred her features. The skin was pale, of course, and cool to the touch. Garrett was a skillful mortician, but although she looked as lifelike as was possible under the circumstances, it was still evident that no spark moved behind those closed eyelids, no breath stirred under that motionless breast. Derek would have it no other way.

There were no outside windows in this room, so he turned on all the lights confident that no one would suspect anything. Crossing to the coffin, he stared down, allowed his gaze to travel the full length of her body. Then he reached out tentatively, his hand shaking, and laid one palm across her breast, squeezing it gently.

"Just tell me if you want me to stop, Betty," he whispered softly, then giggled inanely.

He opened the blouse carefully, folding the material back to expose the white lace bra underneath. This was a bit more troublesome, since he didn't want to chance disturbing the body any more than was necessary, but previous experience lent him enough confidence that he persevered. He gathered the material of the velvet burial dress up to her waist, carefully peeled the panties from around her buttocks and pulled them down to her knees.

Then he began to remove his own clothing.

It was even more difficult to refrain from smiling with satisfaction the following morning. There were no more speeches, and the crowd was somewhat smaller, most of the bereft having chosen to meet the burial party at the cemetery. The family had returned, naturally, and Derek amused himself by imagining that it had been Shannon in the coffin the previous evening and not her mother. Even the unattractive black dress she was wearing could not completely disguise the inviting figure underneath.

The final two hours passed with agonizing slowness. Derek had not left the mortuary until well after midnight the previous evening and had returned by seven; fatigue and a totally irrational but undeniable fear of discovery had combined to make him short tempered and impatient. When the family rose to pay its final respects, he gave an almost audible sigh of relief.

Ben Sanderson and his children rose and approached the coffin. Slowly the man bent down and kissed his wife gently on the lips. Eric appeared to be extremely uncomfortable, but his father gestured briefly with his chin and the boy sighed, set his shoulders, and leaned to kiss his mother's forehead. Then it was Shannon's turn.

She stared into her mother's face for a full minute, the first tears Derek had seen from her now streaking both cheeks. Finally she leaned forward, pressing trembling lips against the cool flesh below.

And almost immediately jumped back, spinning on one heel, her eyes searching the room. Derek was startled to see that her sorrow had been replaced by a new emotion, eyes flashing angrily as she scanned the faces arrayed before her. A few of the latter muttered uncertainly when they noticed Shannon's expression, but her eyes shifted determinedly until, finally, they met Derek's. And stopped, fastened there. She nodded once, very deliberately, and turned away, mouth twisted into an expression of contempt and hatred. Derek realized that somehow, in some incomprehensible fashion, she had obtained some knowledge of what he had done.

Two days passed uneventfully following the funeral, and Derek began to wonder if he'd imagined that icy stare. On the third evening, he received the phone call.

"What?" he answered shortly. His nerves had been on edge these past few days, and the shrill sound of the telephone was almost painful.

"I know what you've done." The words were spoken quietly, but intensely.

"Who...who is this?" He knew instantly even though he'd never actually heard the voice before. "What are you talking about?"

"You've done it before, haven't you?"

How could she know that?

"Whoever you are, you're making a big mistake. Now stop bothering me." Almost, he returned the receiver to its cradle, but something made him hesitate, waiting for her to speak.

"She told me, you know. She told me what you did. I could tell people, tell them what you've done." The voice was still a whisper, but there was an undertone of determination, hatred, resolve.

"What do you want from me?" He realized he was cringing, betraying his guilt, flayed himself internally for this weakness.

"I don't know," her voice came after a pause, thoughtful. "I'll think about it and let you know. You're going to pay for this, you know, pay a lot." And without another word, she broke the connection.

It was intolerable. Derek was content if not overjoyed with his life. At twenty-five years of age, he had a secure if not well paid job despite the fact that he'd never finished high school. Intellectually, he was capable of mastering most of the course material, but he had just never felt inclined to make the effort. His parents had tolerated his presence in their home until he was old enough to support himself, but were absurdly happy to see him move out. He hadn't seen or spoken to them now in six years. But he had found a place for himself, and no teenage bitch was going to ruin it for him.

Derek laid his plans carefully, watching the Sanderson home, which was set far back from the road and surrounded by enormous willow trees, for several days before acting. One evening, while he lay concealed in an adjacent woodlot, Ben and Eric Sanderson drove off, the boy clad in a Little League uniform, and Derek realized his chance had come.

He entered through the unlocked sliding glass door from the rear patio.

Shannon was sitting on a couch in the family room, and the television was loud enough that she never heard him coming. When he threw the loop of clothesline around her throat and twisted it tight, she turned her head, eyes widening with recognition and realization, but he yanked back sharply, cutting off her breath, bracing himself against the back of the couch so that she couldn't pull free. She stopped struggling after a surprisingly short period of time but he held on desperately for several minutes anyway, just to be safe.

When he was satisfied that she was truly dead, he left the rope buried in her flesh and walked around the couch, staring down at the recumbent body. Shannon's eyes were wide open, bulging with pain and terror, her complexion mottled blue, mouth open, drool streaking her chin, tongue swollen and extended. She was no longer attractive at all, and he felt a moment of regret before realizing that all of this was transitory, that Bill Garrett would restore her beauty almost effortlessly. Derek had seen him work wonders in cases far more extreme.

He nodded to himself, preparing to leave. "We'll meet again, Shannon," he promised her in a whisper. "It's a date."

"This is a real tragedy," averred Garrett as he spread the sheet over the body of Shannon Sanderson.

Derek turned from the sink he had been scrubbing, nodded, then realized his employer's back was turned and that he had been unable to see the gesture. "Yeah, I guess so. Wasn't that her mother who died a week or so back?"

"That's right. Betty Sanderson. She was real proud of her daughter. Poor kid was a looker too, just like her mom, but she died a virgin anyway." Garrett sighed. "I know that sounds funny, but it always bothers me somehow when a young girl dies without ever having a lover. I suppose the same thing is true of young boys, but with them you can't really tell, you know what I mean?"

Derek wasn't certain how to answer that, so he remained silent, but Garrett seemed to expect no answer.

"Well, she's pretty much finished. I can't get her mouth right; I wanted them to remember her smiling, but I guess under the circumstances that wouldn't be appropriate anyway. Her father's bringing over the burial clothing in the morning and the wake starts at one o'clock sharp. Is the Rose Chamber ready?"

"Needs to be vacuumed."

"I thought I told you to do that earlier today?"

Derek was prepared for this. "I got behind. The cord on the vacuum was frayed and I had to get some duct tape and fix it. Then you sent me downtown, remember, and that ran later than usual. Don't worry; I'll take care of it before I go."

Garrett looked at his watch. "It's quitting time in ten minutes, Derek. And that sink has to be completely disinfected."

Derek nodded. "I'll stay as long as it takes. I still have the spare set of keys, remember? I'll lock up."

Garrett's anger was displaced once more and he seemed uncertain. "Well, all right. Sorry if I jumped down your throat. It was just, you know, seeing a young girl like this, you never really get used to it even after all these years. The whole world seems to be going to hell lately. You hear about those killings over in Smithfield, the mutilations?" Without waiting for an answer, he sighed deeply and shook his head. "Sorry, Derek. I shouldn't be taking things out on you. Look, I'll stay and help. The two of us can finish up in twenty minutes."

Derek was suddenly alarmed, afraid his opportunity might be slipping away. "No!" he protested, a bit too loudly, then modulated his voice. "I mean, don't worry about it. I know how upset you've been lately. Those weird stories kind of bother me too. I don't mind cleaning up and stuff; it keeps my mind off things."

Garrett was silent for several seconds, then stepped forward and clasped Derek's upper arm. "Sure, I know what you mean, Derek. Look, why don't we plan to have you over for supper sometime next week, okay? You're still living by yourself, aren't you? I'll set up a date with Marge."

Derek nodded nervously. "Sure, Mr. Garrett; that sounds fine to me."

He waited until Garrett's car had disappeared around the corner onto Main Street before locking all the doors. Normally he would finish cleaning up first, but this was a special case. Shannon was easily the most attractive client to show up since Derek had discovered the fringe benefits of his job, and he had already developed an erection just from being in the room while the older man applied makeup to the dead girl's face. He had remained outside his employer's line of sight, afraid that the man might observe and recognize the bulge in his pants.

Derek carefully folded the sheet back, revealing the nude form beneath. Although he had sneaked a few glances in her direction earlier, there had been no opportunity for a thorough examination, and he had a secret fear that she would be marred somehow, an ugly disfigurement always previously concealed by her clothing, some blemish, a birthmark or appendectomy scar.

But she was perfect. Her breasts were still small, but he liked them that way, hips full, thighs tapering gracefully toward a pair of slender calves. Much of her tan had faded, but the cream colored skin was smooth and unblemished wherever he looked, and he left no vista unexplored during the next few minutes, circumambulating the table in order to view his conquest from every possible angle.

"I told you we'd meet again, you little bitch," he breathed softly. "Just couldn't stay away from me, could you?"

He touched her for the first time then, placing one hand on the right kneecap, cupping it briefly, the too cool flesh not dismaying him in the slightest. Then he moved his hand slowly up her body, the tips of his fingers just brushing the flesh of her thigh, through the tuft of hair that marked the line of demarcation of right from left, over the concavity of her belly, across a series of well defined ribs, and on to the slight swell of her breast. He hesitated there briefly, his forefinger a fraction of an inch from her nipple, then moved on, reserving this pleasure for later. Across her now motionless chest, past the larynx that would never reveal whatever it was that she had somehow learned about him, up over the soft chin toward the face.

Her eyes were open!

Derek recoiled as though she had opened her mouth and bitten him, took two rapid steps backward, his motion arrested only when one foot struck a metal waste bin that overturned and went rolling away across the floor with a clatter.

He froze, as breathless and motionless as the corpse, eyes locked with hers, before he realized that she was in fact still dead. For some reason, the eyes had opened, or perhaps Garrett had not yet gotten around to closing them. It was an odd oversight, but perfectly explicable.

"Gave me a scare there, girl," he said aloud, moving back to the table. "I suppose it won't hurt any if you see what's happening; might even make it more pleasant for you, right?"

She made no reply, but Derek wasn't expecting one. He began to remove his clothing, letting it fall to the floor beside the table.

Several minutes later, he slammed his clenched fist down onto her right shoulder in frustration, shifting his weight to a more comfortable position between her unresisting thighs. "Damn it!" His erection had not returned after the earlier fright, and although everything seemed ideally arranged for his enjoyment, he couldn't seem to get back into the mood.

"You could help a little," he said inanely, then giggled. "Show a little enthusiasm."

She stared at him without comment.

It was cruel, he thought, and unfair. There might never be another opportunity like this again; how often did attractive teenage girls die in a small town like Managansett, with their bodies unmangled and their looks unspoiled?

Unless, of course, he helped another along. That was a idea worth considering further. But at another time. There was a matter of more immediate concern.

Derek had never experienced such incapacity before. Even old Mrs. Merkori, overweight, her skin dried to parchment and mottled with age spots, had proved herself adequate to receive what he thought of as his last gift to the departed. There was no reason why his body should fail him now.

Unless it was the eyes.

They had always been closed before. Derek crossed his forearms on Shannon's chest and rested his chin there, regarding her face solemnly. "Am I keeping you awake, dear?" Again the giggle. But Derek felt no real humor, just frustration building to an aching core somewhere below his belly. Abruptly, he became convinced that those sightless but somehow accusing eyes were the source of his problem and he half rose, reaching up with one hand to close them.

The lids seemed inflexible at first, but he carefully exerted pressure until they moved, rubbery against his fingers. When he withdrew his hand, he felt renewed stirring between his legs and smiled with satisfaction. Apparently that had been the problem, easily solved.

Both eyes popped open, the right a split second behind the left.

Derek almost leaped from the body, losing his balance and crashing to the floor with bruising force. Seconds later, simultaneously angry and wryly amused at himself, he stood up, to discover that his erection had wilted once again.

"All right, kid, we'll do this another way." He was standing beside the table again, even more determined to consummate this tryst. "Let's see if you've got eyes behind your head." And with a quick, efficient motion he pulled the body toward himself, then rolled it completely over.

"I'm behind you all the way," he snickered. Derek's interest was immediately rekindled, stronger than before, and he hardly noticed when he scraped his knee clambering up onto the table.

In fact, as the minutes passed, he wondered why this particular variation had never occurred to him before. It was a new high in physical gratification, every bit as wonderful as that first time, almost a year ago now, when he had been left alone while Garrett was recovering from food poisoning. There had been perhaps a score of assignations since then, but none of them had provided nearly as much pleasure as was the late Miss Sanderson. Each thrust seemed to penetrate more deeply, his thighs slapping against her bottom cheeks, and he wondered how long he had grown, felt a passing regret that there was no way to check.

That's when something moved where there should be no movement.

He froze instantly, then laughed and resumed his exertions, dismissing it as a phantom sensation. "Getting you stirred up, am I, baby? Can't get enough of me, can you?"

Something soft but firm moved laterally along his erection. It was unmistakably real, a physical event; Derek broke out into a cold sweat and felt himself shrinking once more. "What the fuck?" Bizarre images flashed through his mind. Could some sort of insect have been trapped inside the body somehow, a spider perhaps? The idea was so unnerving that he shuddered and raised his upper body, preparing to withdraw.

A fiery circle of pain and pressure closed around the base of his penis.

Derek cried out, as much from terror as pain, the muscles in his arms locking, holding him as far back from the cold flesh as his captured member would allow. His mind shied away from contemplation of what might have caught hold of his distended flesh, all it could deal with at the moment was concentration on that intense, unbelievable pain, willing it to recede. And it did diminish slightly, but the grip remained as firm as ever. When he tentatively moved to withdraw, setting his knees down on the table and easing back slowly, her supine form moved with him, one limp arm falling loosely over the side. "Shit!" he cried out, and discovered tears running down his face.

The pain began spreading forward, an eruption of agonizing pinpricks that progressed rapidly toward the glans, growing in intensity. Bellowing, heedless of the consequences, Derek threw himself to one side, unbalanced, crashing down onto his back, jarring the breath from his lungs as he hit the floor.

Shannon Sanderson's corpse went with him, still impaled from behind.

There was no respite from the agonizing pain, which grew in intensity with each passing second. Lights flashed behind Derek's eyes as he struggled to his feet, arms wrapped around the body's ribcage to hold it erect. There was a rack of tools beside the sink, just above the disposal unit, he remembered, including a couple of knives; regardless of the consequences, he was intent upon cutting himself free. He'd have to fake a break-in later tonight, to explain the mangled corpse, but that was the least of his problems right now.

He was terrified that he would pass out and be found here in the morning.

They moved across the floor together in a grotesque dance parody; she was shorter than he and her dangling legs kept getting mixed up with his own, threatening to trip him. Just as he staggered to within arm's reach of the sink, the pressure increased so much that he was certain his flesh must burst.

As Derek reeled back, eyes wide and momentarily blinded, Shannon's body fell away from him, disengaged, landing limply and rolling half over onto its side. Derek lurched toward the sink, one hand raised to brace himself on the counter. Gasping, he turned to the body, realized that her opened eyes were staring at him once more.

"You little pain in the ass," he breathed weakly, close to fainting. "What's gotten into you?"

Then he glanced down, and had his answer.

Bill Garrett was as pale as one of the many clients he had worked on over the years by the time the police had removed the body.

"It just doesn't seem possible," he insisted weakly.

Detective Coyle nodded. "It's unbelievable, that's for sure, but I've seen a lot of things in this job you'd say the same about. If there were any evidence of forced entry, we'd look further, but it's pretty clear your boy there did it to himself, then just bled to death."

Garrett shook his head. "But then where are...you know, the parts?"

Coyle shrugged. "Down the disposal, I suppose. Pretty weird, I admit. He must have been one sick boy. The lab boys will check it out."

"But there was no blood in the sink."

"So he washed it out after he was done. Who knows, Mr. Garrett? When they go over the edge, there's no telling what they'll do."

The body of Shannon Sanderson lay on a table under a sheet in the back room of the Managansett Funeral Home, arms at her sides, eyes closed, mouth...finally...curved in a gentle smile.

LITERALLY SPEAKING

"If I can just make the basketball team, I'll get a little respect," Billy Coleman told himself, speaking aloud as had become his habit. After all, almost no one else was ever willing to listen to what he had to say, so it was understandable that he spent a lot of time acting as his own audience. He paused, leaning forward on the rake with which he had been cleaning up the fallen leaves behind the Sheffield Library. "Jerry Reynolds would like me then, I'll bet, and even Eric Nicholson wouldn't pick fights any more. Susan Fletcher might even go out with me."

He was considering this last thought in rather more explicit detail when his reverie was interrupted by a shout from Arthur Kaplan, the adult sent over to make sure the teenagers hired by the town actually performed the work for which they were being paid.

"Hey, Coleman! This isn't a coffee break. Move that rake!" Billy jumped to do as he was told, face flushed, embarrassed and annoyed that he had attracted the man's attention. Kaplan frightened him a bit; the man was an alcoholic and there had been rumors for almost a year that he was going to be fired from the town maintenance staff. As it was, he had been demoted from Chief Janitor at the Town Hall to a series of progressively more menial jobs, such as this present one.

Billy glanced up at the building that loomed overhead. The library had been closed for years; there just didn't seem to be much public interest in the collection of occult books and art objects that had been accumulated there decades before and the town had finally locked the doors, although the grounds were still maintained in some semblance of order, usually by high school students hired to cut the grass and clean up the trash on Sunday afternoons. Billy found it boring and a waste of time, the Sheffield place had always been kind of spooky and unpleasant, but he was saving up the money to buy a car so that he wouldn't have to keep borrowing his older sister's and every little bit helped.

As he pushed the growing pile of leaves ahead of him, he advanced along the side of the building. There was a sudden tinkling from below and he glanced down into a scatter of broken glass. Puzzled, he scanned the wall above and saw that a window just above eye level was missing one of its panes. Through the open window he could see the edge of a shelf that seemed to have come loose from wherever it had originally been anchored, as it now sloped down at a sharp angle, one end protruding out into the open air. Billy thought he should probably mention it to someone, but a glance at Arthur Kaplan was enough to make him shudder and dismiss any thought of opening a conversation.

"Better just sweep the glass up with the leaves and forget it," he told himself.

That was just precisely what he was doing when Billy noticed the dull gleam of gold. Of course, it might not really have been gold, but the large coin that sparkled in the sunlight when he disturbed it from its resting place certainly appeared to have been fashioned from that precious metal. With a quick glance to be certain that he was not observed, Billy squatted, scooped it up and rose.

It was shaped like a coin, but there were no markings to indicate that it was any kind of legal tender. One side was decorated with a series of symbols, pyramids, sunbursts, scrolls, a disembodied eye, a trident, and other shapes all inscribed in impressive detail. The opposite side, however, was almost completely blank, bearing around its circumference a brief inscription in plain English.

"Be Precise Thrice," Billy read aloud. "What the hell does that mean?" He heard Kaplan shouting at another boy just then, quickly slipped the coin into his pocket and resumed raking. He could examine it in more detail later.

Two hours later, he was doing exactly that, sitting behind the wheel of his sister's convertible at the town lot, the top folded down despite the cooler weather, waiting for the engine to warm up so he could go home. Now that he could examine it more closely, he noticed that the coin seemed worn, less impressive than before, and certainly he could never have been so lucky as to have found a

piece of genuine gold. "I never get a break," he said
sorrowfully. "I was born too unlucky and unfortunate to ever do the
things I want to do. Why did I even think I might have lucked
out this time?"

Finally, he replaced the disc in his pocket. "Maybe it'll
bring me luck," he reflected. "I can use all the help I can get
during the tryouts at school tomorrow."

A few minutes later, it was obvious that his luck had not
improved. Billy had pulled out onto Main Street behind a flashy
red sports car, intent upon getting home and taking care of the
homework he had been putting off since Friday night.
Unfortunately, the woman driving ahead of him seemed to be in
absolutely no hurry and maintained a steady thirty miles per hour
as they headed east, leaving the downtown and heading out into
open country. As Main Street extended east of Managansett, it
opened out into a narrow straightaway through a series of farms,
and most of the time the traffic moved at fifty miles per hour or
more despite the posted speed.

Impatiently, Billy pulled out and attempted to pass. The
sports car immediately speeded up and he was forced to pull back
over into his lane. The woman then eased off the gas pedal and
dropped back to thirty miles per hour. "Goddamn it, lady," he
whined. "Don't be such a pain." He pulled out to pass a second time,
and the same sequence of events repeated itself. "Shit!"
he shouted, then felt embarrassed at his own temerity, though
still angry. "Lady, I wish I could just get ahead for a while.
I'd show you a thing or two."

Billy felt a sudden intense pain in his right thigh, as
though something sharp in his pants pocket had become stuck in
his flesh, but before he could investigate, an even more serious
turn of events pre-empted his attention. The road had taken an
abrupt curve to the left. There was a long, open stretch here and
Billy had automatically moved out to pass. Predictably, the
woman had accelerated sharply again, determined not to let him
by, but with her attention riveted on her rearview mirror, she
had not seen the slow moving flatbed truck ahead. As a
consequence she hit it from the rear at a respectable rate of
speed, and the tailgate smashed through the windshield and
convertible top with ease. It also smashed through something else as

well, and the object that arced through the air
and down into Billy's lap lay there for quite a few seconds
before he recognized that it was a human head. Even then,
someone else had to take it out of his lap; he couldn't bring
himself to touch it.

His parents told him that he could skip school the next day
if he wanted to, but youth is resilient, and he was also determined
not to miss the first round of tryouts for the
basketball team. And so it was that he had dressed for school and
was sitting at the kitchen table the following morning,
disinterestedly picking at scrambled eggs and toast, while his
free hand held the possible good luck charm that he had appropriated
the
previous afternoon.

"Be Precise Thrice," he repeated.

"Did you say something, Billy?" His mother glanced over
from where she sat watching the morning news on television.

"No, Mom, just talking to myself."

"That's a bad habit to get into, you know. People will start
wondering if you keep it up."

Billy frankly thought that his mother's addiction to the
television was considerably stranger, but he tactfully refrained from
making his opinion public. He sneaked a look in
her direction to see if she expected an answer, but she had
a lready turned back to the ongoing interview with Gerald
Lawrence, widely considered the heir apparent to the seat of the
retiring Senator Plunkett from this district in the state
legislature. Lawrence's face filled the screen as he spoke about
the need to lure new business to northwestern Rhode Island, and
Billy made a face.

"I wish someone would defeat the bastard," he whispered
under his breath, so that his mother would not hear him. But she
did hear his yelp of pain as fire lanced across the tips of his
fingers. His lucky coin fell to the table and rolled over to the
opposite end, rattling to a stop.

"What's going on?" Her voice was more annoyed than
concerned.

Billy stared at the ends of his fingers, which were neither bloody nor blistered. Already the pain was just a memory, and fading at that.

"Nothing, Mom, sorry. I bit my tongue." He was lying, but he didn't know what else to say to her.

It was at lunchtime that day when he heard the news announcement over the radio in the cafeteria. Gerald Lawrence, independent candidate for the state legislature from the district that included all of Managansett, had fallen from an Amtrak passenger train into the path of another. Although he had survived the experience, both feet had been amputated at the ankles. Billy never connected the incident with his wish.

The basketball tryouts did not really go badly. Billy had spent a great deal of time practicing and his foul line shooting percentage was close to 75%, second best in the entire school. He was a pretty good dribbler and passer as well and quick on his feet. Basketball was really the only sport in which he stood a chance of making the team and he had concentrated all of his effort on these tryouts. But there was one thing against him, one thing that might make this dream just as ephemeral as all the others he had entertained and finally abandoned in the past. At seventeen years of age, Billy Coleman was still only five foot six, and he was the shortest of the thirty boys to survive the first round of eliminations.

When he arrived home that night, he was animated and enthusiastic, telling his parents how much he was looking forward to the final cut on the following day, how certain he was that he had made the final ten who would make up the varsity team, or at the very least the second ten, who would still be allowed to play some junior varsity games. But when he finally lay in bed, willing sleep to come, the truth hit him with an almost physical force.

There was no way that Billy Coleman was going to qualify for either team. He was probably as talented as most of the rest of the boys, but the fact was that his height just made it very unlikely that he would be selected. As much as the school coaches insisted that it was the game and not the victory that mattered, Billy knew that they were lying, that they agonized over every loss during the year. And the fact was that his lack of stature made it very difficult for him to play effective defense, and he was inevitably going to be eliminated on the following afternoon.

"Just my luck," he said aloud. "If there were twenty-one finalists for the two teams, I'd be the one person they'd drop. If there were only twenty finalists, they'd drop the junior varsity team. Even if I made the team, I'd probably break a leg or something and never play in a game."

The thought of his bad luck reminded him of the charm, and he retrieved it from the pocket of his pants, which lay in their usual spot on the floor beside his bed. He turned it over and over, looking at the inscription, the various shapes and symbols on the reverse.

"If you really are a good luck charm," he said softly. "I need you now." Suddenly angry and depressed by his presentiment of failure, he clenched his hand tightly around the coin. "I wish I could grow another foot before morning. That would solve all of my problems." But he had closed his hand perhaps a bit too tightly, because it felt as though the edge of the coin had cut deeply into his palm. The fingers flexed open reflexively and the coin fell onto the bed. "That's the third time I've hurt myself on you, damn it!" he whispered tensely, and knocked it flying from the bed with the back of one hand. Then, with a resigned shrug, he turned over, fluffed up his pillow, and settled down to sleep.

He did feel better the following morning when he woke, refreshed, less pessimistic, perhaps resigned to the inevitability of rejection. The sun came in brightly through his window and the room was cheery and warm.

"So what if I don't make the team," he said to himself. "There are worse things in the world." And for the first time in a long while, he genuinely felt good. Very good in fact. And the mood lasted right up until the moment when he threw back the bedclothes and looked down and saw what had grown out of his right ankle during the night and counted the fifteen perfectly formed toes that poked up from his sheets.

THE PIGGY BANK

Buster brushed aside the shrunken heads hanging in the window and climbed into Old Man Crenshaw's house. He'd waited until Crenshaw was gone, watching from the bushes as the ancient Ford backed slowly from the driveway and turned toward the center of town.

It was shadowy inside and he waited a full minute for his eyes to adjust to the dim light. Crenshaw never let anyone into his house, kept to himself except for regular shopping trips like this one, every Monday afternoon. He'd lived on this lonely side road in northern Managansett for longer than anyone remembered, and about the only thing people knew about him was that he had lots of money, and didn't keep it in a bank.

Once a week he came into town with two crisp hundred dollar bills and did his shopping.

Buster figured it was time to liberate some of that cash.

The house was crowded with furniture, most of it covered with dust. There were four rooms on the ground floor, and a narrow staircase leading upstairs.

"All right, old man, where do you keep it?" Buster made a cursory search, found piles of books about magic and ghosts and things like that, but nothing resembling cash. He hoped to do this clean, get away with the money before Crenshaw returned. But if he couldn't find it, he had a folding knife in his pocket that he figured would persuade the old geezer to be forthcoming about his wealth.

The second floor was every bit as dark as the first. One bedroom, a full bath, another room full of junk, and the last with a locked door.

"Gotcha!"

It wasn't much of a lock; Buster used the blade of his knife to pop it and entered.

An enormous glass sculpture dominated the room, a vaguely piggish body resting on its haunches, with two batwings raised like a cowl above the head. The face was so ugly Buster involuntarily retreated a step, blunt snout, narrow eyes, oversized jaw stretched wide revealing needle sharp teeth of shiny glass. The entire statue was transparent, so Buster had no difficulty seeing the large pile of hundred dollar bills resting within, as though the creature had swallowed them whole.

"Jackpot!" Once over his initial surprise, Buster wasn't shy about approaching the statue. He used one hand to test its weight, discovered that it was massive enough he wouldn't be able to move it. It might be possible to break the glass if he could find something heavy, but that would cause more noise than he cared to make. The Wilsons next door might not be friendly with Crenshaw, but they were close enough to hear and report any disturbance.

"The old man gets the money out, so I oughta be able to do it."

The jaws were opened wide, but the teeth were so long that there wasn't much clearance. Still, as long as he was careful...

Buster cautiously raised his hand and stuck it down the statue's throat.

Although he brushed the tips of the teeth more than once, he found the task easier than he'd expected. The cash was just at the limit of his reach; he wouldn't be able to get more than half of it this way. But that's all he needed. No reason to be a pig about it; let Crenshaw keep enough to live on.

His fingers closed on a packet of bills and he started to withdraw.

Something stabbed him in the upper arm.

"Damn!" He'd been careless. One of the glass teeth had torn through his shirt and drawn blood. Buster eased away and winced as teeth from the lower jaw penetrated his flesh.

"What the hell?" For some reason, there didn't seem to be as much clearance as before. It was almost as if the jaws were slowly closing. Closing on his arm.

Blood was trickling from his shirt. Buster tried to withdraw at a different angle, and the sudden serrated pain caused him to jump, which only made things worse. He dropped the wad of bills and concentrated on escaping the trap.

It took almost half an hour and another score cuts before Buster's arm was free and he collapsed against the opposite wall, weak from shock and loss of blood.

"Hope I left a bad taste in your mouth, you bastard," he said softly.

Then the statue slowly turned in his direction, jaws opening again, and Buster realized he'd only made it hungry.

WINGS OVER MANHATTAN

Fallon wasn't happy. He didn't like working as a bodyguard under the best of circumstances, and it was even more frustrating when you were trying to protect someone whom you'd never met and who didn't want to be protected. When Lionel Rose had described the job he wanted done, Fallon's immediate impulse had been to pick up his hat and leave, but Rose was offering double his usual rate, and the stack of unpaid bills sitting on his desk were never far from Fallon's thoughts.

He spotted her immediately as she stepped out of a black Studebaker Phaeton in front of the Lamp Post, a speakeasy whose owners were so tight with the local police that they made no effort to conceal their real business. They served food all right, and it wasn't half bad, but their clientele came to drink and to socialize, not for the cuisine. And sometimes there were even less savory reasons. There were rooms on the third floor where poker was played for high stakes and others where visitors could pursue business that would have been impossible even in the tolerant atmosphere downstairs.

It had been easy enough to recognize Selina Rose the first time he had tailed her. She had the same general features as her father, although they were smoothed and softened into a less formidable whole. Selina was twenty-two, although she looked younger, short even in heels, with dark shoulder length hair and a dress that seemed to have been molded to her body. She moved with an easy grace that Fallon admired, and envied. He himself was a large man not entirely comfortable in his own body. The doorman gave her a close look before letting her inside, not because he was worried about her age, but because she was an unfamiliar face. Fallon had received the same scrutiny a day earlier, when he'd come to check the layout in anticipation of tonight.

He dropped his cigarette, ground it out with his heel, and started across the street. It was Saturday night and the Lamp Post was crowded. The doorman nodded, recognizing him as a repeat customer, and Fallon slipped inside. The sound and the lights hit him with an almost physical force, glitter bright, suggesting gaiety with a hard edge. Clouds of cigarette smoke drifted over the bar, an elaborate set-up that spanned the entire rear wall. Tables were arranged in a semi-circle around a small dance floor where perhaps half a dozen couples were moving in something approximating synchronization to the jazz combo who occupied a small stage. There were elaborate staircases to left and right, leading up to the second floor balconies and the terra incognita of the third floor. The murmur of conversation rivaled the music in volume.

There were more customers than chairs and people were milling about like flies on a corpse. Fallon could not immediately locate Selina Rose. He let his eyes wander around the room for a few seconds, then walked over to the bar. It only took a few seconds to catch the eye of the closest bartender – there were three. "Scotch."

The drink appeared almost by magic. Fallon sipped and it burned its way down his throat, but he didn't notice. He turned, leaned back against the bar, and studied the crowd.

Fallon knew in general why Selina had come here, but he didn't know what she intended to do. Almost a month earlier her younger sister, Emily, had disappeared after she and her boyfriend had decided to visit the Lamp Post. The boyfriend had been found late that night lying unconscious in an alley two blocks away, badly concussed. He claimed to have no idea what had happened to Emily, couldn't even remember arriving at the speakeasy. The police looked around a bit and may even have asked a few questions, but they knew better than to ruffle the wrong feathers.

Lionel Rose might have pursued the matter himself if he'd been younger, or healthier, but his star was descending on multiple fronts. His old allies in the city government were dead or out of office, his body was failing so rapidly that he struggled to walk with a cane, and while he still lived a comfortable life style, he only managed to do so by a strict regimen of hidden economies. Fallon suspected that he believed his younger daughter was already dead, or worse, and preferred to live with the uncertainty rather than know a horrible truth.

Selina was another matter entirely. She had harassed the police detective assigned to the case until it became clear that he was not going to be moved by her protests. When she realized that her father was unwilling or incapable of acting, she had decided to pursue things herself. Old Lionel had argued against it, but she had inherited his fabled obstinacy and was determined to discover the truth. Having lost one daughter already, Lionel was unwilling to risk a second, and so he had hired Fallon to keep an eye on her.

"She's all I have left. Please keep her safe."

Fallon had swallowed his misgivings and accepted the retainer. He had spent the first two days following Selina to City Hall and the Department of Records. It had been difficult to discover the exact purpose of her research, but part of it had been to track down the real owners of the Lamp Post. Theoretically, it was managed by Louis "Big Lou" Tablak, but everyone knew he was just a front. It was less commonly known that Tablak worked for Walter and Allison Armitage, siblings rather than husband and wife. Walter Armitage was tight with the mayor, although it was clear that "Holy Joe" McKee wasn't likely to remain in office for very long. His sister Allison was something of an enigma. She moved in exalted social circles in the city, but it appeared that no one actually liked her, although Fallon had never heard just what it was that made her so unpopular. That wasn't a class of people who normally hired bottom feeding detectives like himself.

Selina had also visited the offices of the Herald Tribune where she'd pored through back issues for most of an afternoon, occasionally taking notes. Fallon had lurked in the area throughout her visit, but once again had been unable to learn just what it was that she was searching for.

That evening he'd received a phone call from Lionel Rose. "She's going to…that place…tomorrow. I tried to talk her out of it, but she refuses to listen to me."

"All right, I'll be there. I won't let anything happen to her." Promises were easy to make, not always so easy to keep, but the old man had needed reassurance, even if they both knew how hollow it was.

"I trust you, Mr. Fallon. I don't have any other choice."

In order to protect her, he really ought to figure out just where she was. With half a drink in his hand, Fallon walked slowly along the front of the bar, ostensibly to get closer to the musicians, although his eyes were raking the floor. Despite the crowd, it only took a minute or two to confirm that she was nowhere in sight. Fallon raised his eyes, casually swept them across the line of balconies.

There! She was sitting at one of the small tables, alone, at least for the moment. Fallon breathed a little easier. Although he never liked disappointing his clients, he always warned them that he wasn't infallible, that there was always a risk. That wouldn't make it any less unpleasant if he had to tell old man Rose that he'd lost another daughter.

There weren't enough chairs to accommodate the crowd, about a third of whom were drifting about. Several of the wanderers were unaccompanied women, probably professionals, some of whom undoubtedly held keys to rooms on the third floor which they'd use once they'd attracted the attention of an unattached male. Or an attached one with a tolerant partner. Fallon watched a pickpocket deftly lift a wallet from a passerby and smiled to himself, then started toward the near staircase. There was a second, much smaller bar on the second floor landing and he stopped to freshen his drink. The balcony tables were partially enclosed, but the partitions weren't thick enough to discourage a determined eavesdropper. Selina was at the third table, but the adjacent ones were both occupied.

Fallon decided to walk past, maybe even glance in casually if he sensed she wasn't looking in his direction. It would not be wise to be spotted. However Selina interpreted his presence, she'd do her best to lose him if she knew he was there. Unless, he supposed, she thought he might be one of the parties responsible for the disappearance of her sister. For a moment he considered playing that card. Lionel was paying him to protect Selina, not find Emily. If it seemed best to lead her astray, he would do so, even though he'd feel a twinge of guilt at the deception.

A waiter passed him and stopped at her booth, carrying two cocktails. So she wasn't alone, or she was expecting someone. Fallon inched closer and heard a male voice. During the brief interval in which she'd been out of sight while he'd climbed the stairs, a man had joined her. Selina was facing out over the lower floor so he chanced a lingering look as he walked past and recognized the man's profile. Gimpy Lane. Fallon mentally tipped his hat to the young woman. Gimpy was a roving salesman and his merchandise was information. No one knew exactly how he came by his treasure trove of dirty secrets, but Gimpy was the first person you talked to if you wanted to know who was getting paid off and by how much, or whose star was rising in the underworld, or falling. If he'd been interested in blackmail, Gimpy could have had a lucrative business, but then again, he'd probably have been rubbed out long ago.

Fallon hastily moved on. He and Gimpy had done business in the past. He found a spot to stand where the balcony curved, leaning against the rail so that he could pretend to be interested in what was happening down below rather than cautiously watching Selina's table out of the corner of his eye. He couldn't see much from here, just part of her arm and shoulder, and occasionally the flash of Gimpy's hand. He tended to gesture when he talked, but his low, gravelly voice was inaudible from this distance. Frustrated, Fallon sipped at his drink and allowed part of his attention to diffuse and take in his surroundings.

Fallon had checked out the security arrangements during his previous visit, but he was cautious enough to do so again. There was a heavyset man near the front door, the same one he'd seen the night before when he'd brushed up against him to confirm the presence of a shoulder holster. Another armed guard was positioned near the bar and at least two others worked the floor. The pickpocket would need to be careful. The only illegalities sanctioned here were the ones that benefited management. Fallon was also pretty sure that at least one of the bartenders was armed. There were also men posted on either staircase monitoring visitors to the third floor. Fallon hadn't been up there. They were all low grade goons except for one of the floor men. Pokerface Lansky was a seasoned pro.

The transition was so quick that Fallon might have missed it if he'd glanced away at the wrong moment. Apparently having completed his business, Gimpy Lane was descending the stairs and Selina had moved out of sight. Fallon's pulse quickened as he stepped back, carefully keeping his expression neutral. She was on the move, headed toward the stairs to the third floor, and she wasn't alone.

There wasn't time to be subtle. Fallon moved directly toward them, adding a very slight list to his walk to suggest this hadn't been his first drink of the evening. Selina and her companion had just reached the dour looking guard at the staircase when he caught up to them, catching hold of Selina's arm and half spinning her around. "Mildred! I thought that was you!" He slurred his words a bit, but not too much. "I haven't seen you in a dog's year." He hadn't thought this through but he knew instinctively that it would not be a good idea for Selina Rose to go up those stairs.

Her expression was a blend of anger, confusion, and contempt. "Let me go! You're drunk and I've never seen you before."

She tried to shrug him off but he only gripped her arm more tightly. "C'mon, Mildred. You aren't still mad at me, are you? That was a long time ago." He pivoted slightly, keeping her between himself and the muscle, who looked puzzled rather than angry. So far.

"My name is not Mildred." She freed herself this time, and Fallon was surprised at how easily she'd broken his grip. No dainty flower, this Selina Rose. Maybe she'd inherited more of her old man's toughness than he'd realized. "Please leave me alone."

Her companion was starting to get annoyed and Fallon knew he'd have to cut this short. "Don't be like that, Mildred. It wasn't my fault." He took a step forward, faked a stumble, and fell awkwardly, wrapping his arms around Selina. She was quick on her feet and almost slipped out of his grasp, but he grappled with her long enough to whisper a warning. "It's a trap." Then a firm hand caught his jacket from behind and yanked him back. Muscle had decided to intervene.

"You're drunk, bud. The lady doesn't know you. Now go home."

Fallon cowered a bit. "I know my Mildred when I see her," he pouted. Out of the corner of his eye he watched her face. Indecision. Her eyes glanced toward the staircase, then back toward him. He wanted to say something more, something that would tip the balance, but Muscle wasn't the patient type. He pressed one hand against Fallon's chest and pushed him back a step. He gestured toward the other man, who looked considerably less formidable but just as mean.

"Frank here will see you to the door."

"Wait!" Selina appeared to have come to a decision. "I do know this man."

Frank and Muscle exchanged looks. "He thinks you're some dame named Mildred," said the latter.

"Yes, well, I didn't want anyone to know my real name when we met." She tilted her head coyly. "You know how it is."

Muscle was looking annoyed again. "So what do you want us to do with him?"

"Can't he come with us?"

Fallon suppressed a groan. The last thing he wanted was to join her in the frying pan. Fortunately, Muscle was shaking his head. "That's not part of the deal."

"No one ever said I had to come alone."

Muscle turned toward her, Fallon forgotten. "I have my orders, lady. It's just you and we're running late. You can talk over old times with your buddy here later." There was an ugly note in his voice now. Fallon shifted position slightly in anticipation of having to draw his weapon.

Her voice grew frigid. "I've changed my mind. We'll have to do this some other time."

Muscle moved then, grabbing her by one wrist and pulling her toward him. His head turned to the other man. "Get rid of this lowlife, Frank. I'll watch the stairs until you get back."

Frank wasn't expecting trouble. He came toward Fallon confidently, expecting a pliable drunk. Fallon let his shoulder drop, then brought his fist up in a long arc that terminated at Frank's jaw. The guard stumbled back with a surprised look on his face, his knees buckled, and he dropped to the floor, dazed but still conscious. Fallon spun around to confront Muscle, only to discover that he was doubled over, clutching his groin. The tight dress hadn't prevented Selina from delivering a solid, effective kick.

Fallon sidestepped the other man and caught Selina by the wrist, gently this time. "We have to go."

She didn't argue, followed him downstairs. He moved quickly, not quite running, and the guard at the door didn't give them a second look. No one had sounded the alarm yet and Fallon planned to be out of reach before that happened.

A breeze had sprung up during the last half hour. Bits and pieces of trash skittered across the street. "Where's your ride?" asked Fallon tersely.

"It should be two blocks over that way." She nodded to their left. "I told Paul to wait there for two hours and then come back for me."

Fallon took a step forward, still holding her wrist, but she resisted. "How did you know I had a car?"

"Later," he snapped, but she still wouldn't move.

"You've been following me, haven't you? I thought you looked familiar. You were at the Tribune office."

"Yes. Look, can we talk about this later? We left some unhappy people inside and they're probably going to be looking for us."

"It was Daddy, wasn't it? He hired you to watch out for me."

Client confidentiality be damned. If they didn't move soon, they might lose the opportunity. "Yes, now let's find your car before someone unpleasant finds us."

She allowed him to pull her along then, and after the first block he released her wrist. They scanned the rows of parked cars, but it was so dark that they were just so many humped shapes. They walked another block without speaking. Fallon kept glancing back the way they'd come, but there was no sign of pursuit. Could it be this easy?

"There it is!" Selina was pointing across the street to the next block. A dangling raccoon tail was just visible in the light spilled from the window of a second story tenement. She started across the street, catching Fallon by surprise, and he hastened to follow. They reached the car within a few seconds.

Selina rapped on the driver's window as Fallon tried the rear door. It was locked. "Paul, let us in!" She rapped again.

Fallon's instincts began to shout at him. "Back away, Miss Rose."

She gave him a puzzled look but retreated a step or two. Fallon gripped the handle, took a deep breath, and pulled the door open. The driver, wearing a chauffeur's uniform, was slumped forward over the wheel. A sharp, acrid smell told the story even before Fallon tilted the man's head back. His throat had been cut. Cursing softly, he glanced around. "I don't suppose you have a spare set of keys?"

"No." She must have seen the bloody wound even in the dim light, but her voice was steady. "How would anyone have known?"

Fallon stepped back and closed the door. "I guess I wasn't the only one keeping an eye on you."

Her head turned suddenly, as though she were listening for something. "We're not alone."

Fallon drew his weapon. It might be the girl's imagination, but he wasn't taking any chances and it felt good to have it in his hand. "I don't see anyone."

"No." Her voice faltered slightly. "I think we'd better get out of here. I don't suppose you have a car?"

"Yeah, but it's back the way we came, a block past the club." He looked around. This wasn't the best of neighborhoods. Most of the streetlights were out and they hadn't seen another pedestrian since leaving the club. They could hear traffic in the distance. "We need to find a place with plenty of people around. Come on." He started for the far corner, turned back when he didn't hear her footsteps.

She was standing awkwardly on one leg, wrestling off one shoe. Before he could ask, she had broken off the heel. "I can't run very well in these things." The other heel was already gone and she quickly caught up with him. They reached the corner, but Fallon hesitated, eyeing the alley with misgivings.

"What's wrong?" she asked, whispering now.

"I don't like alleys."

"It's the quickest way." She started into the darkness before he could stop her.

As alleys went, it was pretty unsavory. There was trash and garbage in cartons and barrels along both sides. The lights were distant and indirect and the shadows fell like inky blankets. Fallon heard a furtive sound that he hoped was just a rat. Selina was walking quickly and he had to half run to catch up to her. "Whatever happens, keep right on going."

She glanced at him and he thought she was smiling. Probably just a trick of the light.

They made it half way through without incident. Fallon's eyes were moving all the time, scanning their way ahead, watching for hiding places among the debris, occasionally turning to glance back the way they'd come. There were no fire escapes here so he could perhaps be pardoned for never thinking to look up, and that's where they came from.

His first hint that something was wrong came when something heavy hit him in the back, knocking him from his feet. He twisted his head around and thought he saw something large and dark swoop down on Selina, but he was too busy trying to reach his weapon to worry about anything else. It slid out of his holster but something hit his arm hard as he tried to roll over onto his back. His forearm went numb and the revolver fell from his hand. Then something he couldn't quite see rushed toward his face and pain blossomed in the center of his forehead. Everything went black.

Fallon woke up exactly where he'd fallen. He sat up quickly, then wished he hadn't. His head throbbed and when he touched his face, he felt dried blood on his forehead and nose. He looked around cautiously. He was alone in the alley and his revolver lay just beyond his reach. A wave of dizziness washed over him as he stood up, but he shook it off, retrieved his weapon, and put it away.

Selina Rose was gone. Their assailants were gone. His instinct told him that he'd been left alive because he didn't matter. They hadn't even bothered to kill him. Just like the sister's boyfriend, he realized.

He glanced at his watch. They'd left the Lamp Post about eleven and it was still a few minutes before midnight. His first thought was to go back to the club, but he reconsidered, then turned and continued to the mouth of the alley. There were more lights here and a couple of diners. He chose one at random, slipped inside. It was a narrow, grimy space with only a couple of tables. All of the stools at the counter were occupied but no one even glanced in his direction except the counterman, who frowned with his eyes.

"Getcha something?"

"Scotch." He pulled out a dollar and tossed it onto the counter.

"We don't serve liquor, sir. It's against the law."

Fallon glanced significantly at the other customers. Some of them had half eaten sandwiches in front of them. Most did not. "I'm not a copy and I'm not in the mood. Scotch." Their eyes met and the counterman looked away first, reached under the counter and found a bottle and glass. Fallon pushed the dollar across the counter. "You got a men's room?"

"In back."

Fallon looked at himself in a cracked, badly stained mirror. He didn't blame the counterman for looking askance. There were no towels so he used a wad of toilet paper to wash off the blood.

Satisfied, he returned, drank the scotch quickly, nodded to the counterman and left.

The breeze had grown in intensity, straining to become wind, and the air was cool and moist. Fallon shivered involuntarily and considered his options. "It'd be nice if the Shadow or the Green Falcon showed up about now," he told himself, but he knew he was on his own.

They'd taken her back to the club, of course, whoever "they" were. She was probably up on the third floor somewhere. There was no chance that he could bull his way in; they knew his face now and there were too many of Muscle and his ilk. He didn't have enough to interest the police, and even if he did, they weren't likely to risk the wrath of the Armitages. But if he didn't do something, he was going to have to tell Lionel Rose that he'd screwed up, and his sense of honor would force him to return the advance as well. Except he couldn't, because he'd already paid some of his outstanding bills.

So he'd have to go back, but not just now. The Lamp Post closed at two in the morning. He'd have to wait until then. Wishing that he'd never agreed to see Rose in the first place, Fallon began walking back to where he'd parked his car. First he was going to visit an old friend and then he needed the kit he kept in his trunk.

Ethel Merriam lived in Soho in an aging Victorian monstrosity that had been in her family forever. Ethel hadn't left her house in years, but that didn't mean she was out of touch. She entertained a constant stream of visitors and she didn't discriminate by class, occupation, or any other criteria. Fallon had seen her serving tea to a homeless man, trading recipes with Jimmy Walker's wife, and playing checkers with a retired dockworker. She accepted people for what they were, and everyone trusted her. And talked to her.

With Gimpy Lane, information was a business. For Ethel Merriam, it was a way of life. Technically speaking, she wasn't a gossip because she wasn't profligate with what she knew, but given sufficient motivation, she was a virtual encyclopedia of hidden secrets.

Fallon knew her habits so he wasn't surprised to find lights on when he arrived. He parked his aging Ford out front and knocked on her door, hoping that she wasn't entertaining anyone this evening. The door opened almost immediately.

"Well, if it isn't Mr. Fallon. Where have you been keeping yourself lately? Come inside." She led the way into an elaborately furnished Victorian sitting room. Ethel looked the same as always, not one white hair out of place, dressed elegantly without being ostentatious. Fallon followed her to the elaborate sitting room where she entertained most of her guests. It was like stepping back into the last century.

It wouldn't do to rush her. She offered him brandy which he declined in favor of coffee. Ethel disappeared briefly, returned with a steaming mug and a plate of pastries. "I can offer you something more substantial if you prefer."

Fallon shook his head. "I need some information, Mrs. M."

"Of course you do. That's the only reason you ever come to visit." There was no reproach in her voice, but Fallon felt a twinge of guilt.

"I need to know about the Armitages." He saw the way her face changed, or didn't change, and knew he'd have to offer her something. "There's a girl's life at stake or I wouldn't ask."

Ethel poured herself a brandy and sat down across from him. "Who's the girl?"

"Her name is Selina Rose."

"Ah, Lionel's daughter. Then she's decided to find her sister, I would imagine."

Fallon was used to her nearly prescient flashes. "The sister disappeared at the Lamp Post, and I think that's where Selina's been taken. And nothing goes on there without the Armitages knowing about it."

"Indeed not. I knew Walter's parents, you know. They separated shortly after he was born. Helen went off to Asia somewhere but she was never fond of her son so Walter stayed with his father here in New York. He was a troublesome boy. Not very bright in the normal sense but he had a highly developed survival instinct. He cozied up to the syndicate after his father died and they scratched each other's back a few times. He's a small time snake, but that doesn't mean his venom won't kill you."

"What about the sister?"

Ethel frowned and shocked him by admitting that she didn't know a great deal about Allison Armitage. "She was already an adult when she arrived. Muriel, that was her mother, must have been pregnant when they split up, or she found a lover somewhere. She's only a year younger than Walter, which makes her thirty two if I remember correctly." Ethel always remembered correctly. "She came back to the city about six years ago. Moved in with her brother and is assumed to be the brains behind his recent financial successes."

"I know he owns the Lamp Post and that metal stamping company his father founded."

"They also have speakeasies in Brooklyn and Queens and one out on Staten Island. They bought the warehouse behind the Lamp Post and several small shops uptown. That's what they own outright. Walter has part interest in many other concerns."

"Are they involved in anything," he groped for the right word, "sleazy."

Ethel laughed. "Everything that the Armitages do is by definition sleazy, Mr. Fallon. Bootlegging is probably the least of their sins. Extortion, blackmail, tax evasion, and prostitution come immediately to mind."

"How about murder?"

She hesitated. "It probably would not be incorrect to make that assumption, although I cannot say with any certainty."

"White slavery?"

"I'm sure the provisions of the Mann Act would not deter the Armitages from making a profit. Is that what you think they plan for the misses Rose?"

"I don't know what they're planning, Mrs. M. That's why I'm here."

Her expression, never playful, had grown more serious. "These are dangerous people to cross, Mr. Fallon. They don't like to be interfered with and, I regret to say, they have considerable influence with the authorities."

"I can be dangerous at times myself."

She smiled, leaned over and patted his knee. "I've no doubt that you can. So what more can I tell you?'

Fallon ran his fingers through his hair. "I'm not sure. A set of floor plans for the Lamp Post would be helpful."

She actually seemed to be considering the possibility, but she shook her head. "My late husband was an architect, you know, and he collected such things. But I know that Walter made extensive renovations before he opened his establishment. Anything I might be able to find would be of questionable assistance."

Fallon absentmindedly tried one of the pastries. It was quite good. "What about the sister? I understand she's not well liked among her social peers."

"Loathed would be a more appropriate description."

"Why? I mean, there are any number of society women whose husbands have just as questionable occupations or hobbies."

Ethel's expression told him he was wrong. "Come on. If it was anything that bad, I'd have heard something. People in those circles like to talk about each other."

"Not about this." For the first time since Fallon had met Ethel, he thought she looked uneasy. "When Allison Armitage came back from the Orient, she brought strange new ideas, new perversions if you will. "

There was a pause so long that Fallon was trying to decide how to prompt her when she suddenly gave a little shake of her head and resumed. "Sometimes she'd invite people over to the brownstone she shares with her brother. As far as I know, nobody ever made a second visit, and no one talks much about what happened there."

"Is that all you know?" asked Fallon after another long pause.

Ethel sighed. "All right, I'll tell you the rest. It isn't much and it probably won't help. Several of the visitors were lured in by promises of forbidden pleasures. I have never heard anything explicit, but there have been suggestions of extraordinary sexual encounters, drugs unknown in this country, even hints of Satanic rituals. Only two of her visitors ever talked about their experiences. Arthur Pendleton was one."

"Pendleton? Wasn't he the one who…"

"…was torn apart by his own dogs? Yes, that's him. The dogs were destroyed of course but a gentleman I know on the force insists that they were locked in another room when Pendleton was attacked. Pendleton claimed that Armitage had invoked an actual demon in his presence."

"And the second squealer?"

"Christina Craft."

Fallon blinked. "The actress who disappeared?'

Ethel grimaced. "Only part of her disappeared, remember? They found one leg and some fingers."

He only vaguely remembered the case. His business was primarily skip tracing, following cheating husbands, and finding runaways. Murders were for the police, particularly gruesome ones involving dismembered and missing bodies found in locked penthouse apartments.

"You're not suggesting the Armitages killed them both?"

Ethel shook her head. "I'm not suggesting anything. But after that, no one else ever talked about what happened during their visits. Most people don't even want to be in the same room with them, particularly Allison. Walter is too slow witted to be menacing."

There wasn't much more that she could tell him. Fallon thanked her, promised to visit more often, and took his leave.

Two hours later, he sat on the roof of the rundown hotel next door to the Lamp Post, sheltering behind an oversized funnel. The backpack he had removed from the trunk of the Ford wasn't much of a pillow but it was the best he had, and a coil of rope served as an unsatisfactory seat. The night had grown chill and he had discovered not only that he was hungry but that he only had three cigarettes left. Fallon spaced them out to last until he was ready to move, but the lights stayed on at the Lamp Post for almost an hour after the last customer was chased out. When the security lights were the only ones still burning, Fallon stood up, stretching stiff muscles. He quickly redistributed a few items from the pack, then walked over to the edge of the roof.

The hotel was six stories tall, twice the height of the Lamp Post and the adjoining warehouse. There was a ladder bolted to the side of the building, but it creaked ominously when Fallon tried putting his weight on it and he climbed back up. It only took a few seconds to secure one end of his rope and little more than that to climb down onto the speakeasy's roof. There was an access hut in the center of the roof with a utility door. It would be locked, but Fallon had his skeleton keys and, if that didn't work, a very sharp file.

The file proved to be unnecessary. Fallon slipped inside, found himself on a small landing at the top of a steep staircase. When the door closed behind him, he was left in complete darkness until he turned on his flashlight. Very cautiously, he descended to the foot of the stairs, which ended at a narrow hallway stretching to left and right. There was enough light to see by so Fallon flicked off the flash and waited for his eyes to adjust.

To right and left, numbered doors appeared at regular intervals, so close together that most of the rooms must have been quite small. The wall ahead was unbroken, suggesting a much larger central space. He heard someone speak a few words in the distance, but it was too brief and muffled for him to guess the location. Cautiously, he began moving to his right. He had switched to soft soled shoes so he made only the faintest whisper of sound before reaching the corner. Just as he was about to move forward, he heard a door open and footsteps, so he shrank back, his hand moving toward his revolver.

The door closed and there were more footsteps, fortunately moving away. When he couldn't hear them any longer, Fallon turned the corner. The doors were wider spaced along this wall – larger rooms – and there was one on the left wall as well. He advanced until he was next to the jamb, listening for any hint that the room might be occupied. Once he heard a faint shuffle, although it might have been his imagination. Although he knew that he should finish reconnoitering before doing anything precipitate, there was something about this place that bothered him, something subliminal, and he wanted to find the Rose girl and get out as quickly as possible.

He reached forward and tried the doorknob. It turned.

Fallon drew his weapon and took a deep breath. He hadn't come this far to go away empty handed. The door disengaged from the latch and he opened it smoothly and almost silently, stepping inside with weapon raised.

The lighting was better here, though not bright, and the first thing Fallon saw was Gimpy Lane, tied into a chair. Gimpy's head had fallen backward and there was a small, ugly bullet wound in the center of his forehead. Just beyond, Selina Rose was tied to an identical chair, her head also back, and for a second he thought she was dead as well. The dark spot on her temple must have been a simple bruise, however, because she turned to look at him. Her eyes were bright with alarm but a thick gag made it impossible for her to say anything.

Just beyond Rose, another figure sat on a luxurious Victorian divan, legs crossed, casually smoking a cigarette in an elaborate holder. She had unstylish long dark hair and a pale complexion that was exaggerated by the odd lighting in the room. The divan sat in a pool of moonlight that fell through a skylight directly overhead. It had been opened and the air in the room was distinctly chilly. Although he'd never met her before, Fallon knew this had to be Allison Armitage.

"Come in, please. May I offer you something to drink?" Her voice was thick and more than slightly seductive with not the slightest hint of alarm. She gestured toward an array of liquor bottles on a low table set to one side.

Fallon closed the door and moved closer, but not too close. There was a small, but well equipped bar to his right, two circular tables and chairs to the left that were obviously meant to host card games, a pool table in one corner.

"I don't believe we've been introduced. I'm Allison Armitage." The woman seemed profoundly cool, completely unaffected by his presence, almost amused. "You can put your gun away. I never carry one myself."

"I think I'll keep it handy, if you don't mind." He nodded toward Selina. "Untie her."

Armitage laughed. "Oh, I think not, dear boy. You'll have to do it yourself. I've had quite a tiring day and this is the first chance I've had to sit and relax."

Fallon pointed his weapon at her. "You can relax all you want after we're gone. Now untie her."

A flicker of anger came and went so quickly that it might have been a trick of the light. "Come now. You and I both know you wouldn't shoot me in cold blood. It wouldn't accomplish anything except to attract the attention of Mr. Lansky and his friends, and I assure you they don't share my distaste for firearms."

Fallon knew she was right, that he would have to free Selina himself, then use those same ropes to secure Armitage while they made their escape. He glanced toward the bound girl, who was shaking her head furiously. With his weapon trained on the other woman, he moved to her side, reached out and undid the gag.

"Watch out! They're above us!"

Fallon had time for only a quick glance up toward the open skylight before something heavy crashed into him. His right arm went numb and he dropped his weapon, but as he staggered back he managed to stay on his feet.

Someone had dropped down on him from above. Or something. It was only about five feet tall but its body was squat and powerful. Both legs were slightly bowed and the arms seemed unnaturally short. The face was vaguely human except for two small horns above the ears, a nose that was far too wide for the face, and thick lips that failed to conceal a set of decidedly nasty teeth. The creature was hairless and wore no clothing and its body seemed to be covered from head to foot with bright red leather in lieu of skin. The most unsettling feature was the pair of bat wings now furled behind its back. A rank, metallic smell seemed to fill the room.

"Say hello to Rak," said Armitage softly, a hint of amusement in her voice. "He picked an appropriate moment to drop in, don't you think?"

Fallon retreated a step and looked around for his revolver. At first he couldn't see it, but then he noticed a faint glint of metal visible beneath the chair where Gimpy Lane had breathed his last. "What is this thing?" He was playing for time, moving his feet ever so slightly.

"Manners, my dear sir! Rak is my son, a little Oni I brought back with me from the Orient. Despite his formidable appearance, Rak is actually quite a lovely boy and very protective of his mother. I suggest that you refrain from doing anything that he might construe as threatening. I'm afraid he does tend to be rather impulsive at times. You'll be much better off waiting for Mr. Lansky to return."

That suggestion prompted him to act. The odds were already against him and he didn't relish allowing them to get any longer. He had bent his knees slightly and now he launched himself across the room, landing heavily on his left hip and shoulder behind the inert body of Gimpy Lane. His groping fingers found the revolver easily and he rolled away, stumbling to his feet and turning just as Rak started toward him. He raised his arm, pointing it toward the Armitage woman, and the creature immediately came to a halt.

"There's two of them!" screamed Selina, but it was too late. A dark shadow fell across his arm and he fired reflexively. Then he was lying on his back, his hands empty, and a hideous face stared down into his. It looked just like the first, except that this creature was encased in blue leather rather than red.

"No!" Armitage called out urgently from somewhere out of his line of sight. "Don't kill him yet. We need to know who sent him first."

A second face entered his field of vision. Allison Armitage's expression was no longer relaxedl. Her eyes were bright with hatred, her nostrils flared, and her lips curved into a cruel mockery of a smile. "You should be particularly careful around Sha. He's much more impulsive than his brother."

Only a few seconds passed before Lansky arrived in response to the gunshot but it seemed like eternity to Fallon. The creature, Sha, continued to kneel on his chest and seemed to weigh far more than his relatively small body suggested. He heard Selina speaking sharply, then a slap. "You know, dear, you could scream all night and no one would ever hear you. Ordinarily I might find that rather amusing, but your pointless prattle is just annoying. So remain silent or I'll be force to replace the gag."

Fallon heard the door open and footsteps, two pair. "What's going on?" The first voice was high, thin, and male.

"It's nothing, Walter. Just a troublesome intruder."

Someone came closer but Fallon didn't dare turn his head away from Sha. It was irrational but he was convinced that if he dropped his gaze, those razor sharp teeth would close on his throat.

The second voice was low, rasping. "I know this mug. His name is Fallon."

"Cop?" asked the Walter voice querulously.

"Nah! Private dick. Not a classy one either." Pokerface Lansky's craggy face looked down at Fallon. "So what are you doing here, asshole?"

"Slumming." It wasn't much but it was hard to come up with snappy lines when a horned, winged demon was sitting on your chest.

Lansky turned away. "Want me to finish him like the other one?"

"Certainly not. You might stain the carpet. Walter shouldn't have let you kill Lane here. Take him and the girl and the body over to the warehouse. We'll sort things out in the temple."

A short time later, they had made up a small procession. The two Armitages led the way, Allison looking regal, Walter uncomfortable. Selina followed with her arms bound behind her back and Lansky at her side. They hadn't restrained Fallon because he was carrying Gimpy Lane's inert form over one shoulder. Close behind came Rak and Sha. Sha ran his claws lightly across Fallon's back every few seconds, just to remind him not to try anything rash. There was a gash along Sha's shoulder from which a thick viscous liquid was slowly oozing. Apparently Fallon had managed to nick the creature with the one wild shot he'd fired. Unfortunately, Sha didn't seem particularly bothered by the wound.

One of the peripheral rooms actually concealed an obviously new feature, an exit from the Lamp Post directly into the rear of the warehouse. There were security lights inside but Fallon couldn't see much as they descended a rickety catwalk toward the warehouse floor. The building was one large three story open space, empty except for a large blockhouse in the center of the floor. There were two roll up doors facing the street and three more that opened onto the loading docks on the northeast side. There were a few wooden crates and odds and ends scattered about, but it was obvious that the building was not being used as a warehouse any longer.

When they reached ground level, Fallon noticed another feature. A large rectangular block had been excavated from the floor, leaving a pit ten feet deep. There was an acrid smell that he recognized immediately, the coppery scent of blood. Fresh blood. They proceeded directly across the floor to the rim of the pit, which appeared to be empty. A man stood at the far side, watching them, and Fallon recognized him as the thug he'd named Muscle earlier that evening.

"Throw that garbage in." Allison's voice was crisp and businesslike. Fallon realized that she was speaking to him and - with a silent apology to Gimpy Lane - he heaved the body off his shoulders and let it drop into the darkness.

"Smells like you make a habit of this," he said quietly, looking directly at the Armitages.

Walter looked away but Allison laughed. "I'm afraid the boys are rather messy eaters. I did try to teach them table manners, but they're incorrigible."

"What are these things anyway?" Fallon looked around, was not cheered by what he saw. They were obviously quite alone.

"I told you, they're my children." Allison walked past him and gently stroked Rak's arm. "They're half human and half Oni."

"Oni?" He had never heard the term.

"Japanese demons," said Selina.

"Very good!" Allison Armitage was clearly surprised. "I knew you were brighter than the others."

"Where is my sister?" Selina's voice caught. "Did you feed her to these…things?"

"Of course not, my dear. Your sister is just fine, as a matter of fact. My boys wouldn't harm a hair on her head. They only prey on their own sex. Now if I'd had a daughter, that might have been a different matter." She gave an exaggerated sigh. "But I was never blessed that way. Still, my boys have been a great comfort to me."

Fallon had been considering a rush toward the older woman. If he could secure her before Rak or Sha could react, he might have a bargaining chip. Lansky must have read his body language though because a snub nosed revolver appeared in his hand as if by magic. "Why don't we show our guests to their quarters?" he said quietly. "Unless you want to dispose of this jerk right here and now."

"Don't we need to know who he's working for?" Walter Armitage was obviously uneasy and Fallon noticed that he never looked at either of the two Oni.

"It's not crucial, Walter, but we might as well find out." Allison turned to Lansky. "We don't have much time to finish the preparations. I can only open the gates between worlds at specific times, so we cannot miss this opportunity. You and Walter lock them with the others for the moment. We'll have time to deal with him after the rites are over." She turned to Muscle. "Open one of the doors, Carl. My Lord could arrive at any time."

Carl started toward the nearest but she shouted after him. "Not one of those. It has to be facing northeast. The ceremony won't work if he comes from any other direction. "

Fallon didn't see any more because Lansky was gesturing with his weapon for them to enter the blockhouse. There were no windows except a narrow one inset in the door and only a single light bulb burned inside, but Fallon heard stirring from all around as they entered and when his eyes focused, he realized they were standing between two rows of cells. He counted at least six young women before Lansky roughly pushed the two of them into the nearest cell and swung the barred door closed. Walter locked it and pocketed the key.

Selina wasted no time. As soon as Lansky and the two Oni left the building, she called her sister's name. "Emily! Emily Rose! Are you there?"

A low, shaky voice answered from the distance. "Selina? Is that you? My God, what are you doing here?"

"Looking for you, of course. Are you all right?"

"Yes, I guess so. But I don't know what's going on. What do these people want with us?"

Fallon interrupted. "We need to know who else is here." A handful of voices shouted their names. "Not all at once. Let's start with Emily and go clockwise around the room."

It didn't help much. There were ten women plus Fallon. They were all quite young and none of them knew much of anything useful. Six had been abducted while at the Lamp Post. The others had been grabbed in various places and brought to the warehouse in a kind of "black Maria". The earliest, Velma Walters, had been drugged and kidnapped just over two months ago. "They never touched me but they won't tell me anything. I'd give anything just to be able to take a bath!" None of them had seen the Oni. All of them had been treated reasonably well, under the circumstances. They'd been fed, allowed to wash with a cloth and a bucket of water, and there were crude sanitary arrangements. That didn't keep the blockhouse from smelling of sweat, decay, and fear.

While listening to the stories from the other prisoners, Fallon had been examining the lock on the cell door. He removed a thin metal pick from the sleeve of his shirt and began probing inside, confident that it would only take a moment or two to trigger the mechanism. He was rewarded by a click as the mechanism engaged. Selina's face brightened perceptibly, but he pressed a finger to his lips and she didn't say anything except to whisper to him. "Very resourceful, Mr. Fallon. I don't suppose you have another gun up the other sleeve."

He smiled and shook his head. "Sorry. But while I'm thinking of it, my compliments for the way you handled yourself inside the club."

"The kick?" She grimaced. "Daddy insisted that I take dance lessons even though I'm too short and clumsy to be very good at it. That was the first time I found a practical application."

"Well, let's hope you get another chance." He raised his voice slightly. "Ladies, it's very important that you remain quiet." There was a murmuring and a gasp of surprise when he opened the cell door, but no one cried out.

He crossed to the blockhouse door and looked outside. The interior of the warehouse was much brighter now because someone had set up more than a dozen torches, all of which were ablaze. Fallon had a limited view but he could see that just beyond the pit, a large red carpet had been laid on the floor. The corners were held down by bronze statues of dragons with doglike faces, at least the two corners he could see. One of the Oni moved on the far side but the shadows were dancing and he couldn't tell whether it was Rak or Sha. There was no sign of their human captors.

Fallon jumped as something touched his elbow, but it was only Selina. "What are we going to do?"

He would have liked to be able to answer confidently, but something told him that she'd see through any deception. "I don't know. If I can get the drop on Lansky and get his weapon, I don't think the Armitages will be a problem."

"What about the Oni? I don't even know if they can be killed."

"They bleed. If they bleed, they can die." Or at least he hoped that was the case. "But they're fast and even with a gun I'm not sure I could stop them both fast enough."

There was movement outside and Fallon shrank back. "Quick! Back to the cell! Someone's coming."

They barely made it before they heard the blockhouse door opening. Fallon wrapped his arm around two of the bars, but only to prevent the cell door from swinging open now that the lock was disengaged. Allison Armitage and her brother entered the blockhouse unaccompanied. Even in the dim light, Fallon could tell that the woman was much more animated than earlier. She was excited, exhilarated, could barely stand still.

"All right, ladies, it's nearly time to open the gate. I know that you aren't likely to appreciate the honor which is about to be yours, but I don't want you to approach our Lord in ignorance of his nature and your own purpose." Walter Armitage stood to one side and slightly behind his sister. Contradictory emotions rippled across his face. He was terrified, Fallon realized, but nearly as excited as his sister.

"Many years ago, I uncovered a wonderful secret while I was living in Japan. I I was introduced to a world that exists beyond our own but is also hidden within it. This hidden world is populated by godlike creatures with powers you can only imagine, creatures who would rule this world if they could escape their confinement. I found favor with one of these and discovered a way to release him into our world, at least briefly and at great intervals. My Lord will be here very soon now, and you will all have the opportunity to meet him."

She began to pace back and forth, her face twisted with carnal passion. "I took him as my lover and discovered an ecstasy you could only begin to imagine. Out of that union came my two beautiful children. You will meet them soon, but more importantly, you will meet their father, and he will make you a similar though lesser gift. You will bear his children and, if you serve us loyally, you will be allowed to live and serve as their nurses. If you choose otherwise," she paused for effect, "your flesh will fulfill a different purpose."

There were cries of protest but Armitage raised her voice. "Silence! We have little time left to prepare. You have all been provided with the means to clean your bodies. I warn you now that our Lord is not patient with those who displease him."

She and her brother both began to turn toward the door. Fallon knew he had to act now. With both hands, he swung the cell door violently open. The edge brushed against Allison's shoulder and spun her around. Walter tried to throw an arm up, lost his balance, and was knocked from his feet. Fallon stepped out briskly, turned his body, and lashed out with a foot. He didn't mean the blow to be fatal, but it caught Walter Armitage under the jaw and his head flew back with an audible snap. He fell back without so much as a groan and never moved again.

Fallon turned toward Allison, who might not carry a firearm but who proved to be less fastidious about knives. She was rushing toward him with an ornately decorated dagger in one hand when Selina charged forward with her head down, grapping for the other woman's arm. She was outmatched and tossed aside almost casually, but the distraction gave Fallon enough time to engage her, twist the wrist, and force her to drop the blade. When she tried to slash his face with her nails, he backhanded her and she staggered back. Fallon crouched, retrieved the knife, and stepped in front of her when she started for the door. Once again she tried to claw at him, but this time he caught her wrist, twisted it around behind her back, and then brought the knife up to her throat.

"I'd rather not kill a woman, Miss Armitage, but I'll make an exception in your case if you give me an excuse." She stopped struggling, but her body was tense, like a coiled snake, waiting for a chance to strike.

"Selina, unlock the other cells. The key's in his pocket."

If Selina had any qualms about searching a dead man's clothing, they weren't apparent. She retrieved the keys and worked her way along the row of cell doors, opening each in turn. The women who emerged looked bedraggled, tired, and frightened, but none of them appeared to have been seriously harmed. Not yet anyway.

"We're going out now," said Fallon. "Stay close behind me and watch out above you." He remembered that the prisoners had not seen the Oni. "They have some kind of flying animals trained to attack." It was lame but the best he could come up with at short notice. "They're dangerous."

Outside the blockhouse, Fallon paused long enough to take in the changes that had been made during his brief incarceration. There were at least twenty torches blazing, most of them surrounding the red carpet. Carl and Lansky were standing at a bench facing toward the single open overhead door. Beyond was a large loading platform whose far end was cloaked in shadow. Something must have warned them, however, because Lansky spun around, his hand already reaching for his weapon.

"Hold it right there or Miss Armitage dies!" Fallon turned so that they could see the knife he held at his prisoner's throat.

Lansky eased his arm back and put out a hand to restrain Carl, who looked as though he was going to charge across the floor. "That won't do you any good, Fallon. Let the lady go."

"I don't think so. You, Carl, take out your weapon and put it on the floor."

Neither man moved. Fallon was less inhibited about killing the Armitage woman than he had been earlier, but if he did so he'd probably be dead within seconds. "I'm not bluffing, Pokerface."

"Maybe not, but you don't have the best hand either. "

Help came from a surprising quarter. "Do what he says." It was Allison. She didn't sound frightened either, and that scared Fallon. She ought to be very nervous indeed.

"But Miss Armitage…"

"Do what I tell you. They can't get away. He'll be here very soon. I can feel my Lord's presence."

There was an uncomfortable pause before Lansky turned to his companion. "Put your rod on the floor, Carl."   The other man looked resentful, but complied.

"Now you, Lansky." The hood chuckled, carefully withdrew his own weapon, and set it gently on the floor. "Now both of you back up, all the way to wall."

The only one of the women Fallon trusted to act calmly was Selina. He turned his head. "Go get their weapons and bring them back here. And be careful."

She darted across the intervening space, less cautious than he would have preferred, picked up both weapons and ran back. Fallon forced Allison down onto her knees, then quickly discarded the knife and accepted one of the revolvers. He pointed it at the back of her head. "Where are they?" he asked.

Allison turned her head to look back at him. "My boys? Oh, they're around somewhere. They're very anxious to see their Daddy."

"All right, now this is what's going to happen. You are going to stand up slowly and walk ahead of me, Miss Armitage. We're going out onto the loading dock. Once we're outside and I think we're clear, we'll release you. If anyone tries to stop us, or any THING for that matter, I won't hesitate to shoot you. Is that clear?"

"I understand what you intend to do." There was a hint of amusement in her voice that worried him but he could think of no better course of action.

"Let's go then. The rest of you stay right behind me."

They only made it halfway before the attack came. Although he'd told them to watch overhead, none of the young women had done so after the first few seconds. When a dark shape came hurtling down, they had no warning. Fallon heard screams and was shoved from behind. Armitage pulled free and started to run and he almost fired. At the last possible moment, he couldn't make himself shoot a woman in the back. Then something heavy brushed across his shoulders and sent him reeling across the floor.

Somehow he managed to twist and fall in a sitting position. He looked up and saw something moving straight toward his face. Without hesitation he raised his arm and fired three times. There was a scream that originated in no human throat and he twisted away just before the Oni would have crashed into him. Instead it hit the floor, skidded several feet across the rough surface, rolled over and tried to sit up. Fallon scrambled to his feet, raising the weapon again, but the Oni fell back, jerked a few times, and was still. He recognized it by its coloring. It was Sha.

There was a scream of rage from behind him. Fallon spun and saw that the others had been scattered by the second Oni, Rak, who now stood in his familiar bow legged stance. Two women lay prone and motionless. Fallon raised his arm to fire again but he was too slow. Rak flew toward him as though he'd been fired from a cannon. Fallon barely managed to hold onto the pistol grip as he was thrown backward, landed awkwardly, and skidded across the gravelly floor. He shook his head, blinking his eyes, and saw that misshapen head lunging toward him again. By instinct rather than thought, he swung his arm up, jammed the revolver between Rak's jaws and pulled the trigger, kept pulling it even after he'd run out of bullets.

Rak's inert body fell across his legs. Fallon twisted out from under, exhausted, and let the empty revolver drop from his hand. Selina and a younger girl who looked much like her, probably her sister, rushed over and helped him to his feet.

"Here. Take this." Selina handed him the second handgun, the snub nosed one that Lansky had carried.

Fallon's mind finally began to work again and he looked for the Armitage woman and the two thugs. Neither Lansky nor Carl had moved from where he'd ordered them to stand, but Armitage was crouched next to Sha's body. She stood up suddenly, her face composed, and stared directly at Fallon. "You'll pay for this," she called to him. "You'll answer to their father." She turned toward the open doorway. "He's here now."

A gust of wind rushed through the door, stirring up dust, and then the light from outside was obscured momentarily as something large, bigger than a man by half, filled the opening. Fallon gripped the revolver tightly and took a step backward.

At first it just looked like a larger version of Rak or Sha. The face was much the same although the horns were more prominent and the eyes were larger, almost glowing. The legs were bowed but they were also covered with bony spurs, as were the arms. And there were four arms. Incongruously, this Oni wore a tiger striped loincloth around his hips. Despite its odd stance, it moved with singular grace as it entered the warehouse, the chunky head turning slowly to survey the interior.

Fallon's grip tightened, but the Oni wasn't looking his way. It was staring at the inert body of Sha.

The Oni's entrance had frozen everyone, but Carl had turned pale and suddenly turned to run toward the catwalk, apparently hoping to escape back into the Lamp Post. Lansky was made of sterner stuff and stood his ground, at least until the Oni's head turned toward the unexpected movement. Then Lansky panicked as well and started off in his associate's tracks.

Neither of them made it. The Oni seemed to leap across the intervening space. One sweep of its massive arm lifted Lansky off his feet and sent his broken body crashing into the far wall. Carl made it to the base of the catwalk before a gnarled fist lifted him into the air. He screamed once as the Oni opened its massive jaws and then they closed and a headless body dropped to the floor.

"No, my Lord! Not them! Those are not your enemies!" Armitage screamed the words but it was too late. The two thugs had died so quickly that she hadn't even realized they were in danger. But now the Oni turned and inclined its head toward her, listening. She turned and pointed directly at Fallon. "That's the one who killed our children!"

Fallon had met some pretty evil people in his lifetime, and had faced more than a few who hated his guts including a handful of very annoyed wandering husbands. Nothing had prepared him for the almost physical impact of the Oni's malevolent glare. He stepped back involuntarily and felt a twisting in his guts that wasn't exactly fear. It was more like dread. His hands were shaking and when the Oni began to move toward him, he felt a wave of nausea so intense that his stomach churned.

He emptied the revolver directly at its face. It was too dark to see the actual impact of the rounds, but he knew that he hadn't missed. The Oni had nearly lidless eyes or perhaps it might have blinked, but it didn't slow down. Fallon tossed the useless gun aside and started to run. Perhaps the Oni had expected him to flee toward the door, because it froze momentarily when instead he headed almost directly toward the creature, then veered aside and sprinted through the open door of the blockhouse. He just avoided being caught as he passed and clawed fingers tore the shoulder of his jacket and the flesh beneath. Fallon didn't feel the pain until much later.

He made it inside the blockhouse and stumbled, rolling across the floor. Something grabbed the door and tore it off its hinges with a scream of tortured metal and a heavily muscled arm and shoulder were thrust through the opening, but the doorway was not large enough. The Oni drew back and made its first sound, a shrill roar of rage and frustration. Fallon scrambled to his feet and looked for something he could use as a weapon, but other than Walter Armitage's body and several buckets of water, the cells were essentially empty.

Something hit the ceiling with enough force that some of the boards split or were torn free. One of the support beams cracked and bent slightly and a one of the cell doors fell with a clatter. Fallon realized that he'd bought some time but that he'd also trapped himself. Faintly he could hear Armitage shouting encouragement to her preternatural lover and he wondered if the others were taking advantage of this distraction to escape. If he had to die here, he'd like to think it had at least served some purpose.

Another blow splintered more wood and sent a shower of debris down from the ceiling. Fallon entertained a brief fantasy in which he fooled the Oni into thinking Walter Armitage's body was his quarry, but there was no place to hide and no time to think of anything clever.

There was the sound of rending wood, nails being pulled out by brute force, and the entire blockhouse trembled. Fallon retreated to one corner, waiting for his entire life to flash before his eyes, instead saw one corner of the roof rise into the air, splintering, collapsing, wrenched aside. The Oni wasn't tall enough to reach over and down, but it was strong enough to clasp one hand on the exposed joists and literally pull a section of the wall out of place. The closest end of the blockhouse leaned over and another section of the ceiling split and disintegrated. The air was filled with the smell of dust and soot; something more substantial than the torches was burning.

Through the rent in the wall he could see Allison Armitage now, standing directly behind the Oni, urging him on. Her face had been transformed by rage into a caricature not unlike that of the Oni. Fallon prepared to launch himself toward her. He wouldn't survive, but he might be able to take her with him.

Another sweep of the Oni's arm sent debris flying and widened the gap. Fallon darted forward and had almost reached the opening when he sensed rather than saw the descending arm. He twisted away but not quickly enough and something massive hit him in the left side. He felt ribs break and this time the pain wasn't deferred. He landed on his back, breathless and stunned. Even though it made the pain worse, he raised his upper body. If he was going to die, he was determined to face his death as upright as possible.

The Oni had one foot inside the ruins of the blockhouse. Armitage was even closer, silent now, avidly anticipating his death. Then there was another figure beside her and a sudden cry of pain. Fallon saw the woman stumble but the Oni roared, close enough now that he felt its hot, fetid breath, and he turned back toward the towering creature, prepared as much as he could ever be for death. It reached for him, its claws extended.

But they never touched him.

Fallon watched in amazement as the Oni faltered, drew back, then started to turn. It staggered and put out one hand to grasp the upright portion of the blockhouse for support. Its hand passed through the wall without disturbing it. It roared then, but the sound came from a distance, as though it had been removed to the far end of a tunnel. The head turned back to stare balefully down at Fallon and one hand was extended toward him, but already the Oni's substance was fading, growing more nebulous with each passing second, and then it was gone.

"Come on, Fallon. We have to get out of here."

He had been transfixed by the certainty of his own death and the bizarre image of the vanishing Oni. For a second he didn't recognize the woman pulling at his arm, but then reality came rushing back as her efforts drove a spike of pain through his side. It was Selina Rose.

"What happened?" He felt groggy, almost drunk, and that distancing from the present helped him bear the discomfort as he allowed himself to be dragged to his feet. "Where did it go?"

"Back where it came from, I hope. Hurry, please! It knocked over some of the torches and the whole building is on fire."

"Where are the others?" He took a step and regretted it. Pressing one hand to his injured ribs seemed to help, but not very much.

"Emily's getting them outside. Some of them were hurt, but not too badly. Fallon, we have to go now!"

She had an arm around him but she was so short he couldn't lean on her for support and had to manage for himself. They picked their way through the wreckage of the blockhouse. Fallon move dvery slowly and stiffly and had more than enough time to see that the flames were spreading across the floor, which had become saturated with oil over the course of years. He also saw Allison Armitage's crumpled body, lying on its back, her ornate dagger lodged solidly in her chest.

"What happened?" His voice was slurred with pain.

"I had to do it," said Selina, her voice equally shaky but not for the same reason. "It was the only way. She was the one keeping it here. If she died, it had to go back to wherever it came from, wherever it belongs."

They made it outside, but they had to run – or at least trot – the last few yards and that hurt so badly that Fallon nearly fainted. Flames were crawling up the walls and licking at the ceiling. For a moment or two, he regretted that they wouldn't be able save the body of at least one of the dead Oni children, something to prove what had happened. But then he realized it was best this way. If he was involved with something this bizarre, his life would never return to normal and he liked his life. Oh, he'd prefer to be able to pay his bills a little more regularly, he'd favor a slightly better class of customer than those he usually had to settle for, and it was a bit lonely at times. He'd rather fancy meeting a woman who respected him and whom he could respect, not just another shallow flapper like those he'd dated in the past.

Yes, it would be nice to meet a real woman. He glanced at Selina Rose thoughtfully. Maybe he'd just been granted his wish.

www.ingramcontent.com/pod-product-compliance
Lightning Source LLC
Chambersburg PA
CBHW072056170626
46813CB00004B/1377